WHAT WE DID IN THE WAR

JENNIE WALTERS

BLOODHOUND
— BOOKS —

Print ISBN: 978-1-916978-59-1

For my mother, who lived through these times, and in memory of my late father-in-law, Moss Walters, who was fighting with Allied troops to liberate France during the doodlebug summer of 1944.

PROLOGUE

High Wycombe, November 1952

I 've found her at last: my partner in crime. It's taken eight years but finally I've tracked her down. She's standing with her back to me, looking out of the window. Her cardigan's slung around her shoulders and she holds a cigarette aloft, one hand cupping her elbow and a thin plume of smoke spiralling up into the air. I close the door behind me, suddenly light-headed, and dig my fingernails into my palms.

She turns around, smiles and advances towards me with her hand outstretched. 'Hello. You must be–' She stops when she realises who it really is, the colour draining from her face. 'Good God,' she says, taking a step back.

'Heavens!' I put on a smile, pretending just in time to act surprised too. 'Claude! Can it really be you? What an extraordinary coincidence.'

She stands there, staring at me, dumbfounded. At least I have the chance to take a good look at her, see how she's changed in the time we've been apart. She's become – well, dowdy, that's the only word for it. Her face has filled out, her hair has been tightly and unflatteringly permed, and she's wearing a lumpy tweed skirt and sludge-coloured twinset with pearls – of course. Pearls are part of the uniform, although I sold mine long ago and haven't the heart or the money to replace them. I used to think she could wear anything and look marvellous but now all that panache has gone. Torn between disappointment and relief, I wonder for a moment how this unremarkable figure can have lived inside my head for so long. Then I catch in her eyes a glimpse of the glorious creature she once was and remember what she did to me, and I'm glad she looks a frump, glad I'm perfectly made up and wearing a particularly smart costume in black-and-white houndstooth check, glad she looks afraid.

'You'll never be pretty but you can try to be chic,' she said to me once, and I've taken her words to heart.

'You look well,' I say, since that's the sort of remark people generally make in these situations.

She doesn't return the compliment, although I deserve it more than she does. Instead she says, 'I wondered whether I'd ever see you again,' and gives an odd little smile, her eyes rather glassy and strange. Her accent is more cultivated than it used to be and I wonder whether she's putting it on for my benefit, or whether this is how she talks nowadays.

We don't seem to be getting very far. I prop my briefcase against a chair and push up my sleeves in a businesslike fashion so that my bracelets jangle. 'Well, you have a beautiful home. Have you decided which rooms you'd like to refurbish?'

I usually say something similar to clients but in this case it happens to be true. Her house is charming: a large Edwardian villa with high ceilings and tall, arched windows filling the rooms with light. The garden's lovely, too, from what I can see through the window, with stone steps from the terrace leading down to a sweeping lawn and a parterre formed of clipped box hedges.

She laughs uncertainly. 'Do you seriously think we're going to sit down and discuss soft furnishings?'

'Why not? The company offered a free design consultation – you might as well have it.'

She stubs out her cigarette, walks over to the sideboard and pours herself a whisky from a cut-glass decanter. Pressing the glass against her cheek for a moment, she says, 'So you work at Berridges? That's quite a step up.'

'I'd say we've both done rather well for ourselves. Clever old you, marrying into money.' I won't be patronised by anyone, least of all her. She hasn't even had the decency to offer me a drink.

She flushes. 'This is all rather awkward. I'd like you to leave, if you don't mind. Obviously, I shan't be asking you to do any work in my home.'

She's becoming more sure of herself but I don't appreciate being dismissed like an unsatisfactory servant. 'Don't you think we should talk?'

'No, I do not.' She takes a mouthful of Scotch, clutching the glass so tightly her knuckles turn white. 'What on earth is there to say?'

'I want to explain. You owe me that, at least.' I sit down in the chair beside my briefcase and light a cigarette to show her I'm not going anywhere. She'll have to account for herself, too, though I know better than to say so.

'I don't owe you anything,' she tells me.

'Really? Do you honestly imagine you'd be living in a house like this, were it not for me?' I wave a hand around the room to take in the cut-glass chandelier, the antique furniture, the surprisingly good paintings. 'I bet your husband has no idea what we got up to during the war.'

She opens her mouth and shuts it again, the colour rising in her cheeks. And then right on cue, the door opens and the man himself walks in. He's tall and distinguished in a sports jacket and flannels, greying at the temples; in his early forties, I'd guess, a good ten years older than Claude.

'Hello there,' he says, amiably enough. 'Sorry to interrupt.' And then to her, 'Stella, darling, have you seen my specs? Can't find the damn things anywhere.'

Without a word, she picks up a pair of spectacles from a side table and hands them to him.

'Thanks,' he says, glancing at the two of us. 'Everything all right?'

'Of course.' She smiles automatically, coming back to herself. 'Henry, this is...' She hesitates, no doubt wondering which name I go by these days.

I stand up, reaching out my hand. 'Margot Hall. How do you do?'

'From the interior designers,' she adds. 'Do you remember, I mentioned someone was coming this morning.'

'So you did. Henry Lycett,' he says, shaking my hand. 'Well, I'll leave you to your deliberations. Women's work, ha ha. Not sure I can add anything to the proceedings.' He helps himself to a sherry and wanders off, leaving the door ajar.

Alone again, we face each other. 'This isn't a coincidence, is it?' she says. 'Somehow you've managed to find me.'

'Well, no one can stay hidden for ever. You of all people should know that.'

'So what do you want?'

'I told you; I want to explain. Nothing more.'

She glances towards the open door. Someone is clattering pots and pans in the kitchen – the housekeeper who showed me in, probably – and her husband can't be far away. 'We can't talk here. Let's go out to the garden.'

Round one to me, I think.

1

HOW IT ALL BEGAN

London, July 1944

I shall always remember the first time I saw her, downstairs at La Petite Amie. I only have to close my eyes and I'm back in that hushed, subterranean room, listening to snatches of other people's conversation, punctuated by the creaking wheels of the dessert trolley with its solitary bowl of trifle and the occasional blare of a siren. She and her companion – a blustering colonel with red pips on his shoulder – were sitting at the table to my right and she was facing me, so it was hard not to catch her eye whenever I glanced around. The restaurant was only half full and I felt a little self-conscious, eating alone. Yet I wasn't the sort of person who attracted attention, not then, and that day I was as nondescript as usual in my tweed skirt, twinset and pearls. They were rather good pearls, but it always seemed to me they lost some of their lustre as soon as I fastened them around my neck. The most one could say was that I looked respectable, which was the impression I wanted to give. Anyway, taking too much trouble over one's appearance was frowned upon then; we were meant to have our minds on higher things, like making Woolton pie and winning the war.

This girl was my opposite in every respect. Somehow she managed to make her drab khaki uniform seem glamorous, as though it had been tailored to fit so perfectly. She had a full, old-fashioned sort of figure with an ample bust. Her hair was a vivid reddish-brown, the colour of a conker, scooped into an untidy knot with strands escaping over her collar, and she had a freckled, tawny complexion with lively hazel eyes. She threw her hands about when she spoke – in a piercing, rather affected voice – and her face was extravagantly mobile. Anyone could tell what she was thinking. She was a few years younger than me, I guessed. In her mid-twenties, maybe? She was probably his driver. In other circumstances, I might have amused myself by making up a story about this odd couple embarking on an affair, but I was too distracted that day to let my imagination run riot.

The colonel had a fat, bristly neck that bulged over his collar, and he slurped up his soup like a pig at the trough. He was making a great performance out of eating, breaking a roll into pieces and pushing them around the bowl with his spoon like a tiny bread flotilla while he held forth on various topics. He was declaiming about morale among the other ranks when this girl winked at me over his lowered head, then rolled her eyes with such a wicked expression that I snorted with laughter and had to snatch up a napkin to cover my mouth. My pretend coughing fit soon turned into a real one, which made the colonel turn to glare at me. I daren't look their way again and spent the next ten minutes turning over the empty pages of my engagement diary in an effort to compose myself.

I ordered a glass of red wine from the waiter when he brought my pâté. Under the navy cardigan, my heart was beating fast. It had taken some courage and careful preparation to come to London in that doodlebug summer of 1944, when the Germans were blowing the city to pieces. We were only meant to travel if our journey was strictly necessary, although the trains were already much less crowded than they had been in the spring, when the whole country seemed to have been on the move. Now that our troops were beating back the enemy in France, those petty restrictions were easing a little so I'd taken an uncharacteristic risk and booked my ticket. The solicitor's letter had requested my presence in person and frankly, any chance of a break from the utter dreariness of my life at the time was worth seizing. I debated for ages over what excuse to make at the farm; in the end, I muttered something about having to see a specialist in London, blushing so furiously that the manager must have assumed it was something to do with women's problems. He let me have the day off, grudgingly, on condition that I did the morning's milking first. I'd been in the Land Army for a couple of years by then, up at dawn to herd the cows and home after a long day's work to give Mother her supper and help her to bed, and a week each summer was the only holiday I'd taken.

I told Mother I'd been summoned to the city on Land Army business, and that Ellen would stay to serve her supper in case I was late home. I could tell what she thought about my outing from the way she stood in the kitchen doorway the night before, leaning on her walking frame to glare at me while I laid up the lunch tray: bread and margarine with the crusts cut off, a slice of cheese and a hard-boiled egg. (Yes, a shell egg! I'd been hoarding it for days.) She clearly didn't believe my story about a training lecture for tractor drivers, though of course she didn't say a word. The nurse had said her speech might improve with practice but she hadn't tried to talk since the stroke. She used to write me shaky notes instead: *Fetch commode. Shut window. Leg hurts.* That sort of thing.

I cycled frantically to the farm at first light the next morning, banged my way through the chores, then hurtled back home again to throw off my breeches, scrub the dirt from under my fingernails and spray myself with cologne to disguise the tang of manure before setting off again for the railway station. I smoked and paced along the platform, looking out across the sodden fields while my hair turned to frizz under my hat, expecting Ellen or a policeman to appear at any moment and summon me home. The summer had been miserable so far and I couldn't bear to think about harvest, which would be late and unrewarding. Finally the train arrived to carry me away, and my heart leapt as I climbed aboard. Escape at last!

I sat in a state of nervous excitement as we left the countryside behind and rattled towards London but the closer we got to the city, the more depressing the landscape became. Tarpaulins flapped over roofs and children played in a wasteland of ruined buildings, squeezing through glassless window frames and sliding down piles of rubble. Fireweed already covered older bomb-sites from the Blitz but newer scars where the doodlebugs must have fallen were raw and brutal. A woman pegging out her washing in a grimy backyard turned to watch the train thunder past, her face blank, and I shivered, wondering what I'd let myself in for.

Eventually it was time to brave the noise of Liverpool Street Station, where newspaper boys shouted the latest headlines beneath the shattered roof and soldiers with kit bags over their shoulders threaded their way through the crowds. I'd allowed plenty of time for the journey, but by the time I'd queued for a taxi and that taxi had made several detours to avoid burst water mains and cordoned-off streets, it looked like I might be late for my appointment. As the driver reversed around yet another corner, I could hear a hoarse rur-rur-rur, like a powerful but elderly motorbike struggling uphill.

'There 'e is!' The taxi driver pointed a finger. 'See the bugger go!'

A flying bomb was shooting across the sky at top speed, alarmingly low. I saw the whole length of it: the torpedo-shaped body, the square, stubby wings in the shape of a cross and the funnel on top, with a wisp of smoke trailing out behind. It looked like a snarling dog with its ears laid back. People called them doodlebugs to lessen the horror but there was no disguising they were fiendish things, launched by the Germans from sites in France.

'Shouldn't there be some sort of alert?' I asked the driver, clutching my handbag.

He looked at me in the rear-view mirror, grinning. 'They're too fast. By the time the siren's sounded in Vauxhall, the bomb'll be falling on Hampstead Heath.' He was one of the chatty types, unfortunately. 'It's all right, Miss. You only have to worry if the engine cuts out. That means there's no more fuel and the bomb's about to drop. When everything goes quiet, then it's time to run for cover.' He took out a handkerchief and blew his nose with one hand. When he'd finished mopping up, he added with grim satisfaction, 'They can come at any time. Day or night, full moon or cloud, don't make no difference. First thing in the morning's often bad, when everyone's leaving for work, and then again in the evening, when folk are coming home. Still, you'll get used to them soon enough. Staying long?'

'Just for the day.' I dug my fingernails into my palm, watching the buzzing insect speed on towards the horizon. A pilotless bomb was somehow more unnerving than a plane with a human being at the controls; it was so indiscriminately malevolent, like some devilish invention from the pages of science fiction. All of a sudden I wanted to be back in the countryside, where everything was ghastly in a different way but familiar, at least. I lit a cigarette and stared out of the window, wondering what lay ahead and trying not to build up my hopes in case of disappointment. The taxi dropped me a couple of streets away because the road ahead was blocked by a lorry offloading sandbags, but I was glad of a walk in the fresh air to clear my head. Perhaps I was imagining things but the solicitor's secretary seemed to look at me with some curiosity as I sat outside his office, powdering my nose with fingers that trembled a little. She brought me a cup of tea later, once he had told me what he had to say, with sugar in it although I hadn't asked. For the shock, I suppose. It was all so unexpected. The solicitor told me not to worry about remembering every detail; he'd written a letter which laid out the gist of the matter. I put it into my handbag to read later.

'Take some time to think it all over,' he said at last, shaking my hand to show me our meeting had finished. 'You don't need to take any action straight away.'

I emerged from his office in a daze and leaned against the wall to take stock. I'd been planning to lunch in the nearest Corner House but that seemed inappropriate now, and I decided instead to treat myself to a slap-up meal; a celebration, of sorts, and a chance to plan my next move. La Petite Amie was just around the corner in Sloane Square. My aunt had taken me there for my twenty-first birthday; we'd eaten grouse and game chips, and drunk champagne cocktails with a maraschino cherry at the bottom – like a gallstone, I thought, although of course I'd never actually seen one. It was a meal that had stayed in my mind and which I'd probably embroidered in my imagination, because the place seemed to have gone downhill since then. The carpet on the stairs leading down to the restaurant was threadbare and the dining room smelt of stale cooking fat. The waiter showed me to an unobtrusive table in the corner, suitable for a single woman; I glanced around at my fellow diners, wondering whether to take off my hat. That was when I first saw her, the girl with chestnut hair. She was an unlikely vision among a cast of nonentities: a sprinkling of military types in uniform, two dowdy middle-aged women eating in silence and an elderly man with a copy of *The Times* propped against his beer glass.

The war had taken the shine off everything. We were all tired out after five long years, longing for it to be over now the tide was turning in our direction. We'd been through so much: the inevitable build-up to war and the tense months when nothing seemed to be happening, then the humiliation of Dunkirk and the horror of the Blitz, the grinding years of blockades, losses at sea and shortages of everything at home – before, finally, the joy of D-Day that June, when our troops landed in France to send the Nazis packing. With the Americans on our side, we were getting somewhere; the Germans were abandoning their defences in Cherbourg and retreating inland. The rout had begun.

For me, however, the prospect of victory brought problems of its own, and the letter in my pocket complicated matters further. I drank the vinegary wine in some agitation, and the steak, which might have been horsemeat, stuck in my throat. Laying my knife and fork together, I snatched a look at the next table to find that the girl was staring at me. And then a most appalling sound came floating down the stairs.

'A nice little creature but ruined by the owners,' trumpeted the voice of Marjory Bly. 'They fed it crumpets from the table, would you believe.'

It couldn't be anyone else; no one had a booming delivery quite like Marjory's. But what on earth was she doing in London? She lived ten miles from us in the country and bred cocker spaniels. Horrified, I saw her stout shoes and muscular calves descend the stairs, and then the hem of her drooping skirt came into view, followed by the hideous tapestry bag she carried everywhere, stuffed with newspapers and dog treats. This was an awful coincidence. If Mrs Bly saw me dining alone, Mother would get to hear of it and I'd be in deep trouble. I stood up, panicking, grabbed my handbag and stumbled towards the back of the restaurant, bumping into tables as I passed. Putting my hand on the door that led to the Ladies' cloakroom, I became aware of someone at my shoulder. It was her, the girl with the glorious hair, so close behind she was almost treading on my heels.

Flattening myself against the wall, I held open the door for her and said in a strangled voice, 'After you, Claude': one of the ridiculous catchphrases from that show on the wireless everyone listened to. What on earth had possessed me?

But she only laughed and stood back herself, replying with the stock answer, 'No, after *you*, Cecil.'

I stumbled through, my hands clammy with perspiration, and headed down the passage. She followed me through to the facilities: two lavatory stalls, side by side, and a small room beyond with a washbasin and mirror above.

'After you, Cecil,' she repeated with a grin, nodding her head towards one of the stalls.

I didn't need to go, and the thought of performing in front of an audience was unimaginable. Why was she stalking me? Clutching my handbag, I said stiffly, 'Actually, I only came out here for a breath of air. Don't let me stop you though. I can wait outside until you've finished.' That would show her how to behave.

She laughed – rather coarsely, I thought – throwing back her head. 'Don't worry, no room for finer feelings in the forces. There's nothing I won't do in public. Well, very little anyway. But I don't want to use the lav either.'

'Then why did you come out here?'

'To see if you were all right. And to get away from Colonel

Blimp.' She brought a packet of cigarettes out from her pocket. 'Fancy a smoke?'

I hesitated. Looking back, this was a defining moment, although of course I didn't realise it at the time. If I'd gone back into the restaurant and made up some story for Mrs Bly, who knows how my life would have turned out? It wasn't like me to accept a stranger's invitation, but something in the frankness and warmth of her expression made me lay down my handbag, take a cigarette and light it from the match she had struck. She must have sensed I needed help, and I was desperate enough to accept it. Or maybe she thought nothing of the sort; maybe she was merely bored and wanted some distraction. I shall never know, and I don't suppose it matters now.

'Mind if I take the seat?' She sat down heavily on the one folding chair, loosened her belt and sighed in relief. 'That's better. So come on, spill the beans. What made you rush out of the room like a scalded cat?'

'Because somebody I knew was coming down the stairs.' That truthful answer was out of character, too, but I didn't feel like myself just then. I was unbalanced by the strangeness and intensity of it all: the danger, the opportunity, Marjory Bly appearing like one of the Fates, and now this girl taking an interest in me. She was glamorous, and glamorous people don't usually bother with me. They certainly didn't then, at any rate.

She narrowed her eyes through the smoke. 'And you don't want to be seen, even though you're all on your tod?'

I glanced towards the window and then the door, wondering what to do next. 'Planning your escape route?' she asked.

'Don't be ridiculous.' I'd had enough of these intrusive questions and wanted to be alone so I could think without distractions. A doodlebug was droning in the distance, too, apparently heading in our direction.

She cocked an ear. 'I've done a recce of this place already. Just as well. Sounds like we might need to make a run for it.'

The grating roar was growing louder by the second and suddenly so frighteningly close that the taxi driver's advice wasn't enough to reassure me. My heart pounded, my stomach lurched – and then abruptly the engine cut out, and all I could hear was a sudden, terrible silence.

'Time to go.' Tossing her cigarette in the sink, the girl grabbed my arm and pulled me after her, out of the room and down the corridor. At first I was too astonished to protest, and she ignored my feeble objections when I found the breath to make them. A waiter hurried past in the other direction, turning back to glance at us before rushing on. We ran in awkward tandem to a door halfway along the passage; without loosening her hold on my elbow, she shot back the bolt and dragged me with her, up the area steps and out on to the street through a blue-painted gate at the top.

'Wait!' I cried, twisting out of her grip. 'My handbag!' That was why I felt so naked: I'd left it lying by the cloakroom sink.

She was looking up at the sky and didn't reply. I only realised then how dark the day had become, as though dusk were falling in early afternoon, and followed her gaze. The bulk of a doodlebug hung over our heads, like a huge mechanical hawk with a mouse in its sights.

'Run!' she screamed, and set off, not waiting to see whether I'd follow.

So I ran, the breath sobbing in my chest. She must have been mad. How could we outrun a flying bomb? Why were we skittering about in the open like beads of water on a hotplate? I hated her now, more than I'd ever hated anyone. More than Hitler. More than Mother, even. But I followed her all the same, because I couldn't think what else to do. I had no idea where we were heading or how far we'd gone; we raced around one corner, and then another, for all the good it would do. The bomb must have been falling although I daren't look back to see. The girl was outpacing me, already yards ahead, and despite my loathing of her, I dreaded being left behind.

Yet suddenly a voice called out and arms were reaching from a doorway. A woman was sheltering there, a stranger who pulled me in and pushed me into a corner of the porch. She was wearing some sort of shiny blouse and smelt of April Violets. As we clung together, braced for the explosion, I focused on her hands with their varnished nails, and the crocodile-skin handbag with a cherry-bobble clasp that hung from her wrist. But where was the mad girl, Claude? I lifted my head to see her standing in the middle of the road, gazing upward with her hair dropping back, her hands on her hips. Ten paces or so away, which seemed to take for ever. Leaving the shelter of the porch, I lunged forward, grabbed her around the waist and half dragged, half pushed her towards a shape on the opposite pavement that turned out to be a motorcar. She was mad but I didn't want to see her killed in front of me.

We collapsed in a heap behind the car, and I'd just opened my mouth to yell when the breath was sucked out of my body – in fact, all the air seemed to have been sucked out of the world. The car and the road with its tall buildings on either side rushed together in a jumbled kaleidoscope and then whirled away. The next second I was flying too, swept off my feet, my thoughts blasted into fragments that were scattered on the roaring wind. Missiles were hurled at me: lumps of sharp-edged stone, rough bricks, slicing shards of glass, jagged spears of wood. My eyeballs were being wrenched from their sockets, muscle and sinew torn from my bones. I couldn't hold on any longer, and discovered the exhilaration of letting go.

2

AFTER THE EXPLOSION

London, July 1944

Time must have passed, though it was impossible to tell whether seconds or minutes or hours had gone by. I became aware of lying on my back with something digging painfully under my shoulder blade. Silence rang in my ears, and I could taste the iron tang of blood at the back of my throat. I felt extraordinarily calm. If this was dying, it wasn't so bad. Shifting about to find a more comfortable position, I opened gritty eyelids to look up at a sky that was streaked with rust. The air was thick with smoke and an acrid, rotten stench I would come to know as that of explosives. Turning my head, I caught sight of my left hand; filthy, fingernails broken and rimmed with blood. Around me lay a strange landscape, a dried-up riverbed with banks of brick and stone. The earth billowed, rose and fell, and everything was topsy turvy. An iron bath surfed the debris and a car lay on its roof like an upturned beetle.

After some effort, I managed to sit up. My mouth and nostrils were clogged with dirt and I was wracked by coughing, yet now a wave of euphoria washed over me. I was alive! Sitting on the ground in my tweed skirt, covered in plaster dust, my stockings hanging in shreds round my knees. I still had my hat on, which struck me as extraordinarily funny. Once I started to laugh, I couldn't stop, and soon the tears were running down my cheeks, washing the grit out of my stinging eyes. Do your worst, Hitler! You might have got the car and the bath but you haven't got me.

At last I staggered to my feet. Water was gushing from a broken pipe a few feet away so I rinsed my mouth, bathed my face and looked around. Apart from the car, I couldn't see a single familiar landmark. The boundary between the pavement and the road had gone, leaving me adrift in a sea of rubble. White stucco houses stood on the far shore but there was no sign of life in any of them; I was alone in this strange, silent world. Pieces of metal littered the ground, melted into strange contorted shapes and still warm, I discovered after treading on one. My left shoe was missing and when I put my foot on the ground, the pain made me gasp. Supporting myself with the help of an iron railing, I set about searching for my shoe, poking gingerly among the shattered stone and glass. My spear sank into something soft and messy, laid out on a plank as if presented for my inspection. Bending down to investigate, I found myself staring at a human torso – or rather, part of it. Flesh had been ripped apart and yards of intestines were tumbling out: pale, damp and stinking of rotten meat. There was also an unattached shoulder, and a floppity arm trailing down, with a hand on the end of it that had varnished fingernails.

I turned away and was violently ill, I'm ashamed to say, heaving and retching until my stomach had emptied. Afterwards I felt better: clear and light-headed. I carried on looking for my shoe and amazingly enough, eventually I found it. Yet the heel was broken and anyway, walking seemed pointless. Where was there to go? I sat down on a heap of bricks and waited for something to happen, crossing my arms over my stomach and pondering the miracle of the human body, that could have such a quantity of guts packed so neatly inside it. Perhaps it had all been a dream: my jaunt to London, and then what the solicitor had told me, and now this. A dream that had turned into a nightmare. And then across the wasteland, I saw another figure standing in the ruins. I recognised her instantly, although she was a living statue in the same grey dust that coated me.

'Diddle, diddle, dumpling, my son John,' I sang to myself, remembering the rhyme about the little boy with one shoe off and one shoe on – or maybe I just thought it – picking my way over the rubble towards her.

I tried to call as I approached, but only a feeble croak emerged from my mouth. She turned to look at me, her eyes wide and blank in a face that was smeared with dirt, said something I couldn't catch in a tiny faraway voice, flung her arms around my neck and burst into tears.

'There, there.' I patted her awkwardly on the back, feeling in my pocket for a handkerchief. 'No need to be upset.' Or at least, that was what I meant to say, although I'm not sure any words came out. My head was vibrating like a gong that had recently been struck.

Eventually I sat her down on a heap of rubble and settled myself beside her with an arm around her shoulder. She was clutching a handbag on her lap that looked strangely familiar: imitation crocodile skin with a silver cherry-bobble clasp. I stared as she opened it and took out a packet of cigarettes and a lighter.

'Where did you get that?' I asked, hearing my voice for the first time.

'I found it over there.' She nodded her head somewhere into the distance. 'No one would grudge us a ciggy, would they?'

I cleared my throat. 'She's dead, the woman who owns that handbag.'

Claude gave a small scream and dropped the cigarettes and lighter as though they were burning. 'Oh my God,' she cried, before bursting into tears again and covering her mouth with both filthy hands.

'Enough of that,' I said, gently but firmly. 'Pull yourself together and stop making a fuss. We're lucky to be alive.'

I picked up the cigarettes, lit one and passed it to her. Seeing someone else going to pieces made me marvellously brave and I could still feel the warmth of her arms around my neck. We were showing our true selves to each other, as though we had been friends for years.

She took a few shallow puffs on the cigarette until her breathing calmed and only the occasional hiccupy sob escaped. Her hair was stiff with plaster dust and sparkling with tiny splinters of glass; blood trickled down her neck from a shallow cut beside her ear.

'So what do we do now?' she said at last, wiping her nose on the back of her hand.

'Somebody will come soon,' I said, looking over the blasted rocky heath with more assurance than I felt. Bells were ringing in the distance as the continuous blare of the All Clear siren died away. And then as if I had summoned her, a figure in the green uniform of the Women's Voluntary Service appeared in the distance, manoeuvring a bicycle.

Claude groaned. 'Really? That's all we need.'

'Well, we need something,' I replied tartly. Members of the WVS were inclined to be bossy, but I was relieved to see a cheerful face and let the shrill tones of the Home Counties pierce the fog in my brain.

'Now what are you two doing here?' the woman asked, leaning her bicycle against a shattered wall.

'Waiting for a bus.' Claude sounded like a sulky schoolgirl.

'I shall ignore that remark.' WVS Lady stood with her hands on her hips, inspecting us. 'Can you walk?'

'I've hurt my ankle,' I said, proud of the matter-of-fact tone of my voice. 'I think it's sprained rather than broken.'

'Jolly good.' She produced a bandage from the first aid case in her bicycle basket and knelt with some difficulty to strap it tight. I heard various reassuring phrases: 'better in a jiffy', 'nice cup of tea', 'wash and brush up'. I tried to catch Claude's eye but she wouldn't look at me.

'Come along then,' said WVS Lady, struggling to her feet when she'd finished her ministrations and picking up her bicycle.

'Where are we going?' I asked, as though it made any difference.

'To the relief centre,' she replied. 'It's not far, and they'll soon sort you out.' She smiled encouragingly. 'We're getting rather good at this sort of thing by now.'

We trailed behind her, my broken shoe clacking with every step. Several small fires were burning, and we had to skirt a fallen telegraph pole, festooned with cables. 'Careful,' warned WVS Lady. 'They might not have turned off the electricity yet.' A van crunched past over the rubble, and in the next road we saw an ambulance with its bell ringing, and now various people in uniform passed by: wardens, policemen, Civil Defence volunteers. None of them had any time for us.

The relief centre was indeed not far, only a couple of streets away: a church hall, laid out with various screens, folding chairs, and desks with official-looking people sitting behind them. I also noticed a public telephone. Claude and I were taken first to the cloakroom, where we queued to wash off as much of the dirt from our hands and faces as we could, and attempted to tidy our hair with an unsavoury communal brush. After that, we were directed to the refreshment table, where we queued again for mugs of sugary tea and a corned beef sandwich each, and sat on folding chairs to consume them. We had been stripped of almost everything. I had no handbag, coat, money, identity card or keys – only the filthy clothes on my back and, thank heavens, my hat and my pearls. I put a hand to my throat, feeling their warmth and my pulse beating beneath them.

A baby screamed from the depths of its pram but there was surprisingly little noise apart from that; people waited patiently in line, still dazed. More WVS members were distributing forms, pens and clipboards, and an official at the head of the longest queue was handing over money from a cash box in return. I pointed this out to Claude. 'See? If we give our names and addresses, they'll probably lend us enough money to get home. Or wherever you need to go.'

I glanced at her filthy uniform and then down at myself. My legs were bruised and bare, my skirt was streaked with dirt and a flap had been torn from my jumper, revealing my liberty bodice underneath. I folded my arms across my chest. Fragments of the day were coming back to me in a rush and I swallowed, sick with apprehension. How could I take the train home in this state? I daren't consider the reception I'd get from Mother. Somehow the fact she couldn't speak properly only made her more alarming; imagining all the vile thoughts running through her head was worse than if she'd actually said them out loud.

'I'm beginning to feel a bit better, actually.' Claude licked her fingers and opened the handbag. 'Shall we have another ciggie? I'm sure that poor woman wouldn't mind.'

'We ought to turn in her bag, I suppose,' I said.

We both looked at it, then Claude took out the pack of cigarettes and offered me one. 'There's not much inside apart from these. Ration book, identity card, house keys, purse with a couple of pounds in it.' She took out the identity card and flipped it open. 'Mary Hale, that's her name, and she lived in W1. Piccadilly, maybe. She might have been one of those Piccadilly Commandos. Did she look like a tart?'

'I didn't see her face.' I only remembered her arms reaching out. Mary Hale: the woman who had varnished her fingernails so carefully, who had tried to shelter me in the doorway and been killed seconds later.

'And you're sure she's dead?'

I nodded. 'No doubt about it.'

Claude blew out a plume of smoke, narrowing her eyes. 'The thing is, Cecil, I'm not keen on giving anyone my name.'

'Why ever not?'

'Because if the powers-that-be find out I was in that restaurant, I'll be in even more trouble than I am already. The chap I was with will wriggle out of it but they'll throw the book at me.'

'So what will you do now?' I asked.

'Hang around London for a day or so,' she replied airily. 'See the sights, have a few drinks, find a shelter to sleep in.' She patted the handbag. 'Mary Hale won't mind, I'm sure.'

'But won't people be looking for you? What will you tell them when you get back to barracks, or wherever it is you were heading?'

'I'll tell them we got caught up in a raid and I was in shock, couldn't remember who I was or what I was meant to be doing. It's almost true.' She stretched out her hands. 'Look at the state of my fingernails! I might easily have been concussed.' She glanced at me. 'Don't look so disapproving. Do you fancy joining me?'

'Oh, I couldn't possibly.' But a voice inside my head asked, why not? And I was flattered she'd asked.

'Suit yourself.' She flicked a barrel of ash on to the floor.

'Thanks for inviting me though,' I added, not wanting to sound rude.

'One thing we might do is get some new clothes.' She nodded towards the trestle tables in one corner of the room that were heaped with clothing. 'That shouldn't cause too much of a fuss, so long as we're properly grateful.'

Jumpers, underwear, scarves and hats had been sorted into heaps, while frocks, skirts, suits and coats hung from portable wardrobe rails along the wall, with a sad pile of abandoned shoes underneath. A smell of mothballs and damp wool rose up, as though an elderly aunt had opened her arms to embrace us.

'Those are the items that have been washed and cleared for distribution,' said another WVS helper in charge, pointing to the nearest rail. 'You'll have to go through them yourselves. I'm coping single-handedly at the moment and run off my feet. One garment each, or possibly a two-piece if you can't find anything else. And kindly don't make a mess. It's time for my tea break but I'll be back to check up on you in ten minutes or so.'

With that, she left us alone. Claude rattled hangers along the rail, pulled out a duffel coat with the toggles cut off and made a face. 'Hardly the latest collection from Dior, is it?'

'Well, beggars can't be choosers,' I said. 'And anything's better than what I'm wearing now.'

'That's not saying much.' She grinned, though, and I couldn't take offence. Gingerly, I started at the other end of the rail, wondering where these clothes had come from and if the people who had worn them were dead. I didn't hold out much hope for the ladies' shoes – my feet are on the large side – but stumbled across a pair of boy's plimsolls in good condition that would have to do.

'Now this is more promising.' I turned to see Claude digging into a tea chest, flinging out underwear in a rainbow of colours.

'You can't do that! We're only meant to choose from the rail.'

'The old bat probably wants pick of the best things for herself. Look at these!' She waved a pair of camiknickers at me, then stretched the waistband. 'Heavens, elastic!'

'But you don't even know if they're clean.'

She buried her nose in them. 'Yes, I do. Sunlight Soap. These are respectable drawers from a good home; we can't let Miss Nutcracker get her claws on them.' Glancing about, she secreted a couple of pairs in the handbag, then tossed one to me.

Had it come to this? I thought, inspecting it gingerly. Yet I was currently wearing a pair of cut-down pyjama bottoms and the thought of decent underwear was certainly appealing. I tucked the knickers under my jumper, having nowhere else to put them, and turned back to the clothes rail, wondering whether I'd find anything to fit. I was fairly hefty in those days, despite rationing. Farm work gave me a healthy appetite and I'd been living off a diet of potatoes and porridge, with bread and butter on the side and the occasional jam roly poly to follow.

'Here, this might suit you.' Claude tossed over an armful of creased green fabric. 'Why don't you try it on?'

A screen had been put up in the corner of the clothing area with, I discovered, a full-length mirror propped against the wall. I stood behind the screen with the dress in my arms, staring at the stranger reflected back at me. Instead of being shocked by my wild hair and grimy face, I felt liberated, as though granted permission to step outside myself. Wearing somebody else's clothes seemed appropriate and actually, the frock wasn't so bad once it was on. At least it fitted me. It had long sleeves gathered at the cuff and shirring at each shoulder, and the full skirt flared out to mid-calf: too long to be fashionable, but pleasantly bohemian. I could picture myself lying in this dress on a chaise longue, discussing poetry. Or perhaps a sofa would have been safer, given the size I was then.

Claude appeared behind me. 'Not bad.' She pursed her lips, adjusting the shoulders of the dress so its V-neck revealed more of my bosom. I pulled them back to their original position, but she slapped my fingers away. 'Don't you want to look nice? You have a wonderful bust. Why not make the most of it? Men love that sort of thing, or so I'm told.' She found the belt and knotted it tightly at my waist. 'That's better. Shoulders back, chin up and chest out.'

I stood up tall. *All puffed up like a pouter pigeon*, is what Mother would have been thinking. *And the frock's far too fancy for every day.*

'That's you dealt with,' Claude said. 'Now budge up. I want to see if this'll do for me.' She held up a striped shirtwaister that I immediately coveted.

'Of course. Sorry.' I bundled my torn jumper and skirt into a ball, put on my cardigan over the frock and gave up the changing corner to her.

Leafing through a pile of scarves outside, I couldn't help overhearing ominous noises from behind the screen. She seemed to be having quite a battle: heavy breathing culminated in the sound of fabric tearing.

'Do you need a hand?' I asked.

'It's all right!' came her muffled voice. 'I can manage.'

The screen wobbled alarmingly. I put my head around it to see her thrashing about in the frock, stuck over her head and shoulders like a stripy straitjacket while she fumbled for the sleeves. The laughter died in my throat though, when I glimpsed her body. I could only stand there, staring at the swell of her pale, taut stomach.

At last she managed to free herself and saw me looking. Neither of us spoke for a few seconds. She wasn't wearing a wedding ring and her expression – half defiant, half ashamed – confirmed the awful truth.

'So now you know.' She held the frock against her chest as we contemplated each other. 'Well? Am I in for a lecture, or are you the silent disapproving type? Don't worry, it's not catching.'

At first I couldn't think how to react. The ultimate disgrace, dangled before us all as a terrible warning, and it had happened to her. How could she have ended up in such a mess? Mill girls got themselves into trouble, according to Mother, and although Claude might have been NQOCD, as my parents would have said with a gentle smile (Not Quite Our Class, Dear), she certainly wasn't one of those.

'Poor you,' I said, finding my voice eventually. 'What a pickle.'

'Don't pity me, for God's sake,' she muttered. 'That's even worse.'

'Why don't you wait here while I look for something with more room for growth,' I said, retreating.

I needed time to absorb this extraordinary fact, to rearrange my face in a neutral expression before we spoke again. Actually, I found myself surprised rather than shocked. Sex hung in the air like vapour during the war; even someone leading a life as sheltered as mine couldn't ignore the number of used condoms littering the ground, or the furtive groans and gasps from doorways under cover of the blackout. I'd have thought a girl like Claude would have had the sense to take precautions but, then again, what did I know about lust? Clattering through the hangers, I came across a loose blue dress splashed with yellow sunflowers that looked just the ticket and passed it to her over the screen. At least she could get it over her stomach and the cut was practical, if not flattering.

'What a sight.' She held out the full skirt. 'I feel like a barrage balloon.'

'Well, at least you don't look—'

'Like I'm expecting.' She finished the sentence for me. 'No, only fat and frumpy. So I suppose things could be worse.'

A pang of sympathy ran through me. She seemed so alone and vulnerable; I wanted to look after her and show her that I was still on her side, whatever mistakes she might have made. 'The Gorgon's still not back from her break,' I said. 'Let me see if there's anything else that might come in handy.'

I found a bolero jacket and even a decent brassiere instead of the knitted affair she was wearing, and brought them back in triumph.

'Thanks,' she said, almost shyly. 'You are being decent.'

And my heart swelled. I didn't care what she'd done or how many mistakes she'd made; I just wanted to help her. That's all I ever wanted, despite how things turned out.

'Actually, I don't have to get home right away,' I told her. 'Would you mind if I tagged along with you for a while?'

'That's the spirit.' She tucked her arm through mine. 'Well done, Cecil. We'll make a rebel of you yet.'

3

VICTORIA MANSIONS

London, July 1944

Of course, we should never have kept a handbag that didn't belong to us, let alone help ourselves to what was inside it. I would act differently now but I suppose we must have been in shock, as Claude had so flippantly made out. She suggested heading to the public baths for a proper clean up next, and I persuaded her to make a detour via La Petite Amie on the way, to see whether my own handbag had been found. We set off in our new outfits, retracing our steps along roads that seemed unfamiliar; I wouldn't have known which way to turn. My ankle was still sore but I was able to put my weight on it and managed to keep up with Claude – which was just as well, because she never looked around to see whether I was following. She didn't look frumpy in the slightest, striding through the shabby streets with her coppery hair swinging and the vivid dress billowing behind her. The street sweepers were out already, brushing glass from shattered windows into glistening heaps, and an old man leant on his broom to watch her pass. I wondered how she could be so jaunty and unafraid.

We turned the corner into a street that had been badly damaged, the trees blasted bare as winter, the pavements cratered, the tarmac littered with roof tiles and glass. A tin bath piled with rocks seemed vaguely familiar and I realised with a jolt that I'd come back to consciousness after the explosion in this very spot. I could hardly bear to look around, afraid of what I might see, but some sort of order had been restored. A mechanical digger with fearsome metal teeth was scooping rubble into a skip that was standing on the back of a lorry, and lines of men passed buckets of stone and brick from hand to hand, to be emptied into larger containers by the kerb. The upturned car had been removed too.

We walked on, fear clenching the pit of my stomach. Around the next corner, the sight of a blue-painted gate stopped me in my tracks; I remembered Claude flinging it open and dragging me with her into the road. Yet the building behind the blue gate was no longer there; we looked through thin air to houses across the street. Three storeys of red brick above La Petite Amie had disintegrated into a lake of rubble and roof spars that flowed into the street, crowned by the twisted wrought-iron portico that once surrounded its entrance. Cars parked by the kerb had been buried up to their wheel hubs in debris.

The road had been blocked at each end by a cordon of oil drums and rope, patrolled by a bored-looking policeman. Behind him towered the iron arm of a crane, crooked at the elbow, from which hung a grappling claw that dangled over the wreckage. The antiques shop to the left of the restaurant had merely had its windows blown out, but the ladies' couturier on the right, Madame Elise, had also been destroyed. What I first took to be bodies lying among the ruins turned out to be mannequins, their vacant eyes staring at the devastation, their painted lips in a rictus grin. A team of men were working on the heaps with picks and shovels, cigarettes hanging from their lips; wardens in tin helmets and policemen in uniform, several labourers and a man in pinstriped trousers with red braces, his shirtsleeves rolled up. An ambulance stood waiting on the corner with its doors open, and a crowd of passers-by had gathered around it to watch the proceedings.

We watched the scene in silence. The same thought must have been running through both our minds: if we hadn't run out of the restaurant and into the open, we'd have been buried under the rubble along with everyone else. It was the second time in one day that I'd cheated death. If Claude hadn't pulled me after her, I'd still have been skulking in the Ladies', hiding from Marjory Bly.

Marjory, with her sensible shoes and honking laugh... She had been kind to me when I was younger and recovering from a bout of glandular fever. Meeting me in the village one afternoon, she'd asked after my health and offered me five shillings a week to help exercise her dogs. 'That'll put the roses back in your cheeks,' she'd said, pinching one of them quite hard. She had meant well though. I shivered. It was easier to think of her having been killed outright than buried alive down there and in pain.

'Somehow I don't think your handbag is going to be top of anyone's list of priorities,' Claude said. 'We'd better go – they'll be bringing out the bodies soon. Let's sit by the river for a while and take stock.'

Beyond a line of trees at the end of a grid of streets, suddenly there was the great sweep of the Thames running past. A narrow wedge of garden lay below street level at the corner where Albert Bridge met the Embankment, with a flight of wooden steps leading down to the water. We settled ourselves on the steps about halfway down, out of sight of the road. The sun appeared for a brief moment, turning the river into a glittering sheet of silver. A narrowboat was gliding by, with a girl in slacks leaning against the wheelhouse, her arms crossed and her face held up to the light. Two sagging barrage balloons swayed high overhead, and a line of planes flew downriver like a skein of silver geese.

I sensed Claude watching me and turned to meet her eye. 'Why have you come to London at a time like this?' she asked abruptly.

Suddenly I wanted her to know who I was, and for her to take some account of me. I wasn't ready to tell her the whole story so merely said I was desperate for a taste of city life. Then before I could stop myself, I'd launched into the dreariness of my daily routine: working for the ridiculously named Mr Cheesman, who hated me because his farm was going under and he had no one else to blame, and because I was such a poor substitute for his two older sons who had both been killed, while the youngest, fourteen-year-old Norman, blushed whenever I spoke to him and stared down my shirt when I was cleaning out the stalls.

I told her pigs were clever but a cow could be vicious, so you had to keep one ear against her flank to sense when she was about to kick. How milking turned your fingers into ugly red sausages, cracked with chilblains in winter, and how the pain of swollen feet in damp wellingtons was enough to make you weep as you waded through pools of stinking manure. How you could never get the stench of pig muck out of your skin, no matter how hard you scrubbed, and how deadly the countryside was in winter, lanes squelching with mud and rain running down the back of your mackintosh. What torture it was to get out of a warm bed in what seemed like the middle of the night when you could see your breath in a cloud and your breeches had frozen stiff over the back of the chair, and what a struggle it was to stay cheerful when the only people sharing your day were Norman and his father and a couple of mournful Italian prisoners of war. How brutal you had to be, pulling rats out of the trap and finishing them off with a shovel, wringing the neck of a flapping, bloody chicken the fox couldn't be bothered to kill, tearing the guts out of a pheasant. The constant round of feeding, milking, cleaning, churning, digging, planting, weeding, harvesting, rearing, killing – on and on, day after back-breaking, tedious day, till you could simply drop in your tracks and let the wilderness grow back over your head.

'Blimey,' Claude said when I'd finished, 'I'm surprised you've stuck it so long. Don't you have any friends though? I thought Land Girls went around in a gang.'

'I'm on my own at the farm, mostly.' I wrapped the cardigan more tightly around me, already regretting having talked in such detail. 'Sometimes other girls come to help with the hedging and harvest but I don't stay at the hostel with them. I live at home so I can look after Mother.'

'What's the matter with her?'

'She had a stroke. I need to be there in case she falls out of bed or has an accident.'

'So you slave away all day on the farm and look after your mother at night? You are a good girl.' I sensed a note of contempt in her voice that made me flush.

'What were you doing in London then?' I asked, changing the subject. 'That man you were with, is he your boss?'

'My commanding officer? No, thank God. I only met him today. I was driving him back to barracks when he suggested a detour. I thought I could put up with him for the sake of a decent lunch – turns out I was wrong. Still, I wouldn't like to think of him dead.'

'What about your car?' I asked. 'Shouldn't you retrieve it?'

'I'm in no fit state to do that, remember? The army will send someone along to dig it out.'

Another doodlebug came speeding low across the horizon, with a Spitfire tagging close behind. According to *Picture Post*, clever pilots could flip a doodle off course with their aeroplane wing and send it spinning down to land harmlessly in a field somewhere. As we watched, the bomb exploded into a ball of flame with an almighty crash, followed two seconds later by the Spitfire. The aeroplane plummeted down, leaving a trail of black smoke against the sky. I jumped up, shading my eyes from the glare, then sat down again with a thump. So that was that, and hard luck to anyone underneath.

Claude clenched her fists. 'I'm so sick of this blasted war.'

'Shh.' I glanced around in case there was anyone in earshot.

'Well, aren't you? Being ordered about with no idea what's really going on, expected to grin and bear it no matter how awful things are, never having a moment's privacy. I've toed the line for the past five years, made do and mended, buttoned my lip, and where's it got me? Precisely nowhere.' She gave a bitter laugh. 'Still, I won't be in uniform for much longer. They'll chuck me out of the force once they realise I'm preggers.'

'And then what will you do?'

She shrugged.

I hesitated. 'Does the baby's father know what's happened? Might he do the decent thing?'

'He can't. He's dead, unfortunately.' She stood up, brushing the dirt off her frock. 'Well, this has turned into a morbid conversation.'

'We'll feel better after a bath,' I suggested, trying to jolly her along.

She paused for a moment at the top of the steps. 'Won't your mother be wondering where you are?'

I suppressed a shiver of disquiet. 'I told her I'd be late, and not to wait up.'

There was no point ringing our house to let Mother know I'd been delayed; she wouldn't answer the telephone and even if Ellen happened to be there, what would I say? The prospect of going home filled me with dread. From a distance, the smallness of my life lay revealed in all its petty indignities, the narrowness of its scope; as though I were looking at myself through the wrong end of a telescope.

'And she can manage without you?' Claude asked.

'She'll be all right. We have a housekeeper who can stay if necessary.'

'A housekeeper?' She smiled. 'Of course you do.'

I ignored the mocking note in Claude's voice but was cool with her as we sat waiting our turn at the municipal baths a little while later, having paid extra for the use of a towel and our own taps. Now I felt embarrassed about having spoken so openly. What could have come over me? Yet deep down, I knew the answer to that question: I wanted Claude on my side. Lying back in six inches of hot water with my injured ankle hooked over the side of the tub, I listened to her splashing about on the other side of the partition. She was singing – or rather, massacring – that old music-hall tune about dilly-dallying while following a van and not finding your way home.

The song seemed appropriate. I smiled and set about soaping myself, singing along with her under my breath.

* * *

'As a matter of fact,' I said to Claude when we were outside on the pavement, pink and clean and feeling a great deal better, 'I happen to know somewhere we might stay for the night: a flat belonging to friends of mine. They've asked me to keep an eye on it so I actually ought to drop by.'

'Really?' Her eyes were alight with curiosity. 'Cecil, you are a dark horse. Where is it?'

'Not far from here, I think. Off the King's Road, about halfway down.' I told her the address. 'But the trouble is, the keys are in my handbag and God only knows where that is.'

'Then we'll sweet-talk our way in. I bet one of the neighbours has a key, or there are bound to be wardens snooping about.'

I shook my head. 'We'll have to be discreet.'

'Why? If you have a good reason for being there?'

'Only to visit. Not to stay the night.'

'But surely your friends won't mind.' She put her arm through mine. 'Anyway, they don't have to know. Let's do a recce. The pubs will be open soon and if we can't get in, we'll have a few drinks and find somewhere else.'

* * *

Number 117, Victoria Mansions; that was the flat we were looking for, and a passing taxi driver told us exactly where to find it. I could vaguely picture its location from before the war but Chelsea looked very different now. The streets down which we walked had their fair share of sandbags, surface shelters, pig-swill bins and rubble, and then we would turn the next corner to find immaculate white villas lurking behind overgrown laurels, waiting for their owners to return from exile in the countryside and reclaim them.

Victoria Mansions was a tall building in red and pink brick that formed one side of a square. Prince of Wales Mansions, Hanover Mansions and Trafalgar Mansions made up the other three, with gardens in the middle that must have once been enclosed by railings. The place looked much shabbier than I remembered. The fanlights at each main entrance had been daubed over with black paint, and the brass door furniture was tarnished. Some of the windows had been boarded up but there were curtains hanging at others, and a ginger cat looked down on us from a high windowsill. Yet although dilapidated, each block was intact, which seemed odd now I was becoming used to gaps in a row of houses, or rooms laid open for anyone to see the pattern of the wallpaper. According to Ellen, bombs never fell in the same place twice so it was good luck to live in a bomb-damaged street.

Flat 117 was on the lower ground floor, halfway along Victoria Mansions. We pushed open the main door, which was unlocked, and walked down a scuffed corridor with a flight of steps at the end to reach it. There, though, we were defeated. The corridor lay dark and empty, its stale air undisturbed. A faded notice had been pinned to the door opposite: *The Vitmayer family no longer live at this address. Please return all mail to sender.*

'Why don't we see if there's a caretaker?' Claude suggested. 'He might have a spare key.'

But I daren't risk anyone asking awkward questions. 'Let's have another look from outside.'

At the front of the building, we peered through railings, which had somehow escaped the national cull, on to a shabby area belonging to the flat, where a rusty tin can lay under shattered glass, as though submerged in a frozen pond. The bay windows behind were shuttered from the inside. Next, we explored a narrow service lane at the rear of the flats where dustbins were put out for collection, but the wall was too high to see into any of the backyards, and it was impossible anyway to tell which gate would lead to 117. So we wandered around the square, past a rectangular Air Raid Precautions post at one corner, walled up by sandbags with wardens coming and going. I gazed up at the snaggle-toothed rows of chimney pots until I had a crick in my neck. Two wardens patrolled the pavement, stopping to chat to an elderly man leaning on a walking stick; a taxi drew up outside the building and a couple got out, disappearing inside before we could get a good look at them. Curtains were drawn back by an invisible hand from a window on the top floor.

'Do you live 'ere, Miss? Want your winders cleaned?' A child of about nine or ten had accosted us. Hard to tell if it was a boy or a girl; they had pale wispy hair, narrow eyes and spindly legs clad in long shorts, ending in a pair of sandals with the toes cut out from which grimy feet protruded. The urchin nodded in the direction of a man on the other side of the square who was propping a ladder against the wall of Hanover Mansions. 'My dad'll be free in 'alf an hour.'

I'd recoiled but Claude smiled pleasantly. 'Thanks for the offer, but no thanks. There is something you could do for us though. We've only gone and locked ourselves out of our flat. Don't suppose you might be able to find a way in?' She nodded in the direction of number 117. 'There's a window at the front and it's quite out of the way. We'll keep watch while you do the necessary.'

'I get the picture.' The child gave a ghastly, knowing wink. 'But it'll cost you half a crown, and one of you'll have to give me a hand.'

'A shilling at the most,' Claude said. 'And my friend will help you.'

'There should be a spare key on a ledge above the front door, on the inside,' I added. 'Bring it to us and you can have your money.'

'What's your name?' Claude asked the child, as we strolled along the pavement towards number 117 in a casual manner.

'Florence,' came the reply, with a look that dared us to laugh. 'But everyone calls me Floss. What's yours?'

I opened my mouth and then closed it again. Claude spoke for us both. 'She's Miss Cecil and I'm Miss Claude.'

Floss snickered unattractively, revealing rabbity yellow teeth that she covered with a self-conscious hand. A couple of American soldiers in white helmets with white belts walked by and I shrank back, dropping my eyes. 'Only Snowdrops,' she whispered reassuringly. 'Military police. Don't worry, they can't do nothing to us.'

Claude and I leaned against the railings outside number 117 while the girl vaulted over; when the coast was clear, Claude gave me a piggyback so I could follow with a little more dignity. I dropped down into the basement area, landing with a thud on a burst sandbag. Floss was already kicking through the glass and rubbish that had collected there. She picked up a child's canvas shoe with the upper rotted away and tucked it inside her shirt, meeting my eyes with her impassive stare. And who was I to judge her?

'Give us a leg up then,' she commanded, arming herself with a half brick.

I helped her climb on to the sill. It seems impossible now that I shouldn't have had some misgivings, yet I didn't feel guilty in the slightest. The crack of splintering wood only made my stomach lurch with excitement.

After you, Claude. No, after you, Cecil.

4

FIERCE TIMES

London, July 1944

C laude stood in the middle of the room, looking about. 'I take it they've not lived here for a while, these friends of yours?'

We'd had to force the front door open through a heap of post on the mat inside; a chunk of the hall ceiling lay in grey drifts of plaster which crunched underfoot, and a yawning rectangle where the cellar door should have been revealed steps leading down into the dark. The flat was long and narrow, stretching from the front of Victoria Mansions right to the back. We'd pressed on into the sitting room, where drawing the blackout curtains revealed the mummified corpse of a bird on a heap of soot in the fireplace. Motes of dust floated in the air and grimy cobwebs hung from every corner. Now the drama of getting inside was over, the enormity of us being there together descended on me. Our voices sounded unnaturally loud and I couldn't think of anything to say. We hardly knew each other, after all. Yet still, I was glad not to have come alone.

'It won't look so bad once we've tidied up,' I said, going in search of cleaning supplies.

The kitchen was a narrow galley, with a door at one end leading out to the yard where dustbins stood beside a tangle of rhododendron bushes. A shopping bag and an apron hung from a hook on the back of the larder door and, after further rummaging, I found a broom and dustpan and brush inside. A half-hearted collection of supplies had been assembled on the shelves – candles, a ball of string, a packet of tea, a few jars of fish paste and tins of corned beef, peaches, evaporated milk and butter beans – as though someone had begun to make preparations and depressed themselves too thoroughly to carry on. Most of the crockery lay smashed at the foot of the dresser; only three plates were salvageable, plus a soup bowl and a few cups missing their handles. I didn't come across anything too revolting, apart from cobwebs and a dead spider in the sink. A trickle of sludge coughed its way out of the taps, but when I'd turned the stopcock under the sink, I could fill a bucket and add some soap flakes.

'Why don't you tidy up the sitting room while I tackle the bathroom?' I said, handing Claude the broom.

She didn't take it. 'I'm not touching that bird. Sorry, but I absolutely can't.' She had turned rather pale.

'All right, we'll swap.' And I gave her the bucket and cloth instead.

'I don't see why we're bothering if we're only spending the night,' she said, accepting the cleaning things with some reluctance. 'Can't we go out now and clean up later? I'm starving.'

'We'll be too tired then. Come on, just a quick once-over. You'll thank me, I promise.'

She needed some chivvying but I made allowances, given her condition and the day we'd had. And despite her limitations, I was glad not to be dealing with the mess by myself.

Dusk was falling. As I dropped the dead crow in a neighbour's dustbin, I pictured Mother for a moment, drinking her sherry in the cup with a lid which she loathed, listening to Ellen banging about in the kitchen and devising some punishment for me on my return. I'd told her not to worry if I was delayed in London and, with the trains the way they were, I might well not be back till the next morning. That didn't go down well. She'd never liked me much and the fact I had some measure of freedom while she was confined to the house infuriated her. I was sure she wet the bed or spilt her tea on purpose – always at the worst time, just when I was about to leave for work or in the deepest sleep. We hadn't managed to keep a live-in housekeeper since the start of the war and Ellen, our daily, was constantly threatening to give in her notice. I didn't blame her.

Still, I couldn't waste my precious holiday from Mother by thinking about her. After I'd brushed the carpet, swept away cobwebs, folded dustsheets and plumped up cushions, I was in a better frame of mind. Claude was suspiciously quiet. Heading to the bathroom to investigate, I found her sitting in the downstairs lavatory with the door open – not using it, thank heavens, but staring at the photographs in tarnished frames that lined the walls. Babies wearing pin-tucked gowns sat in prams or were held up by servants; children posed awkwardly in starched pinafores, knickerbockers and long buttoned boots; young men in flannels and straw boaters loafed with their hands in pockets or elbows propped on pillars, studiously ignoring the sporting trophies arranged around them; middle-aged men stood behind the chairs of their lavishly-dressed wives or frowned into the sun under pith helmets, one foot resting on a slaughtered animal.

'Your friends can't be short of money,' she said. 'Are they spending the war in their country estate?'

'Don't be so vulgar,' I snapped before I could stop myself.

'All right,' she said mildly. 'Keep your hair on.'

I wondered then whether I'd made a mistake, bringing her to the flat, but it was too late now for regrets. We were both tired and hungry, I told myself, and would have to be patient with each other.

'Let's make up the beds,' I said, 'and leave the rest till tomorrow.'

'The rest' consisted of a study-cum-breakfast room with a desk in the window and a dining table in the centre, surrounded by Carver chairs with the horsehair padding from their seats scattered in clumps over the carpet, among drifts of ceiling plaster and mouse droppings. This was the room into which Floss had broken; we would need to board up the window and repair the shutter. A heavy oak sideboard leaned up against the wall; empty, except for a single pewter teaspoon and a set of table mats featuring hunting scenes. There were two bedrooms, one a decent size at the back of the flat beside the sitting room, and the other facing on to the street, much smaller, with bars on the windows.

'Shall we toss a coin for the best room?' Claude suggested.

'I don't think so.' There were limits to my forbearance. 'I always stay in the larger room when I come here. It's only for one night, after all.'

'Fair enough,' she said, after a pause.

We used the dustsheets as bedding with cushions in the place of pillows; Claude's room first, with its narrow single bed, and then mine. Footsteps paced up and down in the flat upstairs and somewhere outside, a blackbird was singing.

'Quiet, isn't it?' Claude said. 'At least until the doodles come.' She wandered about the room, pulling out the dressing-table drawers, picking out books from a stack on the windowsill, opening cupboard doors. I wanted to tell her to stop but it was only natural for her to be curious. So I held my tongue, although it took some effort.

'What's that?' She was looking at a suitcase on top of a built-in cupboard in the alcove.

'I've no idea.' And I really hadn't, never having noticed it before.

She dragged over the dressing-table stool and brought the case down to investigate – throwing it on to my bed and streaking the dustsheet with more grime. Inside were layers of exotic, old-fashioned clothes wrapped in yellowing cambric that she shook out and held up for inspection, one by one: shapeless evening gowns, silk scarves, a red fez hat, limply tangled white kid gloves, a velvet cloak with a floppy collar.

'Some more clothes to add to our extensive wardrobe.' She draped the cloak, dark and soft as moleskin, around my shoulders and fastened its diamanté buckle at my throat. 'There, very regal.'

I glanced at myself in the mirror. What did I look like then? There are no photographs to remind me. My face, I think, was a jumble of ill-assorted features – my nose too big, my eyes too small, my jaw too heavy, my cheeks too plump and pasty – my expression probably doubtful and suspicious. I was altogether unremarkable.

Claude stood at my shoulder. Catching her eye, I gave a rueful smile.

'It's your hair,' she said. 'That fringe does nothing for you. Sit here and I'll see what I can do.'

'Oh, don't bother,' I said hastily. I have an unsightly birthmark on the back of my neck and having my hair touched has always been an ordeal.

'It's no trouble.' She dragged the stool back in front of the dressing table and plonked me down on it, then fetched the comb from Mary Hale's handbag and set to work. I didn't want to look at my reflection so I contemplated my hands, lolling in my lap.

'You mustn't worry about that port wine stain,' she said a few minutes later, scooping up a hank of my hair. 'It makes you special. That's where you were injured in a previous life, or so my granny used to say. Might even have been how you died. Just imagine, you could have been a cave woman or a soldier in Roman times, whacked from behind. My sister had a birthmark like that on her arm.'

I asked whether she'd had it removed but Claude told me her sister was dead, in a tone which discouraged any further questions.

'There,' she said at last. 'What do you think?'

She'd given me a side parting and a sagging victory roll (I'd never got the hang of those), scooping up the rest of my hair with a shoelace so that it fell behind my ears. I turned my head this way and that. 'Goodness.'

'Don't you like it?'

'No, I do. It's just... I'm not sure whether I can carry it off. Don't you think it's a bit much?'

She sighed. 'Oh, Cecil. What are you so afraid of? If anyone tries to steal you for the white slave trade, I'll come to your rescue.'

I swivelled around on the stool to face her. 'Aren't you worried people will stare though?'

'Let them. We could be dead tomorrow. Might as well live a little in the meantime, don't you think? We have one night to do as we please – let's not waste it.'

And so I let myself be persuaded. Claude picked out a couple of gowns and went to her room to try them on; she came back to mine wearing a billowing sheath of golden silk, loosely belted at the waist, that reflected the light on to her face. Then she emptied Mary Hale's purse on to the bed and we counted out her money by torchlight: nineteen shillings and sixpence, all told.

'If we take six bob each for expenses tomorrow, we'll have seven and six to spend tonight. That should be enough, don't you think?' She passed me my share and put the rest back in the purse.

* * *

That evening we made our way down the King's Road through the blackout, following a white painted line at the edge of the kerb, crossed it and walked down to Chelsea Embankment to find a café Claude knew: The Green Parakeet. The waitress was old and the menu didn't seem especially appetising, but there was a cheerful hum of conversation and various artistic types could be seen taking the stairs to the first floor. I noticed Claude gazing after them but she seemed content to sit with me for the time being. She was looking very lovely, like a warm, ripe peach, and basked in the attention she was attracting. She drank stout and I had a gin and lime while we waited for our soup.

'I'm surprised you don't know this place,' she said. 'Aren't you in the habit of visiting these friends of yours?'

'They don't go out much.' I took a gulp of gin. 'Well, this is fun.'

A thump followed by shouts and a gust of laughter had floated down from the floor above. 'There seems to be a party going on upstairs,' she said. 'We could pop up there later.'

'I'm not really in the mood for a party,' I said carefully. We were an ill-matched pair, all things considered. Still, after that night we'd be parting company – and then what would I do? 'Got any plans for tomorrow?' I asked casually. 'I don't need to go home straight away. We could take a stroll along the riverbank, or see if there's a band playing in Hyde Park.'

She put her head on one side. 'I can't work you out. One minute you're playing the dutiful daughter, the next you're bunking off like a naughty schoolgirl. You've found out my secret – why don't you tell me yours? You never know, it might be a relief. Come on, we'll have another drink and share the last cigarette.'

Her beautiful eyes looked into mine with such unexpected kindness that I felt suddenly like weeping. I was very tired, and already a little drunk. 'All right,' I said. 'Actually, that flat doesn't belong to friends. It's mine.'

She spluttered on a lungful of smoke. 'What? How?'

I took the cigarette from her fingers and inhaled, to steady myself. 'My aunt left it to me. I had a meeting with the solicitor this morning' – was that really only a few hours ago? – 'and he read me her will and gave me the keys.'

'My God.' She took the cigarette back. 'You lucky cow.'

I winced.

'Well, you are,' she said, drawing back and folding her arms with the cigarette held aloft in one hand. 'What I wouldn't give for a place like that! Now all your troubles are over. You can tell that farmer to take a running jump and get some cushy job in the city when things have calmed down. These fly-bombs can't go on for much longer.'

I caught the waitress's eye and held up my glass. 'So the drinks are on you,' Claude said. 'We ought to be drinking champagne, if they have any.'

'I haven't got any money!' I protested. 'I might own a flat but that's the extent of it.'

'You will have, once you go home.' She stubbed out the cigarette. 'And you can start earning decent wages in London when the war's over.'

She made everything sound so easy. 'It's more complicated than that,' I told her.

'With your mother, you mean? I suppose you could move her up here. Make sure you get the best bedroom though.'

'She'd never live in London, not even after the war,' I said. 'She thinks it's a den of iniquity.'

Claude shrugged. 'Then she'll just have to let you leave and hire a companion instead. What's the name of that agency? Universal Aunts, or something. You can't give up your life to look after her.'

The truth was that Aunt Ivy's bequest, miraculous though it was, put me in a quandary. I'd had some vague idea of using the flat as a bolthole, a refuge to which I could disappear for a couple of days every now and then – perhaps for a longer spell, when the war was over – but I was beginning to realise that was just a pipe dream. Even if I managed to resign from the Land Army and find some part-time war work, Mother would find out about the flat somehow and there would be Repercussions. And how could I afford to keep the place running, what with rates, utility bills and maintenance costs to pay? I could try to rent it out but no one was keen to live in London while the bombing was going on, and there would have to be telephone calls and correspondence about management, which would give the game away. Besides, Ivy had left the flat to me; I didn't want a stranger living there. In the end, I supposed, I would have to sell her home, although I'd have to keep the money a secret so it couldn't be siphoned away. What a spineless, timid creature I was!

Our soup had arrived, Heinz tomato, out of a tin. Claude took one mouthful and laid down her spoon. 'You could have told me, you know. About the flat, I mean. There was no need to make up a story.'

Yet she was a virtual stranger. Still, I wasn't sorry to have confided in her now, to be sitting in this bright, lively place crowded with people talking and laughing, keeping the darkness at bay. The windows were criss-crossed with tape and I had spotted stairs leading down to a basement where we could shelter if necessary. Next to us, an American soldier and his sweetheart in a polka-dot frock held hands across the table. The girl wore a 'V' for Victory badge, gleaming like a bloody wound on her lapel. We were all doing the best we could.

Claude was talking. '...seriously, Cecil. The men will be coming back soon, what's left of them, and you won't catch a husband if you're stuck at home with Mother.'

I laughed and shook my head.

'Tell me about your aunt,' she went on. 'Were you close? What was her name?'

'Ivy. Miss Ivy Percival.' I brought her to mind: a tall, quiet woman with dark, deep-set eyes and grey hair that she wore in a plait coiled around her head. She was a wonderful needlewoman and taught me how to sew my own clothes, how to hand-smock and embroider elaborate patterns in satin- and chain-stitch. I'd stayed with her for a month after my father died, sleeping in that small bedroom with bars on the windows. We went for walks around the Serpentine in Hyde Park and had tea at Derry and Toms; she took me to a concert at the Royal Albert Hall and to see the sculpture and textile collections in the Victoria and Albert Museum. Architecture was another of her interests, and we visited several of the lovely Wren churches in London – including St Mildred's in the City, destroyed by a bomb in 1941. I should have paid more attention.

One evening we attended a spiritualist meeting in a church hall, where a woman in a black evening gown relayed messages from the dead to favoured members of the audience. My father didn't choose to communicate but that was hardly a surprise; we hadn't had much to say to each other when he was alive. Aunt Ivy was his sister. I remember her leaning forward, her bony fingers interlaced, the silk rose on her hat trembling with agitation. She wasn't demonstrative but she was determined to do her duty by me and we rubbed along well enough.

'I suppose we were close, in a way. But then again, she didn't have anyone else to leave the flat to, no husband or children.'

'Just as well, for your sake. Was she a lesbian?'

'I don't think so. She had a fiancé but he was killed in the last war and she never found anyone else. Her parents packed her off to India but she came back empty-handed. There weren't enough men to go around, I suppose.'

'Let that be a warning. Unless you're a lesbian, that is.' Claude smiled encouragingly. 'It's all right, I don't mind.'

'I'm not a lesbian, I'm just big-boned.' I got the giggles and she joined in, both of us laughing helplessly until our stomachs hurt.

'Oh, Cecil,' she said at last, wiping her eyes, 'you're a one-off, that's for sure.'

I took that to mean she thought I was special, rather than odd, and my heart sang.

* * *

We made our way back to Victoria Mansions by the light of Mary Hale's torch, keeping an ear out for the chugging of doodlebugs. It was a fairly quiet night, apart from the odd drone of an aeroplane.

'We ought to find somewhere to shelter if things get hairy,' Claude said, once we were safely inside the flat. 'The cellar, maybe?'

She took the torch and I followed her down the flight of steps – treading carefully because the door that had been blown off its hinges was jammed halfway down. Between us, we managed to heave it free and send it cartwheeling to the bottom. There were other hazards too: a low-hanging pipe with a bolt sticking out, exactly at head height, and precariously stacked tea chests full of crumpled newspaper. The place stank of mice and damp, and there were scutterings and rustlings in the darkness beyond our narrow beam of light. I blundered through cobweb veils that clung to my clothes, my hair, my lips, stumbled over mousetraps and stray lumps of coal, banged my shins on the corner of a trunk.

'There's nowhere to sit, let alone lie down,' Claude muttered. 'We'll have to manage under the dining-room table. Hang on, what's that?'

The torch beam had revealed a wine rack in the far corner of the cellar, with a few dusty bottles sticking out. Clutching the torch between her teeth, Claude scrambled over the piles of junk to reach it, returning in triumph with two bottles tucked under her arm. 'Ivy wouldn't mind, would she? We might as well have a drink before the bottles get blown to pieces – or we do.'

Somehow the threat seemed strangely unreal, despite everything we'd been through. The bombs were always going to fall on somebody else, I thought; goodness knows why. Upstairs, we stuck a candle in a pool of melted wax on a saucer and drank red wine out of teacups. The flickering light threw her cheekbones into sharp relief but I couldn't read her expression. She seemed elusive, unknowable.

'So you'll be going back to barracks tomorrow, to face the music?' I asked tentatively.

'Not bloody likely. Goodbye and good riddance to the ATS. I'm not waiting for them to chuck me out.'

'But you can't just run away!'

'Who says?' She tossed back her hair. 'What are they going to do, throw me in prison? They'll have to find me first.'

I couldn't decide whether to be appalled or impressed. She couldn't be serious, surely. 'So where will you go?'

'I haven't decided. I might flit around London for a while, if I can find a decent shelter.' She yawned. 'At least we can have a lie-in tomorrow morning. Thanks for putting me up tonight and listening to my tale of woe. I'm glad we ran into each other, aren't you?'

There were no words to express how vehemently I agreed with her so I simply nodded. I felt as though we had been destined to meet, that some guiding spirit had brought us together so we could help each other. It seemed inconceivable that we would say goodbye the next day and she'd be gone from my life for ever.

'Be brave, Cecil,' she said, more seriously. 'These are fierce times and we must be fierce, too, or go under.'

I lay awake for a long time that night, listening to the crash of explosions in various corners of the city, wondering whether I had it in me to be brave, and what might happen if I were.

5

THE EXTRAORDINARY IDEA

London, July 1944

Despite a disturbed night, I was too restless to sleep late the next morning. Throwing aside the dustsheet, I dressed quickly and padded down the hall to see whether Claude was awake. She lay on her side in the golden dress, one arm cupping her stomach, her hair a bright tangle on the cushion. I withdrew, closing her bedroom door quietly, took Mary Hale's handbag and went out to see what could be found for breakfast. It was Sunday morning, I realised from the lines of people in their best clothes filing into church, although of course no bells were ringing. Church bells would mean we'd been invaded.

Now, at last, I had to think about what might be happening at home. Ellen was conscientious and would have called in to make sure I'd come back. (She would, wouldn't she?) Mother would be dressed and sitting in her chair by the window, looking out at nothing. She wouldn't be worried about me, only angry that I'd abandoned her for so long. Yet what if I really had been injured or even killed in a bombing raid? What would happen to her then? Some solution would be found; as Claude said, she'd probably have to pay for a companion. She could afford to and really, she'd be much better off with a professional nurse who could care for her more efficiently than I ever had. She was only in her seventies; she'd probably live for another twenty years, just to spite me.

Hearing the drone of a flying bomb, I looked up to see one speeding across the sky to my right, a few miles away. As I watched, the engine cut out and it hung in the air for a second or two, before plummeting to earth to land with an almighty crash somewhere in North London. A billowing cloud of grey smoke marked the spot where it had fallen, causing the kind of chaos and destruction I could picture only too well. I'd stopped in the middle of the pavement and a middle-aged couple stepped around me, tutting. They didn't give the explosion a second glance and neither did anyone else walking past. I stood to one side, so angry that I could have put my fist through the shop window (an inoffensive haberdashery). Injustice has always made me furious. Hitler couldn't possibly have won the war by then; sheer spite, that's all it was. He was simply making us suffer.

My mind in turmoil, I found myself walking towards the bombsite where La Petite Amie had once stood. Work must have been going on there all night and morning: the mountains of rubble we'd seen the day before had been levelled, and pathways carved between them. Men were shovelling debris into a huge bucket that hung from a crane, which was then emptied on to the bed of a waiting lorry. Coming closer, I saw that a crater had been dug below the pavement which had once been piled so high with brick, wood and stone. Shouts floated up from its depths, and several men wearing tin helmets knelt on hands and knees, looking down into the void. There was a ladder propped against the side, I noticed, and a system of buckets on pulleys to carry a load up to the surface. The oil-drum barrier was still in place but it was no longer guarded by a policeman.

No one seemed to be paying me much attention, so I stepped over the rope and walked towards the pit. Various objects had been arranged in rows on the ground beside the edge, like artefacts from an archaeological dig, and a young woman in khaki overalls was sifting through them, breaking off sporadically to write in a ledger. I saw the twisted brass frame of the dessert trolley, minus its glass shelves, rows of shoes, a pile of hats and coats, blood-stained white aprons and tablecloths, several gas-mask cases – and Marjory Bly's tapestry bag. It was lying beside an umbrella with a distinctive parrot's head handle. My umbrella.

'I say! What are you doing?' I turned, as if in a dream, to see a harassed man in a sports coat and flannels hurrying towards me. 'This is the site of a major incident. You can't just wander about, willy-nilly.'

'I'm sorry.' Yet I had to go on looking. Marjory's bag, my umbrella and, a few feet away, my gaberdine mackintosh, also blood-stained, and no doubt my handbag would be–

'You people make me sick,' the man burst out. His eyes were bloodshot and his face was grey with exhaustion. 'This isn't a tourist attraction. Hoping to see a few bodies, were you?'

'No, you've got it all wrong. I was only– ' Suddenly dizzy, I swayed, putting out a hand to steady myself which landed on his arm.

He gave an exasperated sigh, shaking me off. 'As if we don't have enough to do. Pull yourself together and go home.' He called to the girl in khaki, 'Marion, can you spare a moment? Deal with this one, would you?' And with that, he hurried away.

Marion got to her feet and strolled over, wiping her hands

down her overalls. 'Are you all right?' she asked. 'Not going to be sick or anything ghastly? Sit down and put your head between your knees.'

I did as she suggested. 'Thanks,' I said, when I was able to speak. 'I've just recognised something over there that belongs to – friends of mine. They were lunching here yesterday, you see, and I haven't heard from them. I'm simply frantic with worry so I had to come. Have there been many casualties?'

'Seven so far,' the girl said. Crouching down, she took out a packet of cigarettes and offered me one. 'But I'm afraid the number's probably going to rise.'

'And have any names been released?'

'Not officially. They'll probably put up a list in the town hall later in the week.'

She had an open, freckled face with a smear of dirt on one cheek, and looked young enough to be still at school. 'Don't you get queasy, doing this sort of work?' I asked.

'The worst is over by now, thank God. The rescue team gather up body parts and some poor soul in the mortuary tries to piece them together. I'm just cataloguing personal effects.'

I could have given her my name and asked about my handbag. Why didn't I? Because an idea that had been simmering in the back of my mind was now coming to the boil. My old life was over, as truly as if I really had been buried under a ton of rubble. I didn't want that handbag, or the umbrella, or the gaberdine mackintosh; I wanted to walk away and leave everything behind.

'You've been so helpful,' I said. 'Do you think you could possibly find out if there's been any news of my friends? I can't bear the strain much longer.'

'Well, I can ask, but I'm not promising anything. Give me their names and I'll see what I can do.'

I could have hugged her. 'Stella Atkins and Fabia Heythornthwaite. Oh, and Marjory Bly.'

'You'd better write that down. Here.' She produced a scrap of paper and a pencil from her pocket. My fingers were shaking so my writing wasn't the clearest but I managed in the end, and watched her walk over to a knot of men gathered around a desk under an awning. I dropped my head back in my arms, my heart thumping a tattoo.

It seemed an age before she reappeared. She knelt beside me, her face serious. 'Well, Marjory Bly's all right, more or less. A broken arm and some minor injuries – they discharged her from hospital this morning. But I'm afraid there's no word of Stella Atkins and... the other one.'

'What do you mean, no word?'

'They're reported missing. The list says "Missing, presumed killed", but you never know. Miracles can happen, and they've got a dog down there – if your friends are alive, he'll find them. I wouldn't lose hope just yet. Here, let me help you up.' She reached out an arm to pull me to my feet. 'Want another cigarette?'

'No thanks. I'll just go home now, and wait for news.' I took a deep breath and dug my fingernails into my palms. 'Will their next of kin be informed?'

Marion nodded. 'Don't worry, we've found their details. There's nothing you need to do.' She squeezed my arm. 'I'm so sorry.'

'Thank you for your kindness. You've been simply marvellous.' I kept my voice steady, yet excitement bubbled up inside me like a fountain. It was all I could do not to burst out laughing.

* * *

'You're mad. Certifiably insane.' Claude was sitting up in bed, eating the doughnut I had brought for breakfast – yellow dough with a smear of red paste in the middle masquerading as jam – along with a pint of milk from somebody's doorstep. 'How on earth do you think we'd manage? We have hardly any money and only one identity card between us that belongs to somebody else.'

I sat at the end of the mattress. 'I'm going to sell my pearls. They're worth a couple of hundred pounds at least, and that should tide us over until I can find a job.'

'Us?' She raised an eyebrow.

I felt myself blush. 'I thought you'd jump at the idea. Don't you see? It solves all your problems. You can lie low until the baby's born and no one will know it ever existed. How many months until you're due?'

She licked her sugary fingers. 'Between three and four, I think. But the thing is, Cecil, even if we were to get away with this crazy plan, which seems highly unlikely, the whole thing rests on everyone we know believing that we're dead.'

'Our families will be told we are! We don't actually have to lie – we can just sink under the radar and hide away for a while. The war will be over before long, anyway, and then nobody will care who we are or what we've done.'

'And you'd put your mother through that?' She looked at me gravely. 'Gosh, you really don't like her, do you?'

I walked to the window and seized the bars, looking through them at the legs of strangers walking by. 'You've opened my eyes. I've been such a doormat, letting people take advantage of me and doing nothing about it. Life is short, especially these days. This is my chance, maybe the only one I'll ever get, and I'm not going to waste it. You don't have to stay here if you don't want to, of course, but it might be more fun with two. What are you going to do otherwise?'

'I hadn't thought.'

'Oh, come on,' I said, 'you must have had some idea.'

She sighed, folding the greasy doughnut bag into smaller and smaller squares. 'All right then. I was going to go home and tell my parents.'

'And how do you think they'll take it?'

She shuddered. 'Badly. My dad will shout and my mum will cry, but they should calm down in the end. They'll probably pack me off somewhere until the baby's born and then I might be allowed to reappear.'

'Everyone will know though,' I said brutally, 'and they won't forget. You won't catch a decent husband either, not with your history.'

She sat up. 'What if we're caught, though, which we very likely will be? They could throw us in prison for deserting and using somebody else's identity card.'

'But you were the one who took Mary's handbag in the first place! And what was all that talk about good riddance to the ATS?'

'I was only going to go AWOL for the weekend.' She tossed back her hair. 'I'd have telephoned them on Monday.'

So it was all just talk. My heart sank. 'Fine, if that's what you want. Go home and put up with the whispering behind your back, the gossip and pity and snide remarks. I thought you had some guts, that's all. I thought you actually meant what you said.'

She flushed. 'It's one thing to skip about London for a couple of days and quite another to stay hidden for months. I still can't see how we'd manage it.'

I knelt beside the bed. 'We won't get caught, not if we're careful. That girl Floss will help us – I bumped into her just now, hanging around in the gardens. I bet she and her father will know how to get hold of an identity card. Who's going to bother about a pair of nice girls like us, minding our own business?' Although were we nice now? It was hard to tell.

'The police are looking out for deserters,' she said. 'A friend of mine was nabbed the other week.'

'But they won't be looking out for us because we're dead!' I smiled, willing her to believe me. 'Perhaps we actually are. We might be a couple of ghosts, drifting around London unnoticed.'

I was trying to convince myself as much as her, because I'd already learnt the truth of what she said. Walking back to the flat that morning with my head down, I'd seen too late that a lorry had been parked across the road, and a line of policemen and Home Guard officials were holding back the thickening crowd. People were patting their pockets or reaching into briefcases and bags. I'd quickened my pace, wondering whether it might be possible to slip through unnoticed.

'Steady on, Miss.' A tall policeman stepped in front of me, eyes hard under his helmet. 'Where are you off to in such a hurry?' He held out his hand. 'Identity card, if you please.'

It was hard to look casual as I fumbled to open the handbag. 'Oops. Butterfingers!' My guilt must have been written all over my face.

He scanned the card carefully before giving it back to me. 'Look where you're going in future – it's our duty to stay alert these days.'

Sweat had prickled under my armpits. It was disconcerting, being spoken to in that way by a policeman. Was it only because of the simpering voice that had come so unexpectedly out of my mouth, or were London bobbies in the habit of sneering? If you're ever in trouble, find a policeman; that rule had been drummed into me since I was small. PC Harper had once come to call on Mother and me when a German plane had been shot down near the village and there was no trace of the pilot. He had been respectful and reassuring, a comforting presence for two women living on their own, and when the body was eventually discovered, hanging from a parachute in the woods, we had been informed before anyone else. Now I had strayed into another world.

I seized Claude's hands. 'Just a few months and then you can go home, if that's what you really want. Tell them there was a terrible mistake and the authorities muddled you up with somebody else. Think how happy they'll be! Instead of being ashamed of you.'

She'd opened her mouth to speak when a loud knock on the front door made us both jump. I stared at her. 'Well, don't just stand there,' she said, pulling the dustsheet over her head. 'Go and answer it.'

A short, stout woman in a housecoat with a turban over her curlers stood on the doormat, glaring at me like a malevolent Mrs Tiggy-Winkle.

'Hello,' I said pleasantly. 'Can I help you?'

'I heard you yesterday,' she said. 'Slamming the door late at night.' She craned to look over my shoulder into the flat and then tried to peer under my arm, which I kept resolutely in place, obscuring her view. 'I hope your blackout's satisfactory. You've a broken window at the front, I notice.'

'Yes, I was going to deal with that,' I replied. 'It looks as though someone has tried to break in – unsuccessfully, thank goodness. Who should I talk to about repairs? The cellar door has come off its hinges and the ceiling's in a shocking state.'

'You can get a form from the town hall and put your name down on the list. If you're after compensation, it'll take a while.' Mrs Tiggy-Winkle narrowed her eyes. 'You'll have to give me your details. The wardens need to know who's living here in case they need to dig us all out.'

A needle of fear shot through me. 'May I ask who you are, exactly?'

The woman's name was Mrs Hoffman, I discovered, and she was the superintendent of Victoria Mansions; she could be found in rooms on the ground floor, next to the front door. 'Strictly between the hours of nine to five, Monday to Friday. Don't think you can knock on my door whenever you feel like it, Miss–?'

I would have to say something. A few possible names flashed into my head, and then I saw her looking at the handbag which I'd left on the hall shelf. Was she going to ask for my identity card? 'Miss Hale,' I blurted.

'I heard two voices last night. I need the names of everyone in residence.'

'I had a friend to stay,' I told her.

She sniffed. 'A gentleman friend?'

'Certainly not.' I made as if to shut the door.

The old bag put her foot in the way, clad in a tartan slipper. 'I hope you're not going to cause trouble, Miss Hale. We don't want any undesirable types in this block. I never heard a peep from Miss Percival – such a nice lady, and so genteel.'

I drew myself up. 'As a matter of fact, Miss Percival was my aunt.'

Mrs Hoffman sniffed again, not apparently convinced, and I cursed myself for having told her more than necessary. 'Well, I won't keep you. I'm sure you have a million things to do,' I said, pushing at the door again with more conviction.

She withdrew her slippered foot just in time. 'You'll have to take your turn fire-watching,' she called through the crack in the door. 'Up on the roof. There's a rota in the hall.'

'I'll put my name down, just as soon as my diary allows,' I promised. After a short pause, I heard her shuffle away and let out my breath.

Claude was dressed by the time I returned to her room. 'You see?' she said. 'The world is full of nosy parkers.'

'I can tell I'm wasting my breath.' I folded my arms. 'All right then, go back to your life and forget we ever met. You won't tell anyone about me, though, will you?'

'Of course not.' She frowned. 'Why would I do that? And I'm not saying no, I just need a little time to think. This is quite some plan of yours.'

I wished now that I'd kept quiet. She knew all about me and she was about to go off into the world, armed with that information.

She walked past me into the hall, where she took her bolero jacket from the peg and Mary Hale's crocodile-skin handbag from the shelf. 'I'll be back in a tick. You can trust me, Cecil. I'll never give you away, I swear.'

She looked me full in the face as she spoke, reaching out a warm, freckled hand to be shaken, and I was fool enough to believe her.

6

PAM AND MARY

London, July 1944

While I waited for Claude to return – or not, as the case
might be – I decided to carry on setting the flat to
rights. Ivy's home had become an empty, unloved shell and no
matter how long I'd end up staying there, it seemed only right to
sweep the floor, wash the windows and beat the rugs over a line
in the backyard with a walking stick I found in an elephant's
foot umbrella stand in the hall. Dark rectangles on the faded
wallpaper showed where paintings had once hung: the pastoral
scenes of which Ivy was so fond, full of thatched cottages and
hay-carts, peasants labouring in the fields, and disconsolate
horses hanging their heads over a fence. There had been a coiled
rag rug on the hearth, hand-smocked nighties hanging over the
bath to dry, framed cross-stitch samplers in each bedroom,
drawers full of tea cosies, Dorset lace, crewel work and tiny silk
cushions studded with pins – all gone now.

What had become of these cherished belongings? They
must have been sold or given away by whoever had dealt with

Ivy's affairs. All that remained were some clothes from her youth, a few books and a wall of family photographs in the lav that would mean nothing to anyone else. She'd spent her last six months in a nursing home where to my shame, I'd never visited her, not once. I hadn't even gone to her funeral: my train had been delayed by an unexploded bomb on the line and the ceremony had long since finished by the time I'd arrived in London. So I'd done little to deserve my inheritance, all in all.

I wondered what Ivy had been thinking when she'd decided to leave her home to me. I had pitied her when I was younger, maybe even despised her a little; a lonely spinster, withering away in a basement flat. Yet Ivy had had friends; she belonged to a Gilbert and Sullivan choral society, sat on the parish council and took walking holidays each summer in the Tyrol. Now I envied her independence. Leading a comfortable, cultured life seemed not such a bad fate after all. Perhaps Ivy had guessed I would need a refuge one day; perhaps, all along, she had been feeling sorry for me. She had offered me the chance of freedom. Could I find the courage to take it?

The sun had come out. I was tired of cleaning and sick of my own company, so I went out to see if Floss was still hanging around in the gardens of our square. I'd seen her earlier that morning as I returned to the flat, watching a gang of American GIs playing basketball on the tennis court. Their harsh shouting had disturbed the quiet Sunday morning, their thighs bulging like pink hams and their coats piled in a messy tangle over the grass. The game had finished now but Floss was still there, halfway up a tree. She dropped to the ground when she saw me and ambled over, chewing gum with her mouth open.

'Wanna buy some fags?' she asked, pulling the corner of a packet of Lucky Strikes from her shorts pocket.

'Where did those come from?' I asked, although I had a good idea.

'The Yanks give me them. For my dad, but he doesn't smoke. They're yours for a shilling.'

'Sixpence,' I said, and she handed over the Lucky Strikes without further ado. I knew she must have swiped them – despite their uncouth ways, the GIs surely wouldn't give cigarettes to a child – yet I took the packet anyway.

We sat on a bench while I waited for a passing stranger who could give me a light. From the corner of my eye, I could sense Floss watching me. 'Tell me about yourself,' I said.

'What do you want to know?'

'Anything. Whatever you like.'

She began cautiously, leaking out snippets of information in her nasal, whiny voice, although she warmed up with a little encouragement and the trickle soon turned into a flood. She lived down in the World's End, a mile or so away, with her dad. He was a window cleaner, not presently working because he'd fallen off the ladder and hurt his leg. His real name was Reginald but everyone called him Chalkie because they were the White family. Her mam had been killed a few months before – this offered up in the same matter-of-fact tone – and she had an older brother who was away somewhere, whom she hadn't seen for ages. She sometimes went to afternoon classes in the church hall but school had stopped because of the doodles. Anyway, it was nearly the summer holidays. When I asked whether she had any friends, she said she used to go around in a gang but she'd grown out of that now. And she tossed back her straggly hair with an air of adult world-weariness.

I nodded towards Victoria Mansions. 'Do you know any of the people who live there?'

She shook her head. 'Not anymore. Most of them have moved away – 'cept for Mrs Hoffman, and Dad thinks she won't stick it out much longer.'

I ground out my cigarette in a flurry of indecision. It wasn't too late to go back to the country; I could buy a train ticket with the money Claude had left me and make up a story for Mother. There would be all hell to pay for a few days but my life would eventually settle into its accustomed, awful groove. How could I possibly stay in London without an identity card? Unless Claude returned, I wouldn't even have Mary Hale's to fall back on. And was I brave enough to manage on my own? Anything could happen: I might be arrested, or killed in a raid, or knocked over by a bus in the blackout. And yet, and yet... I would be living on my own terms, and wasn't that worth any amount of danger? I knew in my bones that if I went home now, I wouldn't have the strength to get away on my own a second time. It would all have been for nothing.

'Will you be staying?' Floss asked. 'My dad has a special rate for regulars.'

'I'm not sure. Maybe.' I stood up, wrapping my cardigan more tightly around me. 'Bye for now, anyway. And thanks for the cigs.'

I headed back to the flat, wondering whether Ivy might feel inclined to pass on some kind of guidance from the other side. Mrs Hoffman's door was ajar so I tiptoed past, taking a look at the fire-watching rota on the opposite wall. Most of the slots were blank and several of the names that had been written down were crossed out. Rather than taking the stairs down to number 117, I decided on a whim to head upward and explore the building. The blank doors of each flat gave nothing away. A man in a bowler hat carrying a briefcase came through one of them and nodded to me briefly as he passed. I didn't know what I expected to find, yet it felt good to be climbing higher, towards the light pouring down from the atrium.

Approaching the third floor, I heard a voice calling, 'Is anyone there? Please help!'

My first impulse was to run back downstairs and I'd already

turned with my hand on the banister when the summons came again, more urgently this time. 'Whoever you are, I require immediate assistance!'

This imperious demand seemed to be coming from a flat at the end of the landing. I walked hesitantly towards it and knocked on the door. 'Hello! Is everything all right?'

'Obviously not,' came the peevish reply. 'There's a key on a string. Pull it through the letterbox and let yourself in, if you'd be so kind.'

I stepped straight into an airy room, which appeared to be deserted. It smelt of oil paint and turpentine; a half-finished painting was propped on an easel by the window and canvases were stacked everywhere, three or four deep. What looked like a rectangular pillbox about three feet high, its walls made entirely of paintings, stood wedged in the corner against a vast table. One large framed picture had slid off the top and come to rest at an angle. I found myself confronted by swirls of orange, crimson and fuchsia, overlaid with the outlines of bodies in contorted attitudes. It was wonderful, in a garish sort of way.

'I'm in here,' said the voice, somewhere behind it. 'And I can't tell you how much I'd rather not be.'

I took away the canvases one by one; not an easy job, because some of them were heavy and altering the balance of the construction made it teeter alarmingly. Eventually the wire cage of a Morrison shelter was revealed and inside it, an elderly man in a paisley silk dressing gown, sitting on a mattress and glowering like some furious animal at the zoo.

'At last! You took your time.' He unlatched the door and swung it open. I helped him to his feet, apologising despite myself. 'Thank you,' he said, and tottered stiffly out of the room.

Perhaps I was meant to leave then but I couldn't resist the chance to look at the paintings. There were a few still lifes – vases of flowers on hectic tablecloths – but most showed burning skies with the silhouettes of people or ruined buildings against them. I could imagine him working through a raid, looking out over London as the bombs fell.

'And who might you be, may I ask?' He was back, wiping his hands on a paint-stained towel. He looked like an ancient version of the little boy in the Pears soap advertisement: white ringlets, plump cheeks threaded with spidery veins and watery, round blue eyes.

I was stumped for an answer. 'Do call me Cecil,' I managed, when the silence had become embarrassing.

'How charmingly informal.' He offered up a languid hand. 'Feel free to call me Mr Cavendish. Thank you for liberating me, Miss Cecil. I'd just settled down in the Morrison last night when one of those ghastly fly-bombs set off an avalanche. Good thing you came along or I might have been stuck there for days. Care to join me in a coffee?'

Well, I had nothing else to do, and my stomach was growling. My hopes for a biscuit were disappointed, but the coffee was wonderful: rich and fragrant, rather than the ersatz kind made from acorns that I was used to. 'From a favourite place of mine,' he said. 'There are still a few pleasures left in London if one has the money and knows where to look.' He splashed some brandy into his, 'for medicinal purposes,' and waggled the bottle at me, which I declined.

Looking out of the window, I caught sight of a column of smoke rising into the sky behind the hills a few miles north. It was unnerving to be up high, where the doodlebugs roamed. I asked Mr Cavendish whether he'd stayed in this flat through the Blitz.

'My sister urged me to join her in Tewkesbury,' he replied, 'but after a couple of deadly weeks I came scuttling back to London. How can one bear to live anywhere else? So many heavenly creatures in uniform, such alarms and excitements every minute of the night and day, and on top of all that, the blessed blackout hiding a multitude of sins. Most of the Americans have left by now, alas, but there are still plenty of interesting types about. The other day I met a Russian count at the Savoy Grill, would you believe, with a Fabergé egg in his pocket.'

He finished his coffee and blotted his mouth with a spotted handkerchief. 'Find a man to take you somewhere swanky and tuck in. You look like a girl with a healthy appetite.' He took my cup. 'Well, goodbye, young lady. I'm sure you have plenty of worthy things to be doing, like running a canteen or finding some helpless refugees to take care of.'

'I met Mrs Hoffman this morning,' I said. 'She wants me to sign up for fire-watching. Are you on the rota?'

'I take my turn now and then. It's not so bad in the summer, although things have become a little hairy again recently. We used to gather up on the roof to cheer our bombers on their way to Germany but hardly anyone's left these days. They've all scampered away, like rats deserting a sinking ship. It's refreshing to see a new face.' He looked intently into mine. 'Were you heading that way when you heard my call? The view is certainly splendid.'

That was as good a pretext as any. 'Yes,' I said. 'Could you point me in the right direction?'

He showed me a flight of steps at the other end of the corridor, which led to a door opening out on to the roof. A wide, flat gulley ran along the centre, edged with rows of chimney pots like the funnels of a ship. I walked to the far end and stood with my hands on the waist-high parapet, dizzy with the initial lurch of vertigo. Before me lay the patchwork blanket of south London, speckled with moth holes where bombs had landed. The air smelt of cinders, even four or five storeys up, and rubble blurred the sharp outlines of walls and paths.

I fixed my eyes on calming things: trees in the garden square with its tennis court and neatly cultivated allotments, the ARP post with wardens going in and out like worker bees, a milk float clanking down the street like a child's toy. And there was the small but instantly recognisable figure of Claude, walking towards Victoria Mansions with her head down, the handbag on her arm and a knapsack over her shoulder. I hurried back across the roof and ran downstairs to hear what she had to say.

* * *

'You haven't changed your mind?' she asked.

'Absolutely not. I'm going through with this, whether you join me or not.' I lit a Lucky Strike and hoped she wouldn't notice my fingers trembling.

'I meant, you haven't changed your mind about me staying here too?' Claude dropped the handbag on the coffee table and sat on the sofa, glancing around. 'Goodness, this place looks almost homely.'

I'd put some fireweed and dog roses in a jam jar on the mantelpiece, and arranged a few books on the coffee table.

'Not at all,' I replied, my heart leaping. I kept my tone deliberately casual, so she wouldn't realise how desperately I'd been hoping she'd throw in her lot with mine. 'It'll be fun to share, and we don't have to live in each other's pockets. When I find work, I'll be out half the time anyway.'

'And what will I do? No one's going to give me a job when they twig I'm in the family way.'

I shrugged. 'Potter about at home, I suppose. Do the shopping, keep the place tidy, go for walks, have plenty of rest.'

'But I don't want to sponge off you all the time. I wish I had something to sell.' Her fingers went to her throat, and I saw she was wearing a locket that I hadn't noticed before. 'This isn't worth anything,' she added hastily. 'It's only silver plate.'

'I don't mind, honestly.' And I wasn't just saying that. 'You can think of yourself as my housekeeper, if it makes you feel better.'

She laughed. 'Not really. Well, at least there's one thing I can contribute.' She snapped open the handbag, took out an identity card and ration book and laid them on the table. 'Here's a sight to gladden your heart.'

I gasped. 'Where did you find those?'

'They're my sister's.'

I flipped open the identity card: Pamela Atkins, 59 Cedar Lane, St Albans. 'But won't she miss them?'

'She's the one who died.'

'When did it happen?'

'Six months ago. She was working in an ordnance factory, filling mine fuses with TNT, when one of the fuses in her tray exploded and set off the rest. There was nothing left of her to bury.'

'How awful. I'm so sorry.' I looked at Pamela's name, written in a bold, looping hand. 'But how did you come by her papers?'

Claude kicked off her shoes and leaned back, crossing her legs with her bare feet on the table. 'My folks never handed them in – they've carried on collecting her rations.'

I stared at her. 'You went home then.'

'Don't worry, I knew my parents would be out.' She patted my knee. 'Here we are, Pamela and Mary.' She took Mary Hale's identity card out of the handbag and laid it beside her sister's.

I walked over to the mantelpiece and rearranged the flowers, my unease deepening. 'I wish you'd talked this over with me first. What if your parents realise you must be alive because you've taken Pamela's things?'

She shrugged. 'They haven't the faintest idea where I am, so they couldn't give me away even if they wanted to.'

'I should hope not.' She was lounging on the sofa as though she hadn't a care in the world. 'We have to be careful from now on. We can't risk drawing attention to ourselves and arousing suspicion. You understand that, don't you? If someone starts digging into our background, we'll be sunk. Do you promise?'

'Scout's honour.' She held up three fingers.

I walked back to sit beside her. 'This isn't a joke. You can only stay here if you follow the rules.'

'I will.' She rubbed a hand across her forehead. 'Honestly, Cecil, you're doing me a favour and I'm grateful. I won't let you down.'

Despite my doubts, I let myself be persuaded. It was either that or tell her to leave and, for all my brave words, I wasn't sure whether I could actually have gone through with the scheme alone. As long as we stuck together, I told myself, everything would be all right.

We celebrated with the last of the red wine from the night before. 'To Pam and Mary,' Claude said, raising her teacup.

I didn't feel like much of a Mary; the name was too ordinary for someone who was plain enough already. 'I think Margot might suit me better,' I said, looking at Mary Hale's identity book. It would be easy enough to change the 'y' to a 'g' and add an 'o' and a 't'. And then I read the fine print running along the side of the card: *Any alteration, marking or erasure is punishable by a fine or imprisonment or both.* Mary might have to do.

'Whatever you say. Anyway, we can be Cecil and Claude at home.' She chinked her cup against mine. 'Here's to us, whatever we choose to call ourselves.'

'At home!' I rested my head against the sofa cushion and stared up at the cracked ceiling, daring to imagine the kind of life we might lead.

7

FRIENDS AND ACQUAINTANCES

London, July 1944

The next morning, I set off for Mayfair with my pearls in the handbag, wrapped in one of Ivy's silk scarves. There were several jewellers in the area who'd be delighted to get their hands on them, for a better price than I'd get from some backstreet pawn shop. I felt different now, resourceful and resolute. These streets belonged to me, battered though they were; I had a right to be here and a new life to begin. As I walked along Piccadilly, debating whether to pass myself off as an impoverished aristocrat, I noticed a street sign that looked familiar. Shepherd Street, London W1: the road in which Mary Hale had lived. Her identity card confirmed it. I stood for a while on the pavement, distracted. Claude knew all about her sister; if anyone asked about Pamela's background, she would be able to reply. Mary Hale was a mystery to me.

On an impulse, I turned the corner and plunged into the maze of narrow streets, following a sign pointing to Shepherd Market. A hotchpotch of half-timbered buildings and flats jostled for space next to quaint, old-fashioned shops. Their windows were mainly boarded up, with only a small peephole in the centre to display a loaf of bread or a string of papier-mâché sausages. The place had been badly knocked about; there were gaps where whole houses had been demolished, leaving the open walls of cellars staring up at the sky. It felt as though a mad director had decided to shoot a film about a country village in the middle of London, and I was wandering around the half-built set. There were a few GIs around, striding along with their usual brio, and two girls in smart costumes and feather-trimmed hats spoke to each other in French under an awning, one holding a small dog on a lead.

I walked on down Shepherd Street, past what seemed to be the back of the market. The house in which Mary had lived formed a bridge over an alleyway: three storeys hanging over the void. Four bells were set into the wall beside the door but the name plaques were illegible so I pressed them all. Of course, I could have used the keys that were in her handbag but I wouldn't know which door to try once I was inside and that would arouse suspicion. Just when I'd given up hope of any reply, suddenly a window on the middle floor was thrown up and a head emerged, crowned with hair like an upended hearth brush.

'What do you want?' it called.

'I'm looking for Miss Hale,' I began. 'This is her address, isn't it?'

'She's out,' the hearth brush replied. 'In fact, I haven't seen her for a few days.'

'May I come in?' I replied, finding it undignified to be discussing my business in the street.

'I can't stop you – the door's open. Top floor.' The head withdrew and the window dropped shut.

I pushed open the door and entered a dingy hall, pushing

past a bicycle propped against the wall. The stair carpet was stained and each step creaked ominously underfoot as I made my way to the top floor. Two doors at either end of a short landing confronted me: the right-hand one closed and the left ajar. The sound of typewriter keys and the smell of cigarette smoke drifted through the gap.

I tapped on the open door, pushing it a little wider. A young man in a gabardine overcoat turned around from his seat at a desk by the window. 'Yes?' he said, with some irritation, stubbing out his cigarette.

'I'm sorry to bother you,' I began. 'Miss Hale gave me a spare key, so I wonder whether you'd mind if I left a note in her room?'

'Why would I mind?' he asked, frowning. 'That's between the two of you. It has nothing to do with me.'

He was striking to look at: skin so pale it was almost translucent; thick black hair and eyebrows; dark, intense eyes. I wondered whether he might have a fever.

'Fine. I'll leave you in peace,' I said.

'Jolly good.' He was already turning back to the typewriter.

I took a quick glance around the bedsit as I retreated. Books, newspapers and dirty cups were scattered all over the floor, and a pair of fluffy pink slippers poked out from beneath the unmade bed. I walked along the short landing, past a sink piled with unwashed dishes and a fire extinguisher, feeling for Mary Hale's keys in her handbag. Even though I knew she was dead and the young man didn't seem to care what I did, intruding on her privacy made me nervous.

Her room was immaculately tidy. A stack of true romance magazines lay on the bedside table and a gas-mask case hung from the back of a chair beside the bed, which had been made with hospital corners. I caught a trace of Yardley April Violets in the air, or maybe that was only my imagination, and a bottle of crimson nail varnish stood on the chest of drawers. The sight of it nearly did for me. There were no photographs, pictures or ornaments to give me any clues about the enigmatic Mary Hale, and I wasn't about to go rifling through her drawers. I sat on the bed, terribly sad, and shut my eyes to conjure again the feel of her arms around me. I would make the most of my life from now on, I promised, for her sake.

Her grumpy neighbour had abandoned the typewriter, I noticed as I passed his door, and was now standing by the window, gazing out. He clearly didn't want to be bothered but some perverse obstinacy and a desire for information spurred me on.

'I'm rather worried about Miss Hale,' I said, advancing. 'We were meant to meet today but she didn't turn up. Does she have an employer I could contact to see if she's been at work?'

He glanced at me. 'She's a maid for a couple of girls in the Market, but you'd better not go bothering them before lunch.'

'I didn't realise she was in service,' I said, digesting this information and what it meant for my new identity.

He laughed with what sounded like genuine amusement. 'Not that sort of maid! She deals with the punters, takes their money and makes sure there's no funny business.'

I blushed. 'Oh, I see.' The drone of a doodlebug intruded on the silence that had fallen between us and the young man peered out at a tiny slice of sky, just visible between the tall buildings on either side of the street.

'Why did she give you her spare keys?' he asked abruptly, turning to me. 'Considering you seem to be virtual strangers.'

I hadn't expected him to show any interest in me and this question was disconcerting. For the first time, it occurred to me that coming here with Mary Hale's handbag over my arm might have been a mistake. 'I was stuck for somewhere to stay a few days ago,' I said hastily, raising my voice above the throaty chug, 'and Miss Hale offered to let me sleep on her floor, but as a matter of fact, an old friend put me up instead.'

It was a far-fetched story and one that would fall apart under any questioning, but the young man merely nodded, gazing up at the sky which had turned ominously dark.

'Oh Lord, here we go again,' he muttered as the noise became deafening. 'Get away from the window!'

He grabbed my elbow and pulled me with him. We ended up crouched at the foot of the bed, with me shoved against the wall and his arm around my shoulders. His coat smelt of cigarette smoke and stale cooking fat but I appreciated the gesture as we tensed, waiting in a terrible hush that seemed to last for hours rather than seconds, as the engine cut out. The eventual crash set the window rattling in its frame and the floor shuddering.

'That was a close one.' He got to his feet, quite unembarrassed, and dusted off his knees. 'Still, no harm done. Some other poor bugger must have copped it. Cigarette?' He took a packet from the bedside table and offered it to me. 'The name's Fitzgerald, by the way.'

'Thanks awfully,' I said, glad the ice had broken. 'And I'm Cecil.'

'Miss Cecil?'

'No, just Cecil.'

He smiled. 'Then you must call me Jan. Spelt with a J, pronounced with a Y.'

I got the impression he was warming to me a little as we chatted about this and that in the time it took to smoke a cigarette. It would have been safer to have said my goodbyes at that point, but this Jan Fitzgerald was my only link to Mary Hale and he clearly thought I was far too dull to suspect my motives in asking about her. If I'd got myself into a scrape of any sort, he'd assume it would be to do with ration coupons, perhaps, or carelessness with the blackout. And of course he wouldn't recognise the handbag: he'd probably never given Miss Hale a second glance.

'The pubs must be open by now,' I said, glancing at the clock. 'May I buy you a drink to make up for the intrusion?'

'Why not?' He brightened. 'I could do with a break from the typewriter.'

He worked for the BBC, he told me as we walked a few hundred yards to the nearest pub, broadcasting in Polish and helping with odd pieces of translation, and had been living in the Market for a year or so. It suited him nicely. 'A village in Piccadilly, that's what they call it. We all look out for each other.'

The landlord was unbolting the doors of a pub on the corner of an alleyway, like a wedge of cheese with the nose cut off. Sunlight streamed through the tall windows inside, turning sawdust flakes on the floorboards into a scattering of gold. Steeling myself, I approached the bar and ordered our drinks from a barmaid with a sagging bosom and a lazy eye. I could count on the fingers of one hand the number of times I'd been in a pub before, and certainly never with a man I'd only just met. The idea that Mother would have been scandalised only sharpened my pleasure.

'Miss Hale intrigues me,' I told Jan, to his evident surprise, when we were settled with our drinks and cigarettes. 'Do you know her well?'

'Hardly at all.' He drank steadily for a second or two, then wiped beer froth from his upper lip. 'We say hello in passing, you know the sort of thing. In my opinion it's best not to get too tangled up with one's neighbours.'

'So she doesn't have any family that you know of?' I persisted, remembering just in time to speak in the present tense.

'No idea.' He looked at me over the rim of the glass. 'Why are you asking so many questions? Not a policewoman, are you?'

'Good heavens, no.' I laughed in an affected manner. 'She made quite an impression on me, that's all.'

'Really?' He looked into the distance and I wondered what image of Mary Hale was coming to mind. 'I suppose she's quite...' The sentence trailed away for want of a suitable adjective.

'She was kind to me.' I felt aggrieved on Mary's behalf that he hadn't taken more account of her. She'd given me the chance to start again, step away from the disappointments and mistakes of my past and take a better stab at life, and for that I would always be grateful. Changing the subject, I asked Jan about his background. He had a Polish mother and a Scottish father, it turned out, and then he told me a great deal about the current situation in Poland to which I listened with half an ear.

'Well, I've taken up quite enough of your time,' I said, when I could get a word in edgeways, gathering up the handbag. 'Super to meet you, Jan. I might drop by again in a few days to see if there's been any news of Miss Hale.'

'All right,' he said. 'If I see her, I'll certainly tell her you called.'

* * *

I walked through the dark, narrow streets back to the bustle of Piccadilly, hugging my secret to myself. I'd pulled it off! Invented a story that a stranger had believed and made an acquaintance, if not a friend. A supercilious jeweller with an eyeglass in the Burlington Arcade offered me a hundred guineas for my pearls and I accepted, although we both knew they were worth far more. The glee I felt from my escapade in Shepherd Market drained away after this encounter and I was keen to get back to the safety of Victoria Mansions. There was no sign of Claude in the flat. When she didn't reply to my knock on her bedroom door, I opened it to find the room empty, the dustsheets rumpled and tossed aside on her bed. The haversack she'd brought from her parents' house was half open, the sleeve of a green woollen jumper trailing from its jaws. I could feel her presence, see her throwing off the man's shirt she'd used as a nightie and brushing her hair in front of the mirror above the chest of drawers.

I knelt beside the haversack to examine its contents: underwear, a pair of brown leather sandals, a jar of hand cream, an exercise book with poems copied out in childish writing, a framed photograph of a middle-aged couple walking along the seafront on a windy day. Another picture stood on her bedside table: two girls in their teens, their arms around each other's shoulders. One was Claude and the other, I guessed, was Pamela. She had thin lips parted in a self-conscious smile, and a hesitant, guarded look about the eyes.

I sat on the bed, looking at the photograph and thinking about all the people I knew or had heard of who'd died. George and Billy Cheesman, killed within weeks of each other on the Atlantic convoys; Ellen's niece, Sally, machine-gunned in the High Street by a passing Messerschmitt; the five Talbot children, drowned when their ship was torpedoed en route to Canada. And Mary Hale, of course – or an idea of her. There were so many others. Somebody's cousin, fiancé, friend, wife, mother, uncle; bombed, shot, crushed, died of dysentery, run over in the blackout, victim of some horrendous accident in a factory or shipyard. Alive one minute, dead the next. A random decision to take that train, stop by this shop, visit a friend, and in a matter of seconds one might move from the camp of the living to the dead. I heard the voices of the lost, each passing remark now freighted with significance. Sally had always said she would die an old maid; Penny Talbot was frightened of water and had never learned to swim. Had their fate been decided from the minute they were born?

I'd been so sure it had been my destiny to meet Claude, and that somehow, we would survive. And yet I hardly knew her; she could disappear from my life as abruptly as she had entered it. What if the bomb that had sent me diving for cover in Shepherd Street had killed her? She might be lying dead in the street even now, just like Mary Hale, and I'd have no way of knowing what had happened. To distract myself, I ran upstairs to put my name down on the fire-watching rota and then out into the street, to see whether there were any cigarettes to be found. I hadn't gone more than a hundred yards before Floss had joined me, and I was pleased to see her. There was so much to be done: we would have to change the addresses in our ration books, and register at the local shops, and find out about getting the electricity reconnected, and give our details to Mrs Hoffman, and– And besides all that, we would have to make up a story to explain why the two of us should have ended up living together in Chelsea, without any useful occupation. Damn Claude! Where could she have gone, and why?

'I'll take you down the World's End,' Floss said, 'so you can get the lie of the land. Things are cheaper there and we might run into my dad. You can talk to him about getting your winders cleaned.'

I told her we would be cleaning our own winders, but that I was looking for a job and maybe Chalkie could keep his ears open. She gave me an enigmatic look in reply.

We took the number 22 bus down the King's Road. There wasn't much to be seen through the windows, covered in safety netting; we might as well have been travelling by submarine. All I could tell was that the women getting on the bus looked shabbier and more careworn the further we went: office workers and shop girls gave way to housewives with headscarves over curlers, string bags and thick stockings drooping around their ankles. The World's End turned out to be a rackety sort of place. Narrow streets of terraced houses clustered under the shadow of the power station, its tall chimneys disgorging smoke into the leaden sky. There were more children about here: swinging off lamp-posts, crouched over marbles in the gutter or towing ramshackle go-carts. I wondered why they weren't safely in the country – and why Floss hadn't been evacuated, come to that. But she said she didn't fancy the idea and anyway, her dad needed looking after. She led me to a tobacconist's – the front room of somebody's house, with cigarettes, tobacco and sweets stacked on a trestle table – and then we headed to the market, where Chalkie was to be found.

It consisted of a few stalls beside a pub with some forlorn odds and ends for sale: a single sheet with a worn patch in the middle, several saucepans, tins of corned beef arranged in a pyramid, a piece of lino, a few pots of hair cream and bottles of cough medicine. There was a costermonger's barrow, though, with a basket of cherries that shone like jewels among the tat. I bought some as a treat to share with Claude. A man who had to be Chalkie was leaning against the wall, his hands in his pockets and one foot hooked up behind, looking out at the world with the same casual shiftiness as his daughter. She presented me wordlessly, like a dog dropping a stick at its master's feet.

'Hello, our Floss. So this is your new acquaintance?'

He squinted up at me from under a flat cap; a short, pugnacious man, unshaven, in baggy moleskin trousers and a collarless shirt. He looked grimy through and through, as though all the dirt from the windows he cleaned had transferred itself to him by some sort of osmosis. If he was surprised to find someone like me tagging along with his daughter, he didn't show it; he said any friend of Floss's was a friend of his.

I was looking for a job, I told him, and he asked the kind of thing I had in mind.

'I'm not too fussy.' As soon as the words were out of my mouth, I wanted to take them back. 'Waitressing, perhaps,' I added quickly, 'or some sort of shop work.'

He nodded. 'Ever thought about being a hostess? A pal of mine runs parties for people who like a flutter at cards. It's all above board, so long as you keep on the move – go to different houses every few days and that. A nice girl like you could get plenty of tips if she's minded to make herself agreeable.'

'Thank you,' I said carefully, 'but I'm not sure that's quite my forte.'

'Suit yourself. It was only a suggestion,' he replied. 'Something else'll come up soon. I'll keep me ears open and tell our Floss when there's a vacancy.'

I thanked him and said how very much I appreciated his help, and Floss's too.

He glanced briefly at his daughter, kicking stones against the wall. 'We have to look after ourselves nowadays, don't we? Ain't nobody else going to.' It just so happened, in fact, that an elderly aunt had only that morning given him a large quantity of unwanted clothing coupons. 'I could let them go at a rock bottom price to a friend of the family.'

I told him I was only shopping for essentials at the moment but would bear that in mind. It was reassuring to feel accepted; cared for, even. What a joke! Chalkie must have rubbed his hands when he saw me coming.

* * *

The flat was still empty when I returned. I paced from room to room, growing ever more anxious, and by the time I heard her key in the lock a couple of hours later, I was too agitated to feign indifference. I could have throttled her.

'Where on earth have you been? I thought something terrible had happened!'

'If you must know, I went for a walk.' She folded her arms. 'And then I passed a cinema and went in to watch *Gone with the Wind*. It was marvellous. Have you seen it?'

'But didn't you think I'd be worried? And how did you pay for a ticket? I thought you didn't have any money.'

'I took five pounds from home yesterday. I'll put what's left over in the kitty.'

I went into my bedroom, shut the door and lay down on the bed, not trusting myself to speak. She followed me through. 'This is only going to work if we lead our own lives, you know.'

I propped myself up on my elbows. 'Couldn't you at least have left me a note?'

'But I didn't plan on going to the pictures, it was a last-minute thing.' She sat down on the dressing-table stool. 'I've had such a wonderful day – let's not spoil it by arguing. By the way, I got married on the way home.' She waggled her left hand at me to show the ring. 'It was a small affair, just me and the girl on the jewellery counter at Woolworths.'

I lay back without saying a word and closed my eyes. It would take time for us to get to know each other and there were bound to be difficulties at first. Claude had come from the hurly-burly of the barracks and now suddenly she was living under trying circumstances with just one other person, who cared about her and worried for her safety. I ought not to judge her too harshly.

Still, I kept the cherries a secret and ate them all myself.

8

STEALING BY FINDING

London, July–August 1944

I have such happy memories of those early days at Victoria Mansions. I remember laughing with the thrill of it all while we made up our story, as though by inventing a past, we could create a future too. We decided that Claude should have recently lost her husband and be too sad to talk about him, should anyone ask, and that she had been working in the Land Army until recently.

'Which I enjoyed far more than you,' she said, tucking up her legs on the sofa, 'because I'm so terribly patriotic. In fact, I hated having to give it up but the doctor told me I should rest for the sake of my blood pressure. Now, your turn.'

'I've been working in a munitions factory,' I decided, 'but the noise of the machinery has given me migraines so I'm on sick leave and looking for some other useful occupation. That'll do. Factory work is so deadly dull, no one will ask me about it. And I think we should be cousins – third or fourth, so we don't have to share an exact family history – to explain why we're living together. I've inherited some money and property and taken you in, given your widowed state and interesting condition.'

'How very kind of you.' She gave me a wry smile.

Armed with this fictional account, we bearded Mrs Hoffman in her room on the ground floor that smelt of cabbage to give her our details. She looked Claude up and down, and Claude looked back with a haughty expression that made me wince.

'You should be more humble,' I told her later, when we were alone. 'Putting on airs and graces is only going to antagonise people.'

'Act like I'm ashamed of myself, you mean.'

'Not ashamed,' I said gently, 'but not proud, either.'

I think she understood. Certainly, she wasn't nearly so uppity when we were queuing up at the town hall to register our change of address. I was nervous, too, handing over Mary Hale's identity card, although I told myself there was no possibility her death would have been reported by then and even if it had been, no one would have thought to cross-check the death register. Our cards and ration books would be stamped and posted back to our new address, we were told, and we were given emergency coupons to tide us over until they arrived.

'By the way,' Claude said, as we were celebrating with lunch in a British restaurant, 'we'd better ditch Mary's handbag.' She passed me a rolled-up newspaper. 'Take a look at page six.'

It was a local paper, *The Kensington and Chelsea Gazette*, and page six was filled with reports from the magistrates' court. Sandwiched between the accounts of a soldier who walked about Victoria Station in women's clothes and the woman who'd turned her house into a brothel while her husband was away, I read the story of a girl who'd found a US army torch by the side of the road and used it to light her way home. She was charged with stealing by finding, pronounced guilty and sentenced to four months in prison. I gazed at Claude, horrified. *Stealing by finding!* It was a mean-spirited accusation, given the circumstances.

That night, we emptied the handbag, put a brick inside and walked to Hyde Park, where we threw it into the Serpentine. The dark square sailed through the night, its silver bobbles gleaming like tiny bombs, and with a surge of relief, I heard the distant splash as it landed. As if that were enough to keep us out of trouble!

I was in no rush to find a job. My pearl money would keep us going for a while and I wanted to enjoy a hard-earned taste of freedom. Claude wasn't at her best in the mornings and would sleep late while I explored the indifferent city, where nobody knew who I was or cared what I did. The weather was still grey and damp but that didn't matter. I navigated by means of past disasters: the ruined church by the river, its roof spars tumbling into the vestry, a burnt-out jeep, bomb craters from the Blitz already overgrown with fireweed. I had to see and touch and smell, plunge my hands deep into the wreckage of London and find its beating heart. It seemed important to bear witness when the world was so strange and out of kilter. Each morning, the street cleaners swept up a carpet of shattered glass while people went about their business as usual, one eye on the sky and both ears straining for the sound of approaching doodlebugs.

When Claude emerged from her room, we might walk to the National Gallery to hear Myra Hess on the piano, along with half the workers in London, and then eat beside them in one of those restaurants where a two-course lunch cost less than a shilling. If Floss were loitering in the gardens, we'd take her with us. In the afternoons, we spent hours at the pictures. Once an amber warning light flashed halfway through the film and a siren started up outside, but the projectionist carried on regardless and Claude didn't move so neither did I. We stayed in our seats while the cinema emptied around us, until we were sitting alone for a private screening. Her face was lit up in the Technicolor glow of the screen, and when Scarlett O'Hara said, 'Tomorrow is another day,' she caught my eye and smiled. A bomb could have landed on the cinema right there and then, and I wouldn't have cared. Sometimes, now, I wish it had.

I had survived until then by pretending not to care about anything but now emotion was flooding back, like circulation returning to frozen fingers. I lurched from one mood to another like a child being pushed on a swing, higher and higher into thin air, until suddenly the world has fallen away and excitement turns to dread. Beauty could bring me to tears: the sun sinking behind the chimneys of the power station like a great red balloon, or a blade of moonlight slicing through the dark skin of the river. My heart was sometimes so full, it would ache.

Fear was part of the blend too. In the middle of some routine activity, like washing my smalls or going for a walk, I might be overtaken by a wave of panic so strong that it would leave me faint and dizzy, with no idea where – or even who – I was. I don't know whether Claude felt the same; if she did, she never told me. I tried not to think about Mother and most of the time I succeeded, although sometimes I would dream about her and wake up gasping for breath. I had carried that particular burden for long enough; someone else could take over now.

It was Double Summer Time then, and light until late in the evening. We read, or played cards and Monopoly with a set we found at the back of a cupboard. Together we brought up the rest of the wine from the cellar – four bottles – and stumbled across a wind-up gramophone player there, too, along with a box of records. 'The Very Thought of You,' sang Al Bowlly in his golden-syrup voice, and I drifted away on a tide of sentiment.

There was a sweetness about Claude, a sort of innocent

gaiety that she only seemed able to show when we were alone. She would sometimes make a pot of tea and lay up a tray with the embroidered cloth she'd found in a drawer, and we would chat while we drank it. She talked about her time in the ATS, and I particularly remember one story she told about a highly strung girl who slept in the next bunk. The feeble creature was always bursting into tears at the slightest provocation and everyone thought her pathetic, but one night when no one else was around, she told Claude that her boyfriend had been arrested; he worked for MI5 and had been charged with spying for the Germans. She was scared out of her wits because apparently she knew some of the things he'd been up to. Claude wondered whether she was only making an excuse for her lack of nerve but the very next morning, this girl's bed had been stripped and she was gone, with no record that she'd ever existed. Her name was never mentioned again. Claude herself was prone to exaggeration but this time I believed her; there must have been plenty of undercover operations going on that would make our little escapade seem tame by comparison.

After a couple of weeks, the need to earn money became more urgent. Reconnecting the flat's electricity supply had been expensive and Claude seemed to be constantly hungry. We could have got extra rations if she'd registered as a mother-to-be – orange juice and vitamins, and more milk – but she kept putting it off. 'Stop fussing, Cecil,' she'd tell me. 'All in good time.' Yet in the meantime she was eating us out of house and home and the kitty was fast diminishing. I couldn't go to an employment agency without references so instead I patrolled the King's Road with Floss, looking in shop or café windows for postcards advertising casual work. Eventually I found a position waitressing in a milk bar but that only lasted a few days; I broke two cups and the owner said I wasn't sufficiently friendly.

Floss knocked on our door one morning soon afterwards to pass on a message from Chalkie that if I were still not suited, I could try being a fluffer on the Underground.

'What's that?' Fluffing sounded rather jolly, as though one might be plumping up cushions or drifting about with a feather duster.

'Being a char,' she said, brutally. 'You won't like it.'

But I was used to doing things I didn't like. I presented myself at Piccadilly Underground station that evening for the night shift, my hair gathered up in a turban. My fellow fluffers were a tough bunch: mostly middle-aged women, with a few men to pull the trolley carrying giant dustbins along behind us. We were each given overalls and gloves that weren't nearly strong enough for the punishment they had to take. Armed with a Tilley lamp, scraper, and dustpan and brush, we would jump down from the platform and plunge into the dense black tunnels to chisel the day's dirt and dust from the rails and sweep it away. I soon learned to tie a handkerchief over my nose and mouth yet even so, my nostrils were rimmed with black and my hands so filthy that no amount of washing could get them clean – like a proletarian Lady Macbeth, I thought, scrubbing my fingers in the communal sink.

We toiled through the night, our lamps strung out along the tunnel in a lonely constellation, until it was time for tea and sandwiches at dawn. I did my best to keep up with the chat but the conversation would peter out if I joined in. We all looked the same in our overalls and headscarves but as soon as I opened my mouth, the other women eyed me suspiciously. They probably thought I was spying for the management.

'Why's a girl like you doing this sort of work?' one of them asked. 'Couldn't you find nothing else?'

At first, fluffing gave me a strange sense of satisfaction. I didn't mind the squalor. Maybe I was trying to atone for sins I couldn't admit, even to myself, and grubbing about in the dirt was suitable penance. In fact, I worked too hard. The head of our patrol, a wizened little Cockney called Gert, had to tell me to ease off because I was putting the rest of them to shame.

Because I was working all night, it didn't seem unreasonable that Claude should take over the shopping. Finding supplies was a thankless task: one would tag on to the end of a queue without any idea what would be at the end of it, only to find in many cases that the bread, fish, tripe or whatever it was had run out by the time one stepped into the shop. Still, waiting in line might be tedious but it was nothing compared to the rigours of fluffing. I tried not to complain about my lot – as opposed to Claude, who was always moaning about having to stand in line for hours.

'It's making my ankles swell and I'm dying of boredom. If another old biddy asks me when Baby's due, I shall scream. It's all right for you, out and about, having larks with a bunch of other girls.'

Larks? She had no idea. When I tried to tell her about the realities of my job, she said surely it was better than being a Land Girl and perhaps the issue was that I simply didn't enjoy manual labour. 'At least you're safe down there,' she added. 'I didn't get a wink of sleep last night, what with robot bombs and gunfire and then the fire engines tearing past.'

A doodlebug had fallen on a restaurant in Kensington High Street, we found out a couple of days later; later still, we heard that forty-four people had been killed that evening. Casualty figures were kept secret for as long as possible, for the sake of public morale.

* * *

'I'm not sure how much longer I can stick this fluffing business,' I told Claude one afternoon, as she was trying on hats we couldn't afford in Peter Jones while I watched with my ravaged hands in my pockets.

'Is it really so bad?' She pulled down the veil of a straw toque, turning her head this way and that. 'Perhaps you'd better find something else. Beats me why you don't want to work for Chalkie. Running parties sounds like much more fun.'

You do it then, I wanted to say, but of course that would have been impossible. She had become unmistakeably pregnant all of a sudden – much to her dismay. When an American soldier tossed her an orange from the back of a jeep, 'for the kid,' she threw it back at him.

'Actually, I've got myself a job,' she added, jamming the hat back on its stand. 'It won't pay much but it'll give me something to do and a change of scene.'

Her 'job' consisted of posing for life-drawing classes; afternoon sessions for aspiring artists were being held in the upstairs room at the Green Parakeet. 'Well, obviously I'll be naked,' she said, when I asked. 'They want to draw my body, not my clothes. Don't look so shocked, Cecil, it's perfectly natural, even in my condition. Especially in my condition.'

I couldn't bear the idea of a crowd of strangers gawping at her. I held my tongue, though; she could be surprisingly quick to take offence.

Life drawing was only one afternoon a week, which wasn't enough to keep Claude busy. I encouraged her to rest while she could, read a book or maybe spend a little more time tidying the flat, but she said she was going mad, stuck indoors on her own all day, and how would reading help with that? One Friday when she was in a particularly bad temper, I suggested a trip to the pub in Shepherd Market before my shift underground. I thought she'd like the atmosphere of the place and if we bumped into Jan, they might find each other entertaining.

'Just remember not to mention Mary Hale,' I told her as we sat on the top deck of the bus to Piccadilly. 'It's a tight-knit community in the Market and everyone will know her.'

'So she was a tart then?' Claude asked.

'No, she was a maid. A sort of secretary for tarts.'

She snorted with laughter. 'Goodness, Cecil, you have become worldly wise all of a sudden.'

Her mood had transformed at the prospect of an outing; she'd been humming under her breath as she searched for something to wear. We were running out of clothes by then. One lucky afternoon, I'd found Ivy's sewing machine and basket in the depths of the cellar and scoured the flat for any sort of fabric. Cushion covers became a patchwork jacket and I made a frock for each of us out of the sitting-room curtains. Little Miss Sew and Sew, Claude used to call me – affectionately though. Most outfits were cobbled together by that stage of the war and everyone looked more or less eccentric, so at least we fitted in.

Guy Cavendish came to our rescue. I'd taken to calling on him occasionally when Claude was locked away in her room and I was at a loose end. I'd darn his socks or tidy up his flat and he would pay me in cups of coffee and clothing coupons, which he said were no use to him. He took me through to his bedroom one day to explain why ('No need for alarm, I assure you') and flung open the door of a large wardrobe, crammed so full there wasn't space for so much as another bow-tie.

'These tails belonged to my father. Clothes were made to last in those days and this lot should see me out. Gieves for suits, Lock for hats and boots from Lobb, that's the drill. None of this utility tat.'

We spent most of the precious clothing coupons on shoes. I

bought a pair of wooden-soled sandals, and when Claude heard me coming, she used to sing that song about Clementine with her shoes made out of herring boxes. She'd splashed out on a pair of lace-up brogues, which weren't exactly dainty. 'Oh, Cecil, has it come to this?' she'd complain, stretching out her legs to contemplate her feet. 'To think of the heels one used to take for granted! Will we ever see their like again?'

She was wearing the brogues that evening, I remember, and a cardigan over the gold frock, which was becoming indecently tight. She'd have done better in the dress I'd made but she said she wouldn't be seen dead in Mayfair wearing half a pair of curtains. When we reached the pub, she stood for a moment on the threshold, scanning the saloon to see who might be watching and hold their attention. I felt almost sorry for her, waiting in vain to be noticed as a wave of cigarette smoke and frantic Friday-night conversation broke over us.

'Come on,' I shouted, grabbing her arm and steering her through the crowd towards the bar. 'Oh, look! There's my friend Jan.'

He was sitting at a table under the window with an exquisite waif in a Wren's uniform: tiny but perfectly formed, like a Dresden shepherdess. Dark hair sprang from her forehead in glossy curls, her complexion was dazzling, and her jacket brought out the intense blue of her eyes. I sensed Claude stiffen beside me.

'Do you mind if we join you?' I called above the hubbub as we bore down upon them, squeezing past two old men playing dominoes. 'Quite a scrum in here tonight, isn't there?'

'By all means,' Jan replied, without much enthusiasm. He brightened a little when I presented Claude, though, and introduced the vision of loveliness beside him as Pandora something or other. I went off to fetch a round of drinks, leaving Claude to break the ice. By the time I came back, she was in the middle of an anecdote about bed bugs and a butch ATS sergeant. Jan was smiling politely but Pandora had given up any pretence of listening and was looking around the room as if in search of better company, smoking a cigarette. My heart sank; Claude was talking in that silly, affected tone I remembered from the restaurant when we'd first met.

'So how do you two know each other?' Jan asked when Claude paused for breath.

'We're second cousins twice removed,' she said, before I could reply. 'And now Cecil's taken pity on me and given me a home in London while I wait for news of my husband. He's a POW, you know, in the Far East.'

Pandora swivelled in Claude's direction. 'Really? Whereabouts? My cousin's holed up in Malaya. Ghastly rotten luck.'

Claude bit her lip. 'I simply can't talk about it,' she said, after a pause. 'Sorry.'

'So you've found somewhere to live?' Jan asked me. 'You won't be dossing down on Miss Hale's floor?'

I nodded. 'By the way, has she turned up? I'd love to see her.'

Before he could reply, Claude broke in. 'Our Cecil's a woman of means, don't you know. We're sharing a lovely little flat in Chel–'

I trod on her foot, hard, under the table. 'Now then, nobody wants to hear about our domestic arrangements.'

'Oh, but I do,' Pandora said in her silvery, mocking voice. 'They sound perfectly idyllic. You must throw a party and invite us so we can see for ourselves.'

'There's an idea,' Claude said. 'What do you think, Cecil?'

'Don't be ridiculous,' I snapped, finally losing my temper. 'I'm working all night and you're in no state for parties. And besides, we don't know anyone.'

'But you know me,' Pandora said. 'Sort of. I can bring a crowd and introduce you to a few people.'

'That's enough, Panda,' Jan told her. 'Your crowd isn't for the faint-hearted.'

She smiled, and blew a perfect smoke ring. 'Perhaps not. Now drink up, Fitz, or we'll be late.'

'Where are you off to?' Claude asked.

'The Four Hundred,' Pandora replied distantly. 'Private party, I'm afraid.'

An awkward silence fell over the table. I glanced at the clock above the bar. 'Goodness, I must get going, too, or I'll be late for work.'

'Cecil's a fluffer,' Claude said, with a spiteful gleam in her eye. 'Do you know what that is? Someone who cleans the Underground tracks with a bucket and a brush. She toils away all night long and comes home exhausted in the morning, looking like a miner.'

'Good God,' Pandora exclaimed, looking at me in horror. 'What on earth are you doing that for?'

'Because I can't find anything else,' I replied. 'And we need the money.'

'Well, I think it's marvellous,' Jan said. 'Good for you, Cecil. You're certainly doing your bit for the country.'

Pandora stubbed out her cigarette. 'You should try the Gerrard Street telephone exchange. They're always short of staff and you've got the voice for it.' She scribbled an address on the back of a beer mat and handed it to me. 'It's about twenty minutes' walk down the road from here. Tell them Bunty Braithwaite sent you.'

Bunty Braithwaite was a chum of Pandora's, apparently, who had worked at the exchange for a few months before practically dying of boredom and training as a motorcycle despatch rider instead.

'Thanks.' I put the beer mat in my pocket. 'That's really decent of you.'

Pandora flashed me a smile and Jan squeezed my shoulder almost affectionately as they left.

Claude watched them go, glowering. I turned to her. 'Why did you have to tell them about the flat? And what was all that about your husband being a POW? I thought we'd agreed he was dead!'

'Don't start,' she muttered. 'I got carried away, that's all.'

'We have to stick to the story. This isn't a game – it's important.'

'Oh, what does it matter?' She sighed. 'Nobody cares about us.'

Secrecy wasn't as important for her as it was for me. Perhaps I should have told her then what I was really worried about, but she was far too indiscreet to be trusted. And she had been so nasty that evening. I knew she'd only been mean because she was jealous of Pandora but, even so, she had hurt me. Not for the first time – nor the last, either.

9

GOING UP IN THE WORLD

London, August 1944

The telephone exchange must have been short-staffed because I was given an interview on the spot the very next day. I practised my story on the bus to Piccadilly Circus. This is what I had come up with: my mother had recently died and I was in need of a change, so I'd left my previous job in a munitions factory and was staying with a friend in London while looking for alternative war work. The harassed woman who interviewed me wasn't interested in the finer details, however.

'Passed your School Certificate?' she asked, digging out her spectacles from under a pile of letters sliding off the desk. 'I'll need to see the diploma.'

Our house had been bombed, I improvised rather brilliantly, and since my old school had been evacuated to Wales, it was proving difficult to get a replacement.

She nodded and asked me a few general knowledge questions – for form's sake as much as anything, it seemed –

then threw down her pen and sat back in the chair. 'But are you reliable, Miss Hale? Communications are vital at this time of national emergency, and there's no point in the Post Office training up a flibbertigibbet who won't stay the course. Our telephonists must observe the three Ds: discipline, dedication, discretion.'

I said that I would and promised to add a D of my own: diligence. I was an extremely hard worker. Her eyes lit up; I could see her mentally revising the list. 'Marvellous! Can you start immediately? There'll be an initial training period but you should get the hang of it pretty quickly. Follow our rules to the letter and you won't go far wrong.'

I spent a few days in the Mount Pleasant headquarters with a headset and a pretend switchboard and then, because operators were in such short supply, I was set loose on the real thing. Truly, the work wasn't difficult. I started off by connecting outgoing calls. When someone lifted their telephone receiver, a bulb would light up in the lower section of the switchboard in front of me; I would put a plug in that jack to speak to whoever it was, and say, 'Number, please?' in a voice that was brisk yet pleasant.

We weren't allowed to chat with callers and anything we did say had to follow an exact script, word for word. For example, if they were using a public telephone box and exceeded their three minutes, we had to say: 'Caller, your time is up. If you require further time, please put your money in the box.' During a raid, lines had to be left open for the police and the ARP, so if anyone wanted to make a call, we had to ask whether it was of urgent national importance. Mrs Shaw, who sat next to me, said that a woman who'd replied yes, it was, had in fact turned out to be ringing her dressmaker; she'd taken great pleasure in cutting her off.

Mrs Shaw was a stickler for the three Ds. Her hair was

permed into tight curls, her enunciation was crystal clear and she always looked immaculate. The Bakelite headsets we wore soon left me a dripping mess but she'd blot her face with a lace handkerchief every five minutes and dab it with powder in our tea break, scrutinising herself in the small round mirror of her compact. I was meant to learn from her example and she was meant to be keeping an eye on me, along with Miss Ryan, who supervised the five or six girls in my section, and Miss Magee, who stood on her dais like a goddess and watched over us all. Miss Magee could listen in to any conversation she chose and wore an air of perpetual disappointment, as though she'd learned everything there was to know about human nature and found it sadly lacking.

I felt at home in the telephone exchange from the beginning. My duties were simple and well-defined and I loved overhearing snatches of chatter. I'd relay the choicest snippets to Claude after work, discovering a talent for mimicry. 'She only told us it was horsemeat after we'd finished. It made me feel quite queer.' 'Sorry is as sorry does, but you're not the one who'll be left with a consignment of eels and a ruined reputation.' 'So I says to him, I can't walk about in odd shoes – I shall be a laughing stock.' 'Her Reg is back but he's not himself. He sleeps on the floor and he's gone vegetarian, though he'll eat a sausage if it's put in front of him.'

I was too busy to worry about doodlebugs and it felt safer to be in a crowded room with lots of other girls. If an engine did happen to cut out overhead, we would scramble to take cover, falling over each other in an untidy heap behind a wall of filing cabinets. No one could be standoffish after that. One afternoon Mrs Shaw accepted my offer of a cigarette in our tea break and talked for the entire fifteen minutes – nervously, taking frequent puffs with a tiny smacking of her lips like a goldfish, and her protuberant pale-blue eyes darting about the room. She had lost her husband in the raid on Saint-Nazaire but thank goodness, in 1939 their two children had been sent to stay with his sister in America, so they'd missed all the unpleasantness and were thoroughly enjoying themselves. The sister also sent over parcels, which were a godsend. Last month Mrs Shaw had received two tins of butter and a simply enormous ham that she was still eating up in sandwiches.

'I'll bring you some butter tomorrow,' she whispered behind her hand when it was time to go back to work. 'Don't tell the others.'

Life should have been easier now I had a regular job, and in some ways it was. We could go to the pictures again and didn't have to think twice about eating out in the cheaper restaurants. I could also take on more fire-watching shifts to ingratiate myself with Mrs Hoffman. I was given a stirrup pump, a bucket of water and a football rattle, with which I was meant to rouse the remaining inhabitants of Victoria Mansions. The idea of me running up and down stairs with this rattle reduced Guy Cavendish to tears of laughter. I would knock on his door as I passed, and he would often join me up on the roof in his dressing gown and pyjamas for a cigarette and a nip of brandy from the hip flask. When the sky grew dark, we'd hear our planes roar in formation overhead, off to bomb the doodlebug launching sites in France, or factories and oil refineries in Germany. Maybe the war would only end when there was nothing left to destroy.

It was an extraordinary experience, standing up there on the roof at night. Sometimes searchlights would light up the sky and we could see the columns of Battersea Power Station across the river; at others, we could only hear the great bombs as they roared through the dark, chased by the patter of anti-aircraft guns and exploding shells. Chunks of molten shrapnel would rain down, sending me scurrying after them with the trusty stirrup pump, while fire engines careered through the streets below with their bells clanging. I was never as terrified out in the open: there was too much going on and I was too excited to be truly afraid. There was even a savage beauty to be found in the leaping flames of a fire, when seen from a safe distance.

Guy seemed exhilarated by the destruction. 'Blow it all up!' he would crow above the din. 'Tear down the walls and let in daylight.'

'But Mr Cavendish, people are dying,' I shouted back at him after one explosion alarmingly close by.

'Not me, though,' he called. 'I'm actually living at last. Don't you feel it, too, Cecil? Our time will come! No one can carry on in the old way after this.'

I didn't know what I felt, beyond a sense of unease at being claimed by him as an ally. I was hungry all the time; tired and afraid most of the time. Any journey, no matter how short, was daunting: one was never sure what might happen en route. Perhaps that was the reason Claude was so reluctant to go anywhere. She was becalmed, listless. I would come back from work to find her asleep on the sofa, the needle stuck in a record revolving on the gramophone turntable. She hadn't the energy to register at a prenatal clinic. 'All in good time, Cecil,' she'd say. 'Do stop nagging.'

She was no longer posing at the Green Parakeet, since the baby was kicking and making her too uncomfortable to keep still, and she was too tired to do any shopping, so we paid Floss a shilling a week and gave her our sweet coupons in exchange for collecting the household rations. I tried to be patient but it was irritating to see Claude lounging about when I was working so hard. She managed to strew the few possessions she had all around the flat: a trail of crumpled newspapers, dirty cups, cardigans and odd shoes marked her progress through the day. She was only untidy because her bedroom was too small, she said, no doubt waiting for me to offer her mine. She wouldn't even walk to the library to change our books, although some fresh air would have made her feel so much better.

I did my best to cheer her up, giving her the lion's share of what little food we had and often making do with a cigarette instead of a meal. The weight was dropping off me by the day. I wore a belt with the green dress, drawing it tighter every week, and cheekbones had appeared on my face for the first time in years. I was shrinking while she expanded.

'I'm turning into a suet pudding,' she would say, cupping her breasts with loathing and glaring at me as though it were my fault.

I worried about her. Working on the farm had taught me how dangerous giving birth could be; she was over six months' pregnant and hadn't had any sort of check-up, as far as I knew. Spotting a district nurse unchaining her bicycle from our railings one day, I found out the details of the nearest prenatal clinic and called in there to book Claude an appointment. For one thing, she still hadn't claimed her green ration book for expectant mothers and she'd need a medical certificate to be issued with one of those. After a lot of cajoling, she agreed to go, and came home afterwards in a foul temper.

'Well, you won't get me back there in a hurry.' She threw herself into a chair. 'I had to wait for hours in a room full of enormous women and their horrid little children running amok, only to be told I should rest every afternoon and start knitting a layette – whatever the hell that is. People seem to think they have a right to paw over me and pry into my life. It's as though I've become public property.'

'Did you get the certificate though?'

She patted her pocket. 'Extra milk and orange juice, here we come. Not forgetting the joy of cod liver oil and vitamin drops. We must give thanks to Lord Woolton, who appreciates what a marvellous job we preggies are doing for our country. Unwillingly, in my case.'

To cheer her up, we went out for supper that night to an Italian restaurant in Kensington High Street where the owner had taken a shine to us and would hide extra meat under the broccoli, or slip a pat of butter into our baked potato. I wore a peasant blouse made out of napkins pieced together, while Claude was dressed in a shift that I'd sewn from a candlewick bedspread. Giuseppe paid me more attention than usual that evening and I caught Claude looking at me in a way she never had before, for all her talk of making the most of myself. It was rather gratifying.

'So this is the new order,' she remarked. 'A sack for me and a saucy off-the-shoulder number for you. Suppose I'd better get used to it.'

I finally lost patience. 'Buck up, for goodness' sake! I know you're in a jam but things could be worse. Stop feeling sorry for yourself and think about somebody else for a change. I'm run ragged, trying to keep this show on the road, and you're not lifting a finger to help.'

She blushed, smoothing the napkin on her lap before meeting my eyes. 'Sorry, Cecil. I don't mean to be such a misery. I do appreciate everything you're doing, honestly. It's only that sometimes all this feels a bit... overwhelming.'

I put my hand over hers, balled into a fist on the table. 'Just think, only a couple more months and it will be over. If we can hold our nerve, we'll come through.'

* * *

Claude took my words to heart. She went for a walk every day, which was a start. 'Just around and about,' she'd say when I asked her where she'd been. One day when I was working a late shift, I followed her at a discreet distance, just to make sure she was all right. She went up to Kensington Gardens and sat on a bench by herself. A uniformed nanny pushed a pram around the bandstand but the place was relatively empty; people were leaving London in droves by then because of the doodlebugs, and now one hardly saw any children on the streets. Seeing Claude so alone touched me deeply and I resolved to be more patient with her, although my outburst didn't seem to have done too much harm. She was making an effort to cook with what little food we had, and I appreciated the gesture even if the end result wasn't always a roaring success. Nobody could create miracles with powdered egg and potatoes, after all. It would take me ages to wash up after one of her sessions in the kitchen, but that was a small price to pay for keeping her occupied and happy. Happier, anyway.

One day, she repeated something Jan had told her, and I learned she'd been to the pub at Shepherd Market and bumped into him. 'We had a good chat,' she said. 'I didn't take to Pandora but he's nice, isn't he? We got on much better without her around. She's been posted to Scotland, apparently. He doesn't seem too upset so I suppose it's a case of "out of sight, out of mind".'

I was glad to think of Claude having a friend but the fact it was Jan alarmed me. 'Just be careful. Remember not to mention anything about Mary Hale, won't you?'

She only laughed and told me to stop being paranoid. Yet a growing sense of unease had been creeping up on me for days. Mrs Hoffman's door was often ajar and I would sense her standing behind it, listening to my tread. I became convinced that someone had been in the flat when we were out. A newspaper might be lying on the sofa that I was sure we'd left folded on the coffee table, or the top drawer of my chest of drawers slightly ajar when I always make sure every door and drawer is firmly closed. We were having occasional visitors now: Floss often called by with our shopping and Claude was also being seen at home by a community midwife. Our flat didn't feel so safe anymore.

Claude teased me about these suspicions but that didn't mean they were unjustified. I took to looking over my shoulder as I approached Victoria Mansions, and then to entering our flat via the service alley and our backyard rather than the main entrance. Mrs Hoffman was particular friends with one of the wardens, a tall woman with tree-trunk legs and hostile eyes; if I encountered them together, they would stop gossiping to stare at me, unabashed, returning my greeting with a cursory nod.

One evening, I found a knitted scarf that smelt of aftershave lying on the coffee table in the sitting room. 'Oh, that must be Jan's,' Claude said when I asked her about it.

'He's come here?' I couldn't believe my ears. 'Why? How?'

'Because I invited him. Well, not today specifically, but I told him to drop by if he was ever in the area, and this afternoon he did.'

'We shouldn't tell anyone where we live!' I took her by the shoulders. 'How could you have been so indiscreet? What if he blabs about us?'

She wriggled out of my hold. 'He won't do that, he's a friend. Honestly, it's fine.'

'How can you be so sure? He could be one of these Mass Observation types, or even working undercover for the police or MI5. And you know how Mrs Hoffman feels about callers.' The flat was my sanctuary; she should never have issued an invitation without asking me first. 'Besides,' I added, 'Jan was Mary Hale's neighbour and that's dangerous.'

'He already knows about Mary,' she said, rubbing her shoulder where I'd gripped it.

My blood ran cold. 'What do you mean?'

'Well, somehow he's found out you're passing yourself off as Mary Hale. He asked me how you'd got hold of her details so I told him she'd been killed by a bomb and we'd come across her handbag in the debris.'

I sank into a chair, trying to make sense of her words. 'You should have lied, told him he was talking rubbish.' A wave of dread was rising up from my stomach. 'How did he know about Mary? Did you let something slip?'

'Of course not,' she snapped. 'He just knew, I have no idea how. There was no point denying the whole thing; that would only have made him more suspicious.'

I buried my head in my hands. 'That's it, then. We're done for. Or at least, I am.'

'Oh, don't be so melodramatic. He's not going to report us. Why would he? He hardly knew Mary Hale and he likes us; he told me so. Nobody in Shepherd Market talks to the police, apparently – it's against their code of honour.'

It was all right for her: she could carry on using her dead sister's identity card and get away with it. Her parents were bound to stick up for her if the police questioned them and she could blame me for everything. For the first time, I wondered whether I'd be better off without her. But where would she go? I couldn't just throw her out on the street.

'You don't seem to realise how serious this is,' I said, choosing my words with care. 'Gossip spreads quickly and if we're arrested, we could be sent to prison. That's not the worst of it, either. The press will get to hear and then it'll be us in *The Kensington and Chelsea Gazette*, if not *The Mirror*. Can you imagine what your parents will say? Our lives will be ruined.'

She had the grace to look a little abashed. 'It won't come to that, I'm sure. I made Jan promise not to tell anyone.'

'Well, that's all right then.'

My sarcasm passed her by. 'You really don't need to get in

such a state. Jan's on our side – he wouldn't do anything to hurt us.'

I had to ask. 'He didn't make a pass at you, did he? You're not having some sort of... liaison?'

'Don't be absurd.' The colour rose in her cheeks. 'As if any man would look twice at me in this condition.'

'You should be careful,' I said. 'Going to a pub on your own could give people the wrong idea. If you're so desperate for company, wait till I come home and we can go out together.'

She heaved herself off the sofa and lumbered into the kitchen without replying.

10

AN UNEXPECTED GUEST

London, August 1944

'I suppose you think I'm a terrible person.'

'Not necessarily.' Jan drained his beer mug and set it back on the table. 'An intriguing one, certainly. What passions lie beneath that impressive bosom of yours, I wonder?'

'Same again?' I asked brightly.

He nodded. 'Thanks. Don't mind if I do.'

When I'd made my way back to our table with our drinks, he said, 'You should have come clean from the beginning, though, instead of coming up with that ridiculous story about sleeping on Miss Hale's floor. As if I'd have believed that of either of you.'

'I didn't know whether you could be trusted.' And I still didn't, come to that. 'This isn't how I usually behave, but I have pressing reasons for wanting a fresh start.'

'Evidently. Stealing a dead woman's identity is fairly drastic.' He took out a packet of cigarettes and offered me one. 'Still, I suppose everyone deserves a second chance.'

'So you're not going to turn us in?' I bent my head to the match. 'It's not just me – Claude's hiding away as well. I'm sure you can understand why. She was the one who picked up Mary's handbag. In fact, I probably wouldn't have come up with the idea if not for her.'

'My lips are sealed.' He smiled but his eyes were sharp. 'I told you, this is Shepherd Market. We keep ourselves to ourselves.'

'By the way,' I added casually, 'how did you find out I was pretending to be Miss Hale?'

'It wasn't difficult. I had a hunch that's what you were doing, so I went to the Gerrard Street telephone exchange and asked whether a certain Mary Hale had started working there.'

I should have guessed. Why did he have to go poking his nose into my business though? As if he'd read my mind, he said, 'I'm curious about people and I like to know who's sniffing around the Market and why. But you're one of us now and, like I said, we all help each other however we can.'

I took a sip of sherry, bracing myself for what was to come.

'As a matter of fact,' he went on, inevitably, 'there's a small favour you could do for me. A friend of mine from overseas needs somewhere to stay for a few days. Could you put him up in that splendid little flat of yours? He's a lovely chap and wouldn't be any trouble.'

'I'm afraid that's impossible,' I replied. 'We only have two bedrooms and our caretaker's incredibly nosy. Claude wouldn't like it either.'

'She sounded quite keen on the idea when I mentioned it to her yesterday. Come on, it won't be for long. Look at it as a chance to do some good for somebody else. Don't you want to redeem yourself? He can sleep on the floor. You'll hardly know he's there.'

When I asked Jan why this unobtrusive friend couldn't stay

with him in Shepherd Market, he replied that the two of them couldn't be seen together, and his flat was far too public anyway. 'He needs to lie low for a while until we can get him out of the country. You of all people should sympathise, I'd have thought.' He drained his glass. 'And it isn't as though you'll be arrested for hiding a Jew in the attic. We're not under German occupation yet, thank God.'

In the end I had to agree. What choice did I have? Jan knew my secret – or part of it, at least.

'That's the spirit.' He clapped me on the back. 'Think of it as doing your bit for the war.'

Yet I had done enough already – far more than Jan, lazing around the BBC – and was content to let the war go on its merry way without me. Men had started the fight; let them finish it as best they could. I'd lost interest in the news once the thrill of D-Day was over and victory still seemed beyond our grasp. We had no wireless in the flat and only bought a newspaper when the headlines were especially eye-catching: such as the bomb planted in Hitler's headquarters by his own officers that had unfortunately failed to kill him. I'd been working in the Underground then, and the incident had caused much hilarity among my fellow fluffers. 'They say it blew his trousers off,' Gert told us, which inevitably led to a chorus of 'Hitler Has Only Got One Ball'. Singing along, that was the only time I ever felt part of the gang.

Jan was determined to educate me, however. I had to listen to an earnest lecture about the situation in Warsaw, where the underground resistance movement had been fighting German occupation since the city had fallen after the siege of 1939. I couldn't bear any more stories of the Poles' suffering; it had been shocking enough the first time around, when we'd read reports of them eating rats to survive. My life might have been limited but even so, it was as much as I could manage.

The visitor's name was Anatol; he was Polish and hardly spoke a word of English. 'The ideal house guest,' I said to Claude that evening. 'Why didn't you tell me Jan wanted us to put him up?'

'Because I knew how you'd react. Besides, this is your flat – it's not up to me who stays here. Oh, damn this blasted thing!' She threw down a grubby piece of knitting.

I came to sit beside her on the sofa. 'Well, he's coming tomorrow, whether we like it or not. But as you said, this is my flat, and I make the rules. You mustn't invite anyone back here again. Do you understand? If you do, you'll have to leave.'

She gave an angry sigh, the colour rising in her cheeks. 'But I'm so bored! And it's lonely here, day after day all by myself. I'm glad we're having this chap to stay. I don't even care what he's like. Even if he's horrible, at least it'll make a change.'

The arrangements for his arrival were suitably clandestine: I had to wait outside the Peter Jones department store at nine the next evening with a rolled-up newspaper under my arm. A taxi would pull up with Anatol inside; I was to climb in and tell the driver to drop us somewhere close to my flat.

'Better not use the front door,' Jan had instructed. 'Go around the back.'

My heart was racing as I strolled along the pavement as dusk fell that evening, looking at my shadowy reflection in the shop windows. Peter Jones stood like a landlocked ocean liner gazing out over Sloane Square, all those acres of glass miraculously unscathed. The taxi was fifteen minutes late and I was jittery with nerves as it finally loomed out of the dark and an unseen hand threw open the door. I climbed in, to be immediately assaulted by an overpowering smell of sweat, leather, motor oil and tobacco smoke. The taxi drew away with a jerk that sent me tumbling into the back seat and crashing against what seemed to be a stout, firmly upholstered cylinder that felt like the vaulting horse we used to jump over at school. (Or attempt to, in my case; I was never much good at gymnastics.)

'Hello,' said a guttural voice. 'Hello, hello.' And a pair of arms settled me into the few inches of space remaining on the seat. So this was Anatol, although all I could see of him was his teeth as he smiled – which he did a lot, I was to discover.

I told the taxi driver to drop us at the corner of the square and we sat in silence for the rest of the short journey. The fare had been paid, so I led the way along the service alley and through our gate into the backyard, with Anatol breathing heavily behind me. It was a relief to be out in the fresh air.

Claude was waiting for us in the kitchen.

'Welcome!' she said, throwing her arms wide as though she were mistress of the house. She had washed her hair and was wearing lipstick, although it was almost bedtime and there was nobody to see her except us. Anatol sank to one knee and kissed her hand, which delighted her, so perhaps the lipstick hadn't been wasted, after all.

At last I was able to get a good look at our visitor. He was well over six foot tall and solid as a brick wall, his neck as thick as my thigh and his mighty shoulders straining the seams of his leather jacket. He would have been frightening were it not for the good-natured expression in his eyes, half hidden under bushy eyebrows, and his perpetual smile. He had a mane of shaggy dark hair and always looked in need of a shave, although we were to find black bristles in a tidemark around the washbasin every morning.

'Hello, hello,' he repeated, beaming. 'Good!'

Claude turned to me. 'He's lovely, isn't he? Like a big friendly bear.'

That was all very well, but what were we going to feed the man? He probably had a huge appetite and was only carrying a small knapsack, so he couldn't have brought supplies with him. And where was he going to sleep?

'I've made up the sofa with a spare dustsheet,' Claude said. 'He can settle down in the sitting room.' She pulled up a stool and gestured for Anatol to sit at the upturned tea chest we were using as a kitchen table. I noticed the rabbit stew that was meant to last us the weekend simmering on the stove.

'Make him wash his hands first,' I told her. 'He's filthy.'

'You are a fusspot,' she said, though she consented to take Anatol by the hand and give him a tour of the flat, finishing up by pushing him into the bathroom and closing the door so he'd get the hint.

'Will you be all right with him tomorrow while I'm at work?' I whispered as we lurked outside in the hall. 'I'm sorry about this. He'll be gone in a few days, I promise.'

'I'll be fine,' she said. 'It'll be nice to have company and he seems a sweetie. Let him stay as long as he wants. I can teach him English.'

The chain flushed, water ran and we hurried back to the kitchen so he wouldn't catch us hovering. I lay in bed that night, listening to Anatol's rumbling snore from the room next door. What if he hadn't drawn the blackout curtains properly? What if Mrs Hoffman heard or saw him, or the wardens paid us a visit? What if he attracted undesirables to our flat? What if he turned out to be a lunatic and killed us in our beds? The next morning, I put my head cautiously around the sitting-room door to find the dustsheet folded away and Anatol sitting fully dressed on the sofa, frowning over a copy of the *Gazette*.

'Hello!' He beamed, catching sight of me. 'Good! Yes!'

We soon discovered that his vocabulary consisted of a few basic words: hello, goodbye, please, thank you, yes, no, good and sorry. He repeated those last two words endlessly.

I beckoned him through to the kitchen and showed him

where we kept our store of the unappetising, grey national loaf: unrationed, thank goodness, although that was as much as could be said for it. Anatol managed a doleful thank you and I left for the telephone exchange shortly afterwards, guilty yet relieved to escape. Claude would manage him far better than I.

I spent the day fretting about what was happening back at Victoria Mansions, then waylaid Jan in his room on my way home. He was pacing up and down, waiting for the pub to open.

'Look, I'm worried about this Anatol fellow,' I began, without any preamble. 'He's so big and... obvious, somehow. Couldn't he stay in a hostel? I'm sure he'd be much happier in a more cosmopolitan place.' Chelsea was crowded with refugees of one nationality or another, housed in tenement buildings where they cooked strange-smelling food, squabbled and draped their washing over the balcony.

Jan shook his head. 'A hostel is the first place anyone would look. He needs to hole up somewhere quiet with respectable folk.' He grinned. 'Outwardly respectable, at least.'

'Do you mean there are people after him?' Now I was seriously alarmed. 'We can't risk any unpleasantness, you know that.'

'For heaven's sake, buck up and think about someone other than yourself for five minutes,' he told me. 'Anatol is a decent man and a precious asset – you should be honoured to have him under your roof. He'll be gone by next weekend, I promise.'

An unfair comment, to say the least; I was mainly worrying on Claude's behalf. I walked home in a temper and opened our back door to hear gales of laughter from the sitting room; she was sitting on the sofa with her feet up on the coffee table while Anatol capered – there was no other word for it – before her in a twirling dance, his feet flashing almost too quickly to follow. For such a big man, he was extraordinarily nimble. He finished by sinking to his knees with his arms crossed and kicking out each leg in turn, beaming more broadly than ever although his face was alarmingly red.

'Bravo!' Claude shouted, clapping madly. She patted the sofa beside her. 'Come and see the show, Cecil. We've been having such fun!'

But Anatol had collapsed into a chair, mopping his face with a handkerchief, and I wasn't in the mood for high jinks.

'You shouldn't be making all this racket; Mrs Hoffman will hear. And what are we going to give him for supper?'

'Don't be such a grump,' she said. 'Floss brought us an oxtail this afternoon.'

'Did she meet Anatol? We need to be careful. There are people looking out for him, apparently.'

I became aware that he was looming over me and shrank back against the sofa cushion. 'Hello, Cecil,' he said, speaking slowly and deliberately with a guttural accent. 'My name is Anatol. Good, yes?'

'He's such a dear,' Claude said, daring me to disagree. 'I haven't laughed so much in ages. Do try to enjoy yourself, Cecil. Anatol brought up our last bottle of wine from the cellar' – which, incidentally, I'd been saving to celebrate when the war was over – 'and we're going to have a proper supper in the front room.'

I have to admit that meal was special. Anatol had laid the table with candles and after he'd lit them, he started on a haunting lament that brought tears to our eyes. His strangely reedy voice seemed to express the anguish of every wandering soul, far from home (although I didn't understand a word so he might have been singing about catching the bus), while the oxtail cooled on our plates. The song went on for some time; just when we thought it was safe to pick up the eating irons, another chorus would begin. Luckily my stomach rumbled at the right moment and Anatol took the hint. Then after supper, he washed the dishes while Claude and I lingered over the dregs in our glasses.

'This has been the best day for ages,' she said, her face glowing and happy in the candlelight. 'It's all right for you, Cecil, out and about in the world every day. No one sees me anymore – it feels as though I don't exist. I have to matter to someone or I shall disappear.'

'You matter to me,' I said. 'Isn't that enough?'

She sighed and looked towards the door. 'I'd better help Anatol in the kitchen. Doesn't seem right to make our guest do all the work.'

* * *

The next day was a Saturday and my day off, so I could sleep late. It was a shock to wake up and hear a man's voice coming from the sitting room; Anatol was singing again and I was sure Mrs Hoffman would hear. I went in and put a finger to my lips but he didn't take any notice.

Floss usually dropped in at the weekend to collect her money and coupons. 'So you've met our visitor?' I asked when she appeared an hour later, and she nodded in her usual non-committal fashion. 'He won't be here long. Best not to mention him to anyone though.'

She nodded again. 'Don't worry, Miss. There's all sorts of things I know and I never tell.'

'Actually, Floss,' I went on, 'do you happen to know of anywhere else he might stay? Such as an empty flat close by? We don't really have room here and he's sleeping on the sofa, which can't be very comfortable.' I laughed, aware of talking more than necessary.

'I've got this den,' she said, shifting a sweet from one side of her mouth to the other. 'It's not far. D'you wanna see it?'

She led the way to a scruffy tenement building, a couple of streets away. We had to scramble over a tumbledown wall to get in through the back door, which had an ARP notice pasted on it: *Strictly No Admittance! Danger of Collapse.* The communal staircase was covered in rubble and dust, and a pram stood abandoned on the first-floor landing. Floss's secret place was up four or five flights of stairs, behind a battered black door covered in chalk scribbles.

'I used to knock about with this gang,' she said, putting a shoulder to the door, 'but they don't want girls no more and nobody comes here now except me. I've made it nice, you'll see.'

A broom stood against the wall and the floorboards had been swept clean. A variety of odd furniture was arranged around the room: a mahogany plant stand, a steamer trunk, a wooden stool, a brass coffee table with a biscuit tin on it, a small cane sofa with overstuffed cushions, and a stained mattress propped against the wall.

'Sit down,' Floss invited me with a lofty air. 'Go on, make yourself at home.' She went off and I heard water running somewhere.

I looked out of the window at the usual pockmarked, smashed-up landscape laid out below. It took a while to orientate myself and realise that beyond a couple of snaggle-toothed streets, the back of Victoria Mansions rose up like a mountain range. I spotted our dustbin among the rhododendron bushes, and Claude's blue-and-yellow smock hanging on the washing line. I was disconcerted to realise how exposed we were, that we could be seen coming and going. So that was how the girl always managed to appear at the right time. Yet it was only Floss, after all, and she was on our side. I had a look in the biscuit tin; it contained a few pieces of shrapnel, some cigarette cards, several marbles and a postcard from Clacton to the White family, signed by Aunt Bessie and postmarked July 1939.

Floss came back, holding a jam jar half full of milk which she thrust into my hand. 'Sugar?' Nonchalantly, she offered me the packet with a teaspoon stuck in it.

We took turns sipping the milk. I asked her whether she thought the building was safe, and she assured me that it was. The notice was just a ruse to keep the looters out.

'It's a first-rate den,' I told her, 'but I don't think it's quite the right place for our friend. We'd better keep him with us.'

Anatol was my responsibility, after all. Jan wouldn't be happy if he found out I'd moved his precious asset to a derelict building all by himself – and neither would Claude. We were stuck with him, despite the risk he posed.

'You can use the place, if you want.' Floss wiped away a milk moustache with the back of her hand. 'You might find a bolthole handy one day.'

'What makes you say that?'

Unusually, she met my gaze. 'The way you go about, always looking over your shoulder.'

I'd underestimated her, although she must have been used to that. It was strange to think a girl like Floss should have known me better than anyone else.

11

LIBERATION

London, August 1944

So Anatol stayed with us and he wasn't too much trouble – apart from the fact of his mere existence, his vast bulk so often exactly in the way, and his appetite. Claude was content at last during that week with Anatol. I'd fret about her all day at work and come back to a scene of domestic bliss: the pair of them sitting on the sofa while he read the newspaper out loud and she corrected his accent, or Anatol fixing up the flat with borrowed tools while she was busy in the kitchen. He managed to haul our cellar door up from the depths, but the hinges were twisted beyond repair so it had to stay propped against the wall.

'It's so lovely to have someone about the place, taking care of things,' she said. 'I wish he could stay for longer.'

She had to be admired, and preferably by a man. I could see her basking in the warmth of Anatol's attention like a cat; when he gazed at her with that soppy expression, she practically purred. Of course, I was glad that he cheered her up, but also worried to death he would give us away. When I asked Claude whether he went out in the daytime, she said he might have done; she wasn't his jailer and he could do as he pleased. And then one evening, she told me the warden with the tree-trunk legs had knocked on our door and insisted on being allowed into the flat to inspect our blackout arrangements.

My heart leapt. 'Did she see Anatol?'

'He was hiding behind the curtains.' Claude started laughing. 'I could see his great feet sticking out! Goodness knows how she missed him. It was all I could do to keep a straight face.'

I went to Shepherd Street the next day to tell Jan that Anatol had to be gone by the weekend, and to hell with his good opinion.

'Calm down,' he said. 'He'll be leaving on Saturday. Thanks for putting him up.' So casually, as though it were the smallest of favours!

Claude cooked another slap-up dinner on Anatol's last evening, with sheep's hearts the butcher had produced from under the counter – he seemed to have a soft spot for Floss – and candles on the table again. Anatol wore a small round cap pinned at the back of his head, which I took to be part of his national costume. At least we were prepared for a wait before eating this time. Shortly after he had lit the candles and started on a jollier tune, however, we heard a rapping on our front door. I went to answer it and found Mrs Hoffman bristling on the doorstep. Pushing past me with such force that I was taken by surprise, she headed straight for the dining room and stood for a moment in the doorway. I followed, rehearsing possible excuses – although really, the woman had no business invading our home. She took in the scene, and I looked over her shoulder: Claude and Anatol, their faces secretive in the candlelight, and a bottle of beer on the table.

'We have a visitor, as you can see,' I began, bracing myself for the interrogation.

Mrs Hoffman was looking at Anatol, however, and paid me no attention. He rose to his feet and pulled out a chair for her at the other end of the table. To my astonishment, she promptly sat down as though she had been expecting an invitation, and they exchanged greetings in some foreign language.

'Well, this is an unexpected pleasure,' Claude said. 'Do make yourself at home, Mrs Hoffman.'

Realising my mouth was hanging open, I hastily shut it and went to the kitchen for cutlery and another glass. Rattling through the drawers, the next thing I heard was Anatol's warbling tenor with another, deeper voice joining in.

Claude followed me through. 'Mrs Hoffman's taking the bass part,' she said, and we collapsed in a fit of the giggles.

'I told you there was no need to worry,' Claude said eventually, wiping her eyes.

'But how does she know the song?' I whispered. 'And how to say hello in Polish?'

'That was Yiddish,' she replied. 'Haven't you realised they're both Jewish?'

'Oh yes, of course.' Now I felt stupid. 'Jan should have told me.'

'Would it have made any difference?'

'Not necessarily,' I replied, the moment spoiled, 'but I'd rather have known. Forewarned is forearmed, as they say.'

* * *

When we woke the next morning, Anatol had gone. He left behind a note of thanks for me and a small wooden bear for Claude which, she informed me, he'd carved himself. I'd seen him labouring over it in the evenings. She was his favourite so it was natural, I suppose, that he should have given her a present, but I couldn't help feeling a little hurt. I was his hostess, after all. Yet what could a refugee be expected to know about good manners?

Claude slumped into an even greater lethargy once we were on our own again. One afternoon, at my wits' end, I took her upstairs to call on Guy Cavendish. He'd met her a few times with me in passing, but they'd never exchanged more than a few words. Mr Cavendish was in a particularly winsome mood that day and they seemed pleased with each other. When she told him she'd been modelling at the Green Cockatoo, he asked her to pose for him and she agreed, as long as she could use a chair or even lie on the sofa. I was delighted, once I'd made sure he wasn't expecting her to take off her clothes. Although Guy was my friend, I didn't mind sharing him if it would make Claude happier. She was in a jam, I kept reminding myself; no wonder she could be moody at times. Naturally, she complained about climbing the stairs to his flat but at least she had somewhere to go in the daytime when I wasn't there to amuse her.

* * *

Summer had arrived at last and with it, a new wave of Americans, tearing around the deserted streets in their jeeps. Everyone else seemed to have left for the country so we and the Yanks had the dusty, drowsy city to ourselves. I would walk to work on early shifts at first light, past Buckingham Palace and through Green Park, where the deckchair man set up his shrinking circle of seats while rabbits gorged on bolted lettuce in the abandoned RAF vegetable plot. London basked in the sun and my wooden soles sank into the soft, sticky tarmac of fresh street repairs. One morning I might pass a newly painted door on my route; the next, a trough of geraniums on the sill of a boarded-up window.

The weather made us restless and nostalgic. Mrs Shaw showed me a photograph of her children at the seaside in California, and I could smell the salty ocean tang; the time was surely coming when English beaches would be free of barbed wire and crowded with holidaymakers once again. The number of doodlebugs fell sharply from the middle of August and Pathé newsreels showed footage of Allied troops capturing their launch sites in France. The Germans were being chased out of the country and in Italy, the city of Florence was liberated from the Fascists.

Shepherd Market was on my way to and from work in Gerrard Street so I'd taken to dropping by the pub occasionally. I was getting to know the regulars – the two Chelsea Pensioners in their red coats; the tiny Frenchwoman, Françoise, who'd take out her glass eye when she'd had a few drinks; Alf, the costermonger who'd lost a leg in the last war – so even if Jan weren't there, I could sit in the corner eking out a half pint of beer without feeling too self-conscious. Working girls from the Market would call in for a drink between customers and although they were often tipsy and raucous, I enjoyed watching them and appreciated the efforts they made to keep up appearances when everyone else was so drab. They were blowsy but colourful, like a flock of moulting parrots, and usually managed to raise my spirits.

I wanted to keep an eye on Jan, too, so I could reassure myself he was still on our side. I got the impression he visited our flat – I'd find unfamiliar cigarette stubs in the ashtray or a couple of beer bottles in the dustbin – which made me deeply uneasy. Claude swore she hadn't given anyone else our address, but I wasn't sure whether to believe her. The day of reckoning was bound to come, and I felt in my bones it was fast approaching. In the meantime, I bought Jan drinks and listened to his stories, waiting for the moment he would ask another favour or tell me he'd changed his mind about reporting us. He had summer fever, too, reminiscing in the pub about childhood holidays in Poland: riding the horses on his grandparents' farm down to the river, eating rye bread with caraway seeds, flying kites with his cousins in fields of grazing cows. 'And now they're fighting for the Home Army in Warsaw while I busy myself with verb declensions.'

'They also serve who only sit and work for the BBC,' I said feebly.

'But what are we going to contribute, Cecil, when other people brag about their wartime adventures?'

'We'll say ours were so hush-hush that we can't possibly share them. Or we'll make something up.'

'Ah, the stories we tell.' He sighed. 'If only we could believe them ourselves. I tried the cloak-and-dagger stuff once – turns out I wasn't terribly good at it. Yet I still have a yearning for glory. That's the worst thing about this damn war, don't you think? Being confronted with one's own inadequacies.'

* * *

The next day – it was a Friday, I remember – 'La Marseillaise' was playing on the canteen wireless at lunchtime and we heard that Paris had been liberated. Everyone gave three cheers and Miss Ryan embarrassingly burst into tears; somebody said she'd had a French fiancé who'd been killed at the Somme in 1916. Surely Hitler would throw in the towel any minute now.

After our late shift had ended, I stood with Mrs Shaw on the steps of the exchange. It felt wrong to go home as though this were just another day. When two girls wearing the Free French uniform hurried past, I realised where they were heading.

'Let's have a drink at the French pub,' I suggested. 'It's only just up the road.' Claude and I had once gone there in our early days: a crowded place run by an elderly Frenchman with a grey handlebar moustache.

Mrs Shaw glanced up at the sky. 'But they've forecast showers and I want to get to the Underground before it comes on to rain. My hat's only raffia.'

'Then you can take it off.' I put my arm through hers. 'We should be celebrating. I'll buy you a brandy if they have any.'

'Well, Miss Hale, you are in a funny mood,' she said, although she allowed herself to be ushered up the street.

We could hear the hubbub before we saw the place; people clutching glasses and cigarettes had spilled on to the pavement, all laughing and talking at the same time in a variety of languages, with nobody paying the slightest attention to anyone else.

'My goodness, what a throng.' Mrs Shaw adjusted her hat nervously but her eyes were shining; she had risen to the occasion.

There was nowhere to sit in either bar so I left her outside, leaning awkwardly against a pile of sandbags by the wall. When I came back with the drinks (no brandy but they did at least have gin), she made room for me beside her and we clinked glasses. Maybe this really was the beginning of the end that Churchill had promised us two years before – or words to that effect. Maybe we would come through. But then what? A man with wild black hair staggered by, swigging wine from a raffia-covered bottle, and somebody in the pub was playing an accordion to complete the picture. A cloud of pungent smoke from one of those yellow cigarettes drifted past. I closed my eyes and breathed it in. We might have been anywhere. A few drops of rain pattered down through the heavy air and nobody cared, not even Mrs Shaw.

'Just think,' I told her, 'you could have the children back by Christmas.'

Her face fell. 'What is it?' I asked. 'They're all right, aren't they?'

'Oh yes. They're having the time of their lives. Sally's started horse-riding and Timothy plays baseball. I hardly recognise them in the photographs.'

'Still, I bet they're longing to come home.'

'To a one-bedroom flat with a shared bathroom and nowhere to play? I doubt it. They've been living with Jim's sister and her husband in California. She says she can't imagine life without them, they've fitted in so well. She has her own car, Jim's sister, and a refrigerator with a compartment for ice cream, and a room for her clothes. Sally drew me a picture. Can you imagine? A whole room, with a separate cupboard just for shoes. And now she has my children too.'

'Only for a little while. She can't be expecting to keep them, surely?'

'Maybe they want to stay.' Mrs Shaw's teeth chinked against the glass. 'I wouldn't blame them if they did.'

I asked whether she'd thought about joining the children in America after the war, since there was nothing to keep her in England. 'I couldn't go all that way on my own!' she protested. 'I haven't the money and anyway, Jim's sister wouldn't share her kitchen with another woman. She's always had to be queen bee. I'm not living off her charity, thank you very much.'

I could think of nothing remotely cheerful to say.

'We had such a lovely semi in Friern Barnet,' she went on rapidly. 'Three bedrooms and a kitchen looking on to the garden, with a swing under the chestnut tree. Jim knocked a hatch through to the dining room and we put a dresser against the back wall to show off our dinner service. Bone china with a gold trim it was, Royal Doulton. Too good for every day so we only used it twice, and now it's gone. The house was bombed in 1940 and everything blown to pieces. No one can give me back what I've lost, and I'm tired to my very bones. It's all right for you, you're young. I haven't the energy to make a new start.' She glanced at me. 'I expect you think I'm selfish, wanting the children back.'

'Of course not. You're their mother – they belong with you.'

'In Chalk Farm? They don't know what they're in for.' She laughed, and I realised to my horror she was about to cry.

'How about another drink?' I said quickly.

She looked at her watch. 'Goodness, is that the time? I'd better be going. Thank you, Miss Hale. This has been jolly.'

I put my hand on her arm. 'Perhaps we could have supper together one evening.'

'Oh, pay no attention to me. I should be counting my blessings. There are plenty of people worse off than I am.' She reapplied her lipstick, blotting her lips on a hanky. 'My name's on the list for a prefab. Fingers crossed!'

* * *

I walked home in a sombre frame of mind. Of course, we had all been longing for the war to end but peace would bring its own challenges. Claude and I had been living from day to day, not daring to look ahead, and now suddenly the future filled me with foreboding. The flat was empty, so I ran upstairs to see whether she might have gone to visit Mr Cavendish. I could hear them laughing as I approached his door, and then Claude talking in that silly, brittle voice she sometimes affected.

Mr Cavendish took a little while to answer my knock. 'Come in,' he invited. 'We've been toasting the glorious news. I'm afraid the wine's finished but I can offer you a sherry.'

'Don't worry about me,' I told him. 'I've been at the pub with some friends from work.'

Claude was lounging on the sofa, the colour high in her cheeks. 'Cecil's come to fetch me home,' she said, addressing Mr Cavendish. 'It's way past my bedtime.'

'Not at all. Stay as long as you like,' I replied. 'I just wondered where you were, that's all.' Hovering uneasily, I caught sight of an easel nearby, covered with a cloth. 'Gosh, is that the portrait? I'd love to have a look.'

'Sorry, but I never reveal a work in progress.' Mr Cavendish moved to stand in front of it, as though I might tear off the cloth and look anyway.

'Of course, I quite understand.' I made myself smile. 'Well, I'll leave you to it. Enjoy your evening.'

'Wait, I'll come with you.' Claude began levering herself off the sofa. 'I was only teasing, Cec.'

'It is wonderful to think of Paris being liberated,' I said as we traipsed downstairs. 'Perhaps the war really will be over by Christmas this year.'

'I wouldn't get your hopes up.' But she looked at me a little more kindly, and I felt forgiven.

When we were settled in the flat, drinking cocoa with sugar I'd filched from the staff canteen, I risked saying, 'Maybe we should talk about your plans. Do you know where you'll be having the baby?'

'Oh yes, it's all arranged,' she replied. 'I'll be going to a Salvation Army hostel soon so you won't have to put up with me for too much longer.'

That was a shock. 'When, exactly?'

'Six weeks or so. They take you in well before the baby's due so you can settle in.' She yawned. 'I shall have to do chores, apparently: scrub floors and wash laundry to repent my sins. We have to go to church on Sundays and sit in a separate pew at the back. Can you imagine?'

'I'll come and visit,' I promised, but she wouldn't hear of it. She refused even to tell me where the home was.

'I can't bear to be seen in a place like that – despite everyone telling me how lucky I am to be admitted there and how grateful I should be. It's for first-time offenders, apparently. If I get preggers again without a husband, God knows where I'll end up.' She laughed at my face. 'Don't worry, I'm not planning to. This is enough to put anyone off sex for life.'

I couldn't help smiling. We were so comfortable alone, just the two of us, with no need for fibs or affectation. I knew everything about her and she could be honest with me – or so I thought. Six weeks, though; it wasn't long. I wanted to make the time memorable, so she would look back and realise how special it had been. In years to come we might reminisce about the hard times we'd endured but the thrill and fun we'd had too.

She kicked off her shoes and put up her feet on the coffee table. 'I'd better get on with that blasted layette. And all for a baby I'm going to give to somebody else. She can knit a dozen vests and shawls – I don't see why I should.'

'I'll help,' I offered. 'We'll soon have it finished between the two of us.'

'Thanks.' She fanned her skirt against her legs. 'Sorry to be a grump but I'm not sleeping well. It's so damned hot in the city. Wouldn't it be wonderful to go to the seaside?'

When I pointed out we couldn't get within ten miles of a beach for barbed wire and lookout posts, she sighed and said of course she knew that perfectly well, but a girl could dream, couldn't she?

'Let's go to Hyde Park at the weekend,' I suggested. 'We can sit by the Serpentine and pretend we're in the country. Buck up, things could be worse.'

'You're right.' She yawned again and got laboriously to her feet. 'Well, it's up the wooden hill to Bedfordshire for me. Or rather, along the wooden corridor. Nighty night.'

'Don't forget your shoes,' I reminded her.

She sighed. 'It's such an effort to bend over. Would you be a darling and pick them up for me?'

'Of course.'

I didn't mind doing little things for her, or even bigger ones. There were many evenings when I sat up late after a long day at work, straining my eyes over fiddly scraps of knitting without much expectation of thanks. One day, when all this was behind her and she had time and space to think, I hoped she would realise just how much I'd helped her. I thought we would always be friends; I couldn't imagine my life without her in it.

12

DOWN AT THE WORLD'S END

London, August 1944

It was a Monday morning, I remember, and I had the day off because I'd worked at the exchange all weekend. Claude had gone down to the World's End with Floss, who'd heard a rumour that a consignment of rabbit was due in from Kent; I was knitting a yellow baby bootee and listening to *Music While You Work* on the wireless. A doodle went over and my cup rattled on the coffee table but it was gone before I'd even thought about taking cover. The explosion came more quickly than I'd anticipated and it was louder too. I laid down my knitting needles, apprehension growing in the pit of my stomach as I waited for the All Clear. I couldn't help worrying if a bomb should land when Claude and I were apart, even if she was nowhere in the vicinity.

Just as I was putting on my outdoor shoes in the hall to go out and look for her, Floss knocked on our back door and came rushing through without waiting for an answer. 'Come quick!' she called, her face stricken. 'Miss Claude's in trouble!'

I got the gist of the story out of Floss as we hurried towards the King's Road. Claude had been waiting in a queue outside the butcher's while Floss went off to choose her sweets. They could hear the bomb approaching but no one was particularly worried as the engine was still going. Something strange happened next though: before it cut out, the doodle exploded in mid-air. Its tail fin had apparently crashed through the front of the butcher's shop before coming to rest in the cellar. Several people had been trapped inside the premises and one of them was Claude.

'She was out in the street when I left her, not long before,' Floss said, 'but they must have let her go to the front of the queue, on account of her being in the pudding club.'

'And you're sure she's in there?' I asked, remembering our flight from La Petite Amie. 'It's not always easy to tell straight away.'

'I called to her and she answered,' Floss replied. 'She's alive but the building's unsafe, it could come down at any moment. They're waiting for the Heavy Rescue men. They told me to clear off but they might listen to you.'

Oh, heavens. Hold on, Claude. I broke into a run, my heart pounding. We managed to jump on the platform of a passing bus which took us a mile or so before the road was blocked by a jeep, just past the turning to Old Church Street, and we had to run the rest of the way. The scene outside the butcher's shop was sadly all too familiar: a gang of ARP wardens, firemen and civil defence workers in tin helmets, hands on hips, looking up at a heap of pulverised wood, glass and stone, while a few curious bystanders stood watching from the other side of a barrier. I could hear someone screaming, though it was hard to work out where the sound was coming from.

'He's the one in charge.' Floss pointed out a tall man in a siren suit, helmet pushed to the back of his head, who was backing out from what looked like a cave mouth in the mountain of rubble. 'I told him about Miss Claude but I'm not sure he was paying attention.'

'He'll listen to me,' I said. Every nerve in my body was straining towards one end: getting Claude out of that place before it collapsed. I ducked under the barrier and strode towards the man, summoning my best impression of Marjory Bly.

'My friend is trapped in there and she's pregnant,' I told him, nodding at what had once been the shop. 'I should like your permission to rescue her, sir. I'm currently off duty but I've done this sort of thing before.'

He looked me up and down. 'I've just been talking to her. She's in a funk and nothing we can say will make her move. It's too risky to go in there until the building's stabilised but you can have a shot at persuading her to come out. She doesn't seem to be hurt.'

I nodded. 'Jolly good.'

'I'll show you where to stand,' he said. 'Don't do anything stupid or the whole lot could come down on top of you. You'd better take my torch.' He handed it over. 'And don't light a match, for God's sake. The place stinks of gas.'

He helped me climb to the spot where a fallen roof timber at a slant had created an opening, then slithered back down the slope. Crouching unsteadily on a pile of bricks, I put my head inside the gap. Immediately that pungent, hideous smell – fresh blood and old dirt, overlaid with gas and explosive – hit me in the face. The shop floor was now a crater with a vast sheet of jagged metal in the centre, sticking up from the cellar like a shark's fin. Shining the torch briefly into the pit beneath the shattered floorboards, I caught a pair of eyes staring blankly at me from a face that had no jaw. I found myself looking at a medieval painting of hell: a pig's head lay next to a man's naked leg, and there were other human body parts scattered among the strings of sausages, spongy blankets of tripe and sides of bacon. An agonised howl rose from the depths of the pit, on and on without stopping; the noise was hardly human. I swallowed the urge to gag. Please God, let me not be sick.

'Claude?' I called, raising my voice. 'It's me, Cecil.'

Playing my torch around the room, at last I saw her about fifteen feet away in the far corner, on her hands and knees. There wasn't space for her to stand upright: the ceiling had collapsed and a latticework of laths supported huge blocks of masonry piled on top of each other a foot or so above her head. Her face was chalk white in the torch beam, her eyes glittering.

'Claude, you have to get out of here,' I called again. 'Come on now, there's a good girl.'

A stray rock fell from somewhere above, ricocheting against the wall before falling into the depths of the cellar; the mass of stone grated and settled in a shower of pebbles and dust.

'I can't move,' she said.

'Yes, you can.' I tried to sound encouraging. 'One foot in front of the other, a step at a time. Stay close to the wall and keep looking straight ahead. Fix your eyes on me.'

She could manage it: the floorboards around the edge of the room were still intact, creating a path perhaps a foot wide. I reached through the gap and leant gingerly on the timber, which creaked but held firm.

Claude looked down at her hands. 'There's glass everywhere.'

'That doesn't matter. Brush it away.' And I swept the floor with my sleeved arm to demonstrate. 'Just hurry!'

At that moment, I was jostled from behind and a figure pushed past me, scrambling over the rocky threshold and dropping to the ground.

'Floss?' I'd forgotten all about her. 'What are you doing?'

She ignored me, not even bothering to turn around but running surefootedly ahead, bent double, leaping over gaps in the floorboards; a pale sprite flitting through Hades. In a matter of seconds, she'd reached Claude, had grabbed her arms and was bundling her up in a makeshift fireman's lift.

'Come back!' I shouted ineffectually. 'We're not supposed to–'

But whatever we weren't supposed to do, Floss had already done it. I held the torch steady to light the way as she half dragged, half pushed Claude back towards me, her face contorted with effort. Claude's foot slipped off the boards at one point and she screamed and almost lost her balance, but that seemed to bring her to life and finally she crawled behind Floss with some sense of urgency. Just in time: with a groan and a gentle sigh, the ceiling laths gave way and an avalanche of stone thundered into the exact spot where she had been kneeling, moments before.

'Run!' I screamed to Floss, only a couple of feet away. As she threw herself to safety, I reached in to grab Claude and drag her through the opening. Together, we slithered down the pile of rubble and into the arms of rescue workers as the building roared behind us, imploding in a cloud of dust. When it had settled, and the last reverberations died away, an uncanny silence descended. The poor soul who'd been screaming in such agony was finally out of his, or her, misery.

* * *

'Don't ever pull a stunt like that again,' the incident officer told Floss. 'It's a miracle you weren't killed.' He ruffled her hair. 'You were jolly brave though.'

'I'll say,' Claude put in. 'A lot braver than us grown-ups.'

Which hurt a little, I must confess, because it had taken

some courage for me to climb up there and see those awful things, and I had been warned specifically not to enter the building. And I was actually the one who'd pulled Claude out before it collapsed, so Floss and I had saved her life together. Still, Floss had been extraordinary, and no one could begrudge her the attention she was getting now: hot chocolate and custard creams from the WVS refreshment van, and the promise of a ride in a fire engine when things had calmed down. She and Claude were treated at the first aid post for the cuts on their hands and legs, and Claude was given a tot of brandy for the shock. The baby was jumping, apparently, but a nurse listened to its heartbeat through a trumpet, took Claude's pulse and pronounced them both fine.

When she had gone away to attend to somebody else, I took Claude by the arm. 'Let's go. Quick, while no one's looking.'

'Why?' she asked. 'I'm enjoying sitting here. It's a bit of life, isn't it?'

Yet the knot of people that had gathered around Floss was growing larger and a man with a camera around his neck was positioning her for a photograph. 'Do you want to end up with your picture in *The Gazette*?' I hissed. 'Come on, I'll buy you a hot chocolate on the way back.'

She grumbled but let me usher her away, leaning on my arm as we started to walk along the river; I couldn't face the hectic King's Road after what we'd been through. The colour had come back to her cheeks but her hair was so grey with plaster dust, she looked like an old woman.

'That's the second time I've almost had it,' she said, as we sat on a bench midway home. 'Maybe I shouldn't push my luck. The maternity home might take me in now if I ask them nicely.'

'Could you bear it though? Two months of chores and begging for forgiveness?'

She sighed, cradling her stomach. 'I might have to put up

with that. You know, I was absolutely terrified back there, simply paralysed with fear. I've never felt anything like it. But I was frightened for the baby, not myself. I suppose that's what being a mother is all about: one's priorities change.'

'Possibly.' But I only had experience of my own mother to contribute and I'm not sure she ever felt that way about me.

We sat for a while in silence, watching the murky Thames flow past. It had recently occurred to me too that staying in London, no matter what, might have been foolish. Where could we go though? There might have been fewer bombs in the country but everyone knew each other's business and a couple of women like us were bound to attract attention. I'd have to scrabble to find work on a farm or a factory and even then, we probably couldn't afford to stay in a guest house or rent a flat. No, we were settled in the city, with our routines and a community that accepted us. I didn't see how we could leave.

'Give it a few more days,' I said. 'These doodles can't go on for ever.'

I didn't sleep well that night and neither did Claude; I heard someone moving around at dawn and went out to find her in the kitchen, making a cup of tea.

'Every time I close my eyes, I see such terrible things,' she told me, and I knew how she felt because I saw them too.

It would have done us both the world of good to get away from London for a few days, even if a permanent escape was impossible. The idea lodged in my head like a grass seed, tickling away at me, and a few days later, I happened to overhear a telephone conversation at the exchange that made my ears prick up. By then, I was allowed to snoop: trusted employees were asked to listen out for indiscreet or suspicious individuals and report them to Miss Magee. Anyone mentioning place names or talking with a foreign accent, for example, was an immediate cause for concern. Sadly, nothing particularly juicy had ever come my way.

That afternoon, two cultured ladies were conducting delicate negotiations about a cottage in the country belonging to one of them. At first I listened to the chat with half an ear, connecting other calls, but soon I was giving it my full attention. A friend of the cottage-owner had been planning to stay there for the weekend with her husband – only now she was having to postpone the trip because his leave had been cancelled and she couldn't possibly go without him, since he would be using the car for truly official business, rather than pretend.

'You could go by train,' the owner lady had wheedled, 'and then take a taxi or the bus from Didcot station. Just ask for Thumb Cottage, everyone knows where it is, and pick up the key from the farm. They're expecting someone to call. The house is such a precious little place, especially at this time of year, and you've been working so terrifically hard on the committee, Edith. You need a break.'

'But how would I pass the time, stuck in the country without Michael?' Edith had said. 'I'm sorry, darling, it's simply out of the question. Can't you go?'

'Sadly not. It's Nigel's birthday and we've had a table booked at the Savoy for weeks. Next weekend is fairly frantic too.'

The call had already exceeded its allotted time and I should have disconnected, but the discussion was far too intriguing. Eventually 'Darling' had lost patience. 'To be honest, Edith, a visit from you would be terrifically helpful. What with one thing and another, I haven't been able to get up there for weeks and we've lost our gardener.' She made it sound as though he'd been carelessly misplaced. 'You have such green fingers, dear. Couldn't you drop by and give the lawn a quick trim? There's a mower in the shed.'

Edith said in other circumstances she would have loved to but her back was playing up, and her friend would have to find somebody else to do the gardening. With that, she put down the receiver.

'Well, really!' I heard Darling exclaim before the line went dead.

It was far too good an opportunity to waste. I hurried home when my shift was over, rehearsing what I would say to Claude.

She took some convincing at first. 'It's a long way to go, just for two days. And what if this woman turns up unexpectedly and finds us there?'

'She won't. But if she does, we'll say we're gardeners sent by Edith as a lovely surprise. All she cares about is getting the grass cut and I'll mow the lawn so we can earn our keep. Imagine her face the next time she sees it! She'll think the fairies have paid a visit.'

Claude wrinkled her nose. 'Pretty unlikely fairies.' But I could see the idea was growing on her.

It was an extraordinary scheme, really, and I'd never have suggested it if I hadn't been so desperate for a change, and so worried about Claude. 'Think how marvellous it'll be to get out of London,' I said. 'To be honest, I need a break, stuck in that stuffy office without being able to hear myself think. I'd love some peace and quiet.'

'All right then,' she said finally. 'As you're so keen, I'd better come along and keep you out of trouble.'

13

THUMB COTTAGE

Oxfordshire, August 1944

Thumb Cottage was certainly small, we discovered. Downstairs consisted of one room with a pot-bellied stove in the corner and a pantry tacked on at the side, while an open staircase led up to a couple of tiny bedrooms under the eaves. The furniture consisted of two beds upstairs, a table with three wooden chairs, a sofa under the window and a bench against the wall outside. A tin bath hung from a hook beside the stove and, after an increasingly desperate search, we found a privy at the end of the vegetable garden. The journey had taken four hours altogether, including a fifteen-minute walk after the bus had dropped us off.

Harvest was well under way and the roads were clogged with tractors and haycarts, the fields on either side dotted with Land Girls toiling under felt hats. The sight of them didn't make me nostalgic, only relieved to have escaped. I wore my hair short now – Claude had cut it for me, despite my misgivings – and my head felt light and free. We'd sung as we wandered along: 'Don't Fence Me In', 'Bye Bye, Blackbird' and 'Lili Marlene', making up the lyrics we couldn't remember.

When we reached the farm, I left Claude sitting on a grassy bank and went by myself to call for the key, pushing open the gate on to a yard straight from a children's storybook. A cat slipped out of the barn with a kitten in its mouth, chickens pecked the dirt and an elderly collie dozed in the sun. I could hear the rasp of a broom and smell the sweet scent of hay and freshly strawed stalls. It was a far cry from my old workplace. The hulks of dead tractors had littered the Cheesmans' yard, while rusty machinery overflowed into the neighbouring fields. The barn had been patched repeatedly over the years with corrugated iron and its gaping doors would rumble and clang in the wind. A dirty white farmhouse had added to the general gloom, curtains drawn at every window as though reluctant to witness the decline. Behind them, Mrs Cheesman had drifted about like a wraith, one hand on a bottle of gin in the pocket of her housecoat and the other clutching a cigarette. I would find her empties everywhere: buried in the compost heap or stuffed under bales of straw.

'Can I help you?' somebody called, and I turned to see a girl in familiar uniform standing at the mouth of the barn, bare-headed, her shirtsleeves rolled up over tanned arms. She stared at me, wiping the sweat from her forehead with the back of her hand. I knew exactly how she would be feeling. Those heavy breeches were unbearable in the heat; if no one were nearby in the fields, I would tear mine off, leave them under a hedge and work bare-legged. 'I've lived your life,' I wanted to tell her. 'I'm just like you!' Yet she wouldn't have believed me. I was a city girl now, pale as an uprooted stalk in my summer frock and plimsolls.

When I explained my business, she said Mrs Jones was in the house and told me to call at the kitchen door. I picked my way across the yard and Mrs Jones spotted me from the window, opening the door before I could knock. She was younger than I expected, with a chubby toddler on her hip and a calm, unquestioning face. Her hands were white with flour up to the wrist and a stockpot bubbled on the stove. My mouth watered.

She looked me up and down. 'You must be Mrs Patterson's friend from town. Hold on, I'll get the key.'

It was so easy! I hardly had to say a word. She gave me directions to the cottage and asked whether I wanted to stop by the dairy for milk and butter and eggs, as visitors usually did; the girl would take my money and I could return the jug before I left.

'You'll have to pump water from the well, did Mrs Patterson mention that? It's sweet and safe to drink though. The cottage is fairly remote but there's a pub across the field if you feel like company. The locals are friendly enough.'

Claude was asleep by the time I came back with supplies, her arms crossed under her head, and grumbled when I woke her about having to slog another half mile down a rutted track. We were both ravenous, that was the trouble. After I'd got the stove going and we'd shared a dish of scrambled eggs so fresh the yolks were orange, she perked up a little. In the afternoon, she went upstairs for a rest while I tackled the garden. The grass was too long for the mower, which had run out of petrol anyway, but I found a scythe in the shed and a whetstone to sharpen it. I was rusty too, and inappropriately dressed, yet I tucked my frock into my knickers and soon found my stride. The flash of the blade and the sweep of grass fell into a comfortable rhythm, and I remembered the pleasure of working outside in the open air, pouring all my strength into the swing of an axe or the thrust of a shovel. It was good to discover my body still knew the old dance, and the old songs were still in my head.

I finished the lawn and moved on to a patch of jungle

beneath the plum trees, where wasps crawled over rotting fruit in the long grass, rising in irritated swarms as I disturbed them. It was a relief to see Claude walking down the path towards me and to have an excuse for resting on the scythe.

'In your element, aren't you?' she said with a smile. 'Enough, now. Let's explore.'

Beyond the small orchard, the sound of running water led us through a fringe of woodland to the river; more of a stream at this point. She scrambled down the slope and splashed through the shallows, carrying her shoes under her arm. The river meandered along for another couple of miles and we meandered with it, lulled by the sound of birdsong and rustling branches instead of keeping an ear cocked for doodlebugs. We had the place to ourselves, apart from an old man asleep with a fishing rod and a dog at his feet. The bank was lined with trees on either side; we caught a glimpse of fields beyond, dotted with sheep, and a view of the pub Mrs Jones had mentioned. Then rounding another bend, we emerged from dappled shade into the full sun. The river had widened into a broad stretch of water, bordered by reed beds and the overhanging branches of a weeping willow.

A snippet from some long-forgotten geography lesson came back to me. 'That must be an oxbow lake.'

'If you say so.' Claude was already taking off her frock. 'Shout if anyone's coming. And shut your eyes till I'm fully submerged. I can't bear to be seen in my current condition, even by you.'

From behind, no one would have known she was pregnant. Her figure was perfectly proportioned: lean and long-legged, narrowing at the waist before swelling out into the curve of her hips. A breeze lifted her hair as she walked; I could see the bony indentations of her spine and the muscles flexing beneath her skin. She waded into the water until it had reached mid-thigh and dived in, carving a path through clumps of green weed. After a few strokes, she turned to wave, flinging a shower of glittering droplets against the sky. 'Come on! What are you waiting for?'

To hell with it. I kicked off my plimsolls, wriggled out of my clothes and stumbled over the tussocky grass, my arms crossed over my chest as though I were cold rather than sweatily self-conscious. She was already heading for the centre of the lake with strong, determined strokes. Silky mud oozed between my toes and the water felt deliciously cool against my sunburnt skin. Desperate for cover, I threw myself full-length into the shallows. The initial shock left me gasping for breath and my bottom bobbed ridiculously in the air, but I managed to push off with my feet and was soon afloat: gliding like a swan rather than wallowing like a hippopotamus, or so I pretended, drifting between water lilies and clumps of weed. A pair of dragonflies skated over the surface in a blur of gauzy wings, disturbing the reflections of clouds, trees and sunlight. I kicked out, laughing for sheer happiness. Who'd have thought my life could be so full of wonder?

We stayed in the water till we were shivering, then dressed and sat in the sun to warm up. 'Back on dry land and I'm a beached whale again,' Claude said, settling herself against a tree trunk.

The leaves were already turning from fresh young green to yellow; summer would soon be over. 'It's going to be all right, you know,' I said. 'The war will be ending soon and we'll be free, God willing, to make decent lives for ourselves.'

She looked at me gravely. 'You really think so?'

'I'm sure of it. Look, you've made a mistake but you can pick yourself up again and no one need ever know. I won't tell a soul, I promise.'

She reached over to take my hand and press it against her

stomach. 'Feel that? He's been kicking me all afternoon. I shall have to call him Stanley.'

'Why?'

'After Stanley Matthews, of course! Surely you've heard of him? Britain's greatest footballer.'

I took my hand away, disconcerted by the sensation. I didn't want to think about the baby squirming beneath her skin, a living creature trapped in flesh. 'How do you know it's a boy?'

'I just do.' She cradled her stomach. 'Not such a bad mistake to have made, all things considered. His father and I were mad about each other. Of course, we should have waited until we were married but there wasn't time – he was a fighter pilot and every goodbye might have been the last. I'm glad we slept together, that he knew something about love before he died. And I'm not sorry about the baby, either. Someone will watch him grow into a wonderful man, just like Peter, even if I can't.'

She gave a sentimental smile. 'It's the best thing in the world, Cecil, having a man who's crazy about you. One day you'll discover that for yourself. I'm not sure I shall ever be so lucky again.'

* * *

That afternoon, I raked the grass into heaps and dug up potatoes from the vegetable patch; we ate them boiled for supper in a slick of butter, fragrant with mint, and drank a jugful of stout Claude had fetched from the pub across the field while I was working. Afterwards we lounged outside on the bench, our backs against the warm stone wall, eating plums filched from the wasps until our skin was sticky with juice, talking late into the evening. Dark trees were silhouetted against a sky full of light with a faint disc of moon hanging there, round and pale as a communion wafer.

'So tell me about yourself,' she said. 'What were you like, growing up? Any brothers or sisters?'

I shook my head. 'No, it was just me and my parents.'

'And now it's just you and your mother.' She looked at me with her head on one side. 'I bet you were a daddy's girl.'

'Not really. I was always rather frightened of my father. He'd been gassed in the last war and was pretty much an invalid. It might have been different if I'd been a boy; he never had much time for girls. The only person I really loved was my nanny.'

'Your nanny? Seriously?'

Nanny Roberts, who smelt of camphor and Pond's cold cream and slept in the bedroom next to mine: the only person who would have run into a falling building without a second's hesitation to save me. Such an ordinary, unprepossessing-looking woman in the photograph I kept for years beside my bed, and yet the very centre of my world – until I came home from school one afternoon to find her room empty and the bed stripped. According to my mother, big girls of five didn't need nannies. I didn't even have a chance to say goodbye; my parents would have done anything to avoid a scene.

'Poor Cecil.' Claude patted my knee.

'All that was a long time ago. It probably did me a favour, actually, taught me to rely on myself.'

'Even so...' She hesitated. 'Aren't you worried about your mother? Don't you want to find out how she is, even from a distance?'

'I daren't risk it. This probably sounds awful but I'm just so thankful to have got away. She has plenty of money and she's good at making people do things for her. She'll be fine.'

We sat without speaking for a while and then Claude said, 'You know, I've been thinking. My boyfriend Peter was an only child too. His parents live in north London and they have a pretty distinctive name. I might look them up in the telephone directory when we get back and write them a letter. Don't you think they'd want to know about the baby? It'll be their flesh and blood, after all.'

The idea seemed risky to me but the harder I tried to talk her out of it, the more determined she became. 'They can ignore me if they want, but at least I'll have given them an opportunity.'

'To do what?'

She shrugged. 'Meet their grandchild, at least. Imagine if I presented them with a son to carry on the family name!'

Which was Blenkinsop, apparently – not exactly rarified.

I could tell she was dreaming up some improbable fairy-tale ending to her story, but we were getting on so well that I daren't risk antagonising her. 'You must do whatever you think is best,' I said eventually. 'I don't want to see you hurt, that's all.'

She gazed up at the stars. 'You were right, suggesting we get away. It's been marvellous. Thanks, Cecil. Thanks for everything. You're a pal.'

And I felt closer to her than I'd ever felt to anyone, before or since. Apart from Nanny Roberts, of course.

14

A PRIVATE MATTER

London and Surrey, August–September 1944

The idea of writing to Peter's parents seemed to fill Claude with new purpose, and she was almost her old self in the days following our return to London. I tried to suggest the Blenkinsops might not be overjoyed by a bolt from the blue, telling them their dead son had fathered an illegitimate child, but she wouldn't listen. Seeing she wouldn't budge, I offered to read the letter over but she declined, saying it was a private matter. Yet I was involved, because she was presumably going to give away our address. In the end I decided this wasn't too much of a risk since Mr and Mrs Blenkinsop were unlikely to write back, let alone turn up at the flat in person, and so I left her to her own devices, glad at least of her renewed energy. She was still making the laborious trip upstairs to pose for Mr Cavendish.

'Goodness knows what he'll make me look like,' she said with an affected laugh, 'but it's something to do.'

I kept my head down, bracing myself for her inevitable

disappointment. I usually left for work before she got up in the morning, but I would come back at the end of the day to find her increasingly despondent, and there was no need to keep on asking whether a reply had arrived. One afternoon, however, she greeted me with the news that she'd called at the Blenkinsops' flat – my heart jumped – only to discover they weren't living there. The housekeeper had given her the address of their main residence in Surrey, where they were spending the summer.

'So they probably never got my letter, which explains why they haven't replied.'

It was on the tip of my tongue to say that surely the Blenkinsops would have arranged for their post to be forwarded, but I managed to restrain myself. When I asked her whether she was going to write again, however, she told me she'd decided to pay them a visit instead.

'The facts look so bald in a letter. I want to look Peter's parents in the face when I tell them how much we loved each other.'

I took off my hat and laid it on the hall table. It was so difficult, always having to be the sensible one. 'Are you sure that's such a good idea? It might be a shock for them to be confronted by evidence of his' – I gestured at her stomach – 'you know, activities.'

She laughed. 'Oh, Cecil, you're such a prude! In their position, wouldn't you be overjoyed to think your child could live on in some way? Wouldn't you be so desperate to remember him that the usual rules wouldn't apply?'

I'd thought Claude was the height of sophistication when I first met her, yet she was hopelessly naïve under all that surface glamour. All I could do was pick up the pieces when her dreams were inevitably shattered. I told her that if she were absolutely determined to go to Surrey, I'd come with her. She wasn't keen at first, but I managed to convince her that she could do with some moral support. There'd be two Blenkinsops, after all, so my presence would even up the numbers. I could act as her second in the conversational duel.

'All right,' she said eventually. 'But you must promise not to say a word. You can leave the talking to me.'

I promised in the end although, frankly, she was wasting her best asset. As soon as I opened my mouth, the Blenkinsops would realise the calibre of person they were dealing with.

* * *

We set off for Surrey the next Saturday morning. It was a sweltering day and I felt uncomfortably hot in my finery: a two-piece that had belonged to Guy Cavendish's mother. Claude wore the sunflower smock, which still just about fitted and had faded to a delightfully soft blue and cream, set off by a wide-brimmed straw hat. She could have stepped out of an Impressionist painting. I hoped for the best. Maybe Peter's parents hadn't received her letter; maybe they would be polite, even if they had. Maybe they were the raffish, liberal sort who didn't care about convention. Claude was too preoccupied to make conversation, constantly fiddling with the locket around her neck as she stared out of the taxi window. We were driven away from Godalming through the rolling countryside to a village about fifteen minutes away. The fare was more than I'd expected – we'd have to walk back to the station if there wasn't a bus – but there would be time to think about that later. For now, all my energy was concentrated on the encounter to come. Dear God, I prayed, please let the Blenkinsops be out.

The taxi dropped us by a gate at the bottom of the drive. A name plaque set into the wall read 'The Willows' and, as we crunched our way over the gravel, we could see various specimens trailing their fronds over the velvety emerald lawn.

'Well, this is nice,' I murmured, stopping to gaze at the house. It wasn't what I'd expected, not at all. Built of mellow red brick with timber-framed windows and a tile-hung roof, it shimmered in the heat like a mirage, a vision of comfort and serenity. Only the cooing of birds fluttering in and out of a white dovecote and the faint sound of water running somewhere disturbed the silence. Claude stood beside me, wide-eyed, drinking everything in. I could see her picturing a child running over the grass, and that gleaming front door opening, and welcoming arms reaching out to scoop him up.

I took her elbow. 'Let's get this over with.'

A maid came to the door, dressed in a black frock and white apron with a cap. Keeping my word, I hung back while Claude told her who we were.

'Why did you tell her your real name?' I asked, once the girl had gone off to see if the Blenkinsops were available, but Claude only shook her head.

The maid seemed to be gone a long time, giving me a chance to look around the airy hall in which we'd been abandoned. A vast ingle-nook fireplace and basket of logs took up most of one wall, while a grandfather clock in the corner ticked away the tense, interminable seconds. Then suddenly we became aware of raised voices deeper in the house and the sound of approaching footsteps. A few seconds later, a tall man in a sports coat emerged through a door to our left and stood for a moment, staring at us. His expression was not friendly.

Claude stepped forward. 'Good morning, Mr Blenkinsop. Thank you for–'

'Colonel Blenkinsop,' he barked.

'Oh, I'm so sorry.' She was flustered now, her voice cracking.

'Of course, Colonel Blenkinsop. My name is Stella Atkins, and I–'

He held up one hand. 'That's enough. I know exactly who you are – or rather, who you're pretending to be. You had the audacity to write to us, didn't you? My wife opened the letter. It upset her for days.'

Claude lifted her chin. 'It wasn't my purpose to upset anyone. I only wanted to–'

'Not another word! Let me speak plainly, Miss Atkins: if you continue repeating these scurrilous accusations against my son, I shall have you arrested and prosecuted for slander. Is that clear?'

'But I'm telling the truth,' she protested, gaining confidence. 'These aren't accusations. I'm carrying Peter's child. We loved each other and if he were still here, he'd say so himself.'

A whimper of distress came from somewhere behind the colonel. A faded middle-aged woman in a tweed costume was standing in the doorway, her hand to her mouth.

'Stay back, Daphne!' her husband commanded, as though we were wild animals about to charge.

Claude fumbled at her neck. 'Look. Peter gave me his photograph, and this locket to put it in.' She snapped it open, although the picture inside was far too small to make out. 'And he wrote to me, more than once.' She took an envelope out of her handbag. 'You can read his letter. I don't mind. It'll prove he wanted to marry me just as soon as it could be arranged.'

Colonel Blenkinsop took the envelope from her, his face a mask of distaste. Instead of opening it, however, he reached into his pocket and brought out a cigarette lighter.

'No!' Claude sprang towards him. She was too late – he'd already set fire to one corner and held the letter easily out of her reach, brandishing it like a torch and fending her off with his other arm as she tried in vain to rescue it.

It was unbearable to see her so distraught. I stepped forward to restore some dignity to the situation, and the faded woman also approached, laying a hand on her husband's arm. 'Gerald,' she said. 'Really?'

He broke away and strode to the fireplace, tossing the last burning scrap into the grate before turning back to us: three women standing there like a Greek chorus, in various states of distress.

'Let *me* tell you the truth,' he said, addressing Claude. 'Peter had no intention of marrying you. He was engaged to a lovely girl we've known for years. The poor thing is heartbroken and your trumped-up story would only cause her further distress. She must never get to hear of it.' Puffing out his chest, he gazed at us with narrowed eyes and nostrils flared, the image of manly chivalry.

'Anyway,' he went on, collecting himself, 'it's natural for a young man to sow his wild oats, especially in wartime. But that is a matter of physical attraction: lust, not love.' Turning to his wife, he added, 'Forgive me for speaking plainly, darling. I didn't want you to hear this.'

And then, back to Claude, 'Besides, we only have your word that our son is responsible for your condition. You might have picked him as a convenient scapegoat, for all we know. Dead men can't deny anything.'

I stole a glance at her. Her breathing had become quick and shallow, and she'd turned deathly pale, a bright spot of colour burning in each cheek.

'We can consider the matter closed.' Colonel Blenkinsop folded his arms. 'Goodbye, Miss Atkins. I trust we shall never see or hear from you again. The police take a dim view of blackmail, you know.'

Claude merely stared at him. 'Time to go,' I said, laying a hand on her arm, but she shook it off and stepped forward.

'Please,' she begged. 'You have to listen–'

'Get out of my house,' Colonel Blenkinsop roared. 'Immediately, before I set the dogs on you.'

I had to manhandle Claude away from that terrible scene and virtually carry her over the threshold. What would have happened had she been alone, I shudder to think.

'What an absolute bloody swine,' I said, once we were safely outside. 'Why don't we find a pub and treat ourselves to a stiff drink?'

She didn't seem to hear me. Her eyes were wide and she was trembling from head to foot.

'It's not true,' she said. 'I never slept with anyone else. It was the first time for both of us, that's why it was so special. Peter didn't tell me he was engaged. He'd have broken it off, I know he would. We were madly in love.'

I put my arm around her shoulder. 'Of course. Don't believe anything that awful man says.'

I had no idea how I was going to get her down the drive, let alone back to Godalming, but then the front door opened behind us and the faded little woman emerged.

'Our driver will take you back to the station,' she called, keeping her distance. 'It's too hot to be walking in the midday sun.' A man in shirtsleeves and braces was already heading towards a garage at the side of the house, wiping his hands on a rag.

'That is kind of you, Mrs Blenkinsop,' I replied. 'Thanks.'

She nodded, and an imperceptible wave of sympathy passed between us. I could tell she didn't entirely agree with her husband, although she daren't express her reservations openly. So that was something.

We spent the journey back to London in silence. I could have reminded Claude that I'd told her this would be a wild goose chase, could have pointed out that I'd given up one of my precious days off to accompany her, but I held my tongue. As the train pulled into Waterloo station, I merely patted her knee and said, 'Don't let that dreadful man upset you.'

She looked at me as though I were her enemy. 'Please, if you care for me at all, forget about what happened today. I won't refer to it again and neither should you – not to me or anyone else. Do you swear?'

I should have let Claude go to the Blenkinsops' alone, I realised too late. She would never forgive me for having witnessed her humiliation.

15

THE MERMAID CLUB

London, September 1944

As I'd feared, Claude withdrew completely after our disastrous excursion to Godalming. Her bedroom door was always shut and she would look at me so coldly if I put my head around it that I left her to her own devices. I worked all the overtime possible in an effort to keep busy and away from the flat, becoming Miss Ryan's pet in the process. She'd never seen such a keen worker, she said, and worried that I'd wear myself out. In my spare time, loneliness stalked me, waiting to pounce. When the need for company became overwhelming, I'd go looking for Jan, or even Floss, or invite Mrs Shaw to tea at the Corner House off Piccadilly Circus. An orchestra used to play on the top floor and it was sedate up there, away from the scented and powdered boys who gossiped in a shrieking mass below. She asked me to call her Sylvia when we were alone, but I had to steel myself and it didn't seem worth the effort.

Near the end of one long Saturday afternoon, I went upstairs to call on Guy Cavendish, under the pretext of wondering how Claude's portrait was coming along. An armchair with a green shawl draped over the back had been placed by the window and an easel stood opposite, the canvas propped up on it covered by a dustsheet.

'Almost finished,' he replied. 'I'm ready for you to have a look now, if you'd like?'

And suddenly she was there with us: leaning back in the chair with her head resting against a paisley shawl, hands clasped loosely together in her lap. He had caught her exactly: the bright tangle of hair, those hungry eyes, her freckled skin and wide mouth. The brushstrokes were bold and quick, laden with paint, and the picture vibrated with energy although the pose was so still. It wasn't a large canvas, maybe only eighteen inches square, yet it filled the room.

'I'm trying to pin her down for one last sitting,' he said, 'but she seems to have gone off the idea. Perhaps you could give her a nudge in my direction?'

'We're not spending so much time together these days,' I said. 'And I'm not sure she'd listen to me anyway.'

He was about to replace the dustsheet but I stopped his hand for one last look.

We stood together for a little longer, and then he said, 'Life can be hard, Mary,' (we were on first-name terms by then) 'especially for the young, when feelings are so intense. Yet somehow we all muddle through. Years that bring the philosophic mind, et cetera. You're looking very chic these days, if I may say so. Why don't we toddle off for a drink in Shepherd Market?'

I'd met him by chance one evening in Piccadilly, emerging from the downstairs bar of the Ritz. When he'd asked what I was doing in the area, I'd told him I'd been visiting a friend in the Market, and he'd given a knowing smile that had puzzled me at the time.

'You could take me to that club of yours,' he added now.

I had no idea what he was getting at. Women didn't belong to clubs, as far as I knew – or only the YWCA variety, and I couldn't imagine Guy Cavendish wanting to go to one of those.

'So you don't frequent the Mermaid?' he asked. 'Oh well then, you're in for a treat. I shall take you! If you have no other plans, that is. I'll call for you downstairs in an hour and we can make our way there in a leisurely fashion on the bus.'

He looked so pleased that I hadn't the heart to refuse. Let Claude be the one wondering where I was, for a change. We got off the bus in Piccadilly and headed away from the pub, into Market Mews and down an alleyway I'd never taken before.

'Here we are,' he said, stopping in front of an unobtrusive blue door. 'Shangri-La, otherwise known as the Mermaid Club.'

We headed downstairs (they were always downstairs, these places) and I let myself be inspected by a woman on a bar-stool, legs crossed, puffing on a cigarette in an ivory holder. After a brief glance, she nodded us through into a room just big enough for a bar at one end and a dance floor at the other, where someone was playing dance tunes on the piano. As the crowd shifted, I caught glimpses of a mural painted along one wall: a bosomy Botticelli-inspired Venus, with a mermaid tail curled around her scallop shell.

'I'll get the drinks,' Guy called somewhere behind me. 'Go off and mingle.'

I found a side table with a couple of chairs and a shell for an ashtray, lit a cigarette and looked around. There was something odd about the place – or rather, the people – though I couldn't immediately pinpoint what. At last the truth dawned: those effeminate types on the dance floor were actually women with cropped hair, wearing men's clothes. One of them was smoking a pipe. I caught the eye of a platinum blonde in shirtsleeves and braces, drinking beer from a pint mug, and quickly glanced away. Worse still, a couple of girls I knew by sight from the Market were singing along at the piano, glasses in their hands. Any minute now, they would spot me.

A buxom woman in a low-cut frock leaned over from the next table, plucking at my sleeve. 'Haven't I seen you somewhere before? At Gina's, perhaps? Wait a minute and I'll remember.'

I fixed my gaze on the dance floor. Arms around waists, hands clasped, fingers intertwined, cheek against cheek – and such furtive, longing eyes. A note of desperation undercut the cloud of cheap perfume. 'Give us a kiss, darlin'. You weren't so standoffish last week.'

'This isn't really my kind of thing,' I told Guy when he returned. 'Let's drink up and I'll take you to the pub instead.'

'Oh dear.' He looked anxious. 'I hope I haven't offended you.'

'Not in the slightest.' I knew he meant well. 'These aren't my sort of people, that's all.'

Yet in truth I was fairly horrified: he had looked inside me and found something that wasn't there. As if I would be so overt, parading my feelings in public with women like these! And in such a tawdry place, too. Did everyone who met me jump to the same conclusion? Perhaps I should invent an imaginary boyfriend, like Claude's imaginary husband. Jan might be persuaded to step into the breach, or perhaps I could just pretend he was my beau without telling him.

I was hoping Jan might be in the pub that evening so that I could try flirting with him in a way that might throw Guy Cavendish off the scent, but there was no sign of him. It occurred to me that I hadn't seen him for a while and Claude said she hadn't either. When I asked whether they'd had an argument, she said of course not, and why was I always so quick to jump to the wrong conclusion?

'Because I thought you were close,' I said. 'No need to fly off the handle.'

Jan was on my mind over the coming days: the news trickling in from Warsaw was so bad that even I could no longer ignore it. Instead of liberating the city, the Russians had halted their advance and sat back, allowing the occupying Germans to crush the Polish resistance. Warsaw had been destroyed and over thirty thousand civilians killed, while remnants of the Home Army fled through the sewers.

When at last I plucked up the courage to visit Jan's flat in Shepherd Street, curtains had been drawn across the upper-floor windows and there was no reply when I knocked on his door, which was locked. Martin behind the bar in the Grapes had heard a rumour he'd gone overseas, though he didn't know exactly where. It was just another of those sudden, unheralded wartime departures. I felt relieved, as much as sad. I'd miss Jan in some ways but his company had always been a mixed blessing. He was always judging me, I felt, and finding me wanting.

My friends were drifting gradually, irrevocably away. Mrs Shaw and I no longer met for tea. She had started taking days off from the exchange, claiming migraines, her eyes stared more wildly than ever and the Friday perms were forgotten. Undarned ladders ran down her stockings and her cardigan was often wrongly buttoned; if I pointed it out, she didn't seem to care. And then leaving Victoria Mansions early one morning, I passed Guy Cavendish being delivered home in a police car. A muddy footprint stood out on his immaculate camel coat, one eye was swelling shut and blood trickled from a graze on his cheek. I turned to follow him inside, wanting to help, but he wouldn't hear of it.

'A minor misunderstanding, that's all,' he said, hurrying upstairs. 'Please don't concern yourself.'

I let him lick his wounds in private. We all have our pride, after all. He had managed to finish Claude's portrait and generously given it to her as a present, but I got the feeling she wasn't overjoyed with the end result. She certainly looked pregnant – either that or enormously fat. The painting was now leaning, unloved, against our sitting-room wall.

* * *

An autumnal tang sharpened the air and the first golden leaves were falling as I walked home along the edge of Green Park. There had been no sign of a doodlebug for days and the battle for London was declared officially over. *'Mighty London has shown she can take it,'* proclaimed the newsreels, and now I was glad Claude and I hadn't abandoned the city. We should all have been rejoicing, yet a sense of unease hung in the streets. It was as though buzz-bombs had been the glue holding us together and now they had gone, we didn't know what to do with ourselves. We listened to the eerie silence overhead, wondering what was to come.

Rumours spread of another revenge weapon, more fiendish even than doodlebugs, although that was hard to imagine. Elsie on the switchboard had a cousin who was a bomb disposal expert and knew the truth behind the mysterious blasts we'd been told were down to faulty gas mains. The latest rockets were said to fall silently, with no warning chug-chug to announce their arrival, and were packed with so much explosive that they could reduce a house to rubble in seconds.

'Much easier to deal with,' Mrs Shaw had said gaily. 'You won't even know what's hit you. Boom! And all your troubles are over.'

The date of Claude's departure was growing frighteningly close. I presented her with the finished layette – three bonnets, cardigans and pairs of leggings, two shawls and umpteen tiny socks and mittens – which she received with a distinct lack of enthusiasm. Knitting the fiddly things had taken me hours, let alone the time spent traipsing around shops for wool, and her lack of gratitude was hurtful. She wallowed in misery, not lifting a finger around the flat or appreciating the efforts other people made on her behalf. Floss took care of our chores while I worked like a dervish to pay for everything, and all Claude could manage was to lie on her bed and mope. She didn't even tease me anymore. I felt sure the old sparky Claude was still there somewhere, buried beneath her present lethargy, and that in time we would become as close as we'd been before, but time was a luxury I didn't have.

One day I happened to come across a letter from the maternity home, which had been relocated to a country house near Leamington Spa. Remembering our magical weekend in the country, it occurred to me that another short break from London was my best hope (perhaps my only hope) of getting Claude to like me again. We might be able to find a guest house near the home where I could stay when visiting her after she'd been admitted. I knew she'd change her mind about letting me see her; the other residents weren't likely to be kindred spirits and she would want to see a friendly face. I could wangle some time off from the exchange without too much trouble; the main problem was how to pay for a week or two away. My pearl money had long since been exhausted and with nothing left in the flat to sell, we were living hand to mouth.

The V-2 rockets were dropping more regularly now: on average, one every day or so. They travelled faster than the speed of sound so one only heard the explosion and sonic boom after the damage had been done, and that terrifying noise travelled all over the city. Anderson and street shelters offered no protection against these monsters: only the deepest Underground shelters could withstand their blast.

'I can't bear to stay in London much longer,' Claude said one evening. 'These bloody rockets are more than I can stand.' I couldn't blame her, though the idea of her leaving was hard to contemplate.

And then out of the blue, the idea of escape became a necessity – at least, for me. I'd been working an early shift and came home mid-afternoon to find a subtle but definite change in the atmosphere. Claude seemed invigorated. I heard her singing – off-key as usual – when I walked into the hall, and found her wandering around the sitting room with a duster.

'Thought the place could do with a freshen-up,' she said. 'How was your day?'

I'd been delighted to see colour in her cheeks and a gleam in her eye, but now something in her expression alarmed me. 'What have you been up to?' I asked, glancing around the room. Our few possessions were in their usual places – the jam jar of fireweed on the mantelpiece, the *Guinness is good for you* ashtray stolen from a pub we'd taken against, the stirrup pump standing ready by the grate – yet a faint, intangible difference hung in the air. I sensed a whiff of the outside world.

'Nothing much,' she replied. 'I went to the library this afternoon and found you a new Angela Thirkell. It's in your room.'

'Gosh, thanks.' My suspicion grew.

'Oh, and we had a visitor this morning,' she added casually.

'What do you mean? Who?' I spoke more sharply than I'd intended.

'Don't worry, it was nobody official. Just a man who'd sold your aunt a painting some time ago and thought she might want another by the same artist. He was very sorry to hear she'd died.'

A roaring sounded in my ears. 'What did he look like?'

She laughed. 'What a funny question! He looked perfectly ordinary, actually. Middle-aged and not especially artistic, but then I suppose he was only a dealer. He was nice though.'

'And did you let him in?' I could hardly bring myself to ask.

'Of course not. We spoke on the doorstep.'

I knew from her face she was lying. 'You didn't mention me, did you?'

'Why would I do that?' Now she was getting irritated. 'You don't occupy my every waking thought, you know. I can actually hold a conversation without bringing your name into it.'

We regarded each other with mutual dislike. She had no idea what she'd done and I couldn't tell her. I clamped my mouth shut and hurried out of the room, the sour taste of panic rising in my throat. That was a made-up story if ever I heard one; Aunt Ivy had inherited all her pictures and she wasn't one for contemporary art. I had to get away before this man came back, even if it meant leaving Claude behind. He was going to come back, of that I was certain, and his return visit would have nothing to do with paintings. She'd obviously fallen for his pretence and would think my fear was merely the old paranoia, and I couldn't waste time trying to convince her otherwise. I had to get as far away from the flat as possible, without a moment to lose. How, though? I hadn't enough money for the train fare out of London, let alone anywhere to stay.

In the end I wrote a note for Floss to deliver to Chalkie, apologising for my lack of success in the fluffing line and saying I was in urgent need of cash. Would he consider a loan? I'd pay him back in instalments and he could obviously charge a healthy rate of interest, as long as I could get my hands on the funds quickly. Scruples were a luxury I could no longer afford.

16

CHALKIE'S PLAN

London and Cheltenham, September 1944

There was a slim chance this man who'd come calling might have been an investigator on Claude's tail, rather than mine. And even if he had been looking for me, she might have stuck to her word and kept my existence a secret. Yet I couldn't be certain about either of these possibilities, and that uncertainty was enough to send me running. I wasn't going to sit in Victoria Mansions and wait to be found. I tried to make Claude aware of the danger we were in but she laughed off my fears, as I'd predicted. That night, I kept a walking stick beside me in the bed and didn't fall asleep for hours.

Chalkie replied the next morning with a message via his daughter that I should meet him after work that day at Victoria station. Floss would escort me to the chosen spot for an audience. Her dad liked to conduct his business at railway stations, she told me; they were anonymous places with everyone in a hurry and intent on their own affairs. That evening we bought platform tickets and sat on a bench on

Platform Three to wait for Chalkie, watching the passers-by. Eventually I spotted his characteristic gait: head held forward and low, as though he were balancing a weight on the back of his neck, shoulders hunched, feet scuffing the ground. Leaving Floss behind, we strolled further down the platform for a private talk.

'I'm short of ready cash at the moment, Miss Cecil,' he began, peering at me shiftily from under his cap, 'but there is a job you could do for me, in exchange for a cut of the proceeds.'

I steeled myself. 'Does it involve parties?'

He chuckled. 'Nothing like that. I can count on your discretion, though, can't I?'

I told him he could rely on me, and he nodded. 'We're friends, aren't we, you and me and Floss, and friends don't let each other down. Floss has helped you, and you and Miss Claude have helped her. Taught her how to behave an' that.' He turned to look at his daughter, munching her way through a sherbet dab. 'She's always going on about what the pair of you have been up to. Thinks the world of you, she does.'

'I don't want to seem rude,' I interrupted, 'but could you tell me a little more about this opportunity?'

'All in good time. I need to know you'll play straight with me, cos I'll be trusting you with a large amount of money.'

That sounded promising. 'Certainly.'

'Course you will.' He clapped me on the back. 'Got too much to lose, haven't you? Right, down to business.'

Friends of his had fallen on hard times, he said, and were sadly being forced to part with a magnificent sable coat. 'You could go all over Russia and not find another to match it.' A furrier would only pay half what it was worth and charge a fortune in commission, so they were looking for other ways to sell it. No one left in London had the cash or inclination to buy a fur whereas, according to Chalkie, the provinces were teeming with rich women falling over each other to get their hands on one. Cheltenham was the perfect spot. As a matter of fact, he'd already advertised the coat in a local newspaper but the young lady who'd agreed to help with negotiations had dropped out at the last minute. All I had to do was take the coat there, show it off to prospective buyers, then wrap up the deal and walk away with a cut of the proceeds. The coat had been advertised at four hundred guineas but any offers over three hundred and fifty would be acceptable.

'All right, I'll do it. I need to leave right away though.'

If he was surprised by my eagerness, he didn't show it. 'Suits me. The ad's going in the paper tomorrow.'

I told him I could take the first train the next morning.

'Good girl. I'll ring the hotel to book you a room. Walk about in the fur, show it off a bit. If anyone asks, say it belonged to your auntie. And then come straight home once it's all done and dusted.' He gave me the key to a left-luggage locker in Paddington station where the fur was currently stored, and some petty cash for expenses and the return train fare. 'First class, to show the sort of person you are. Sell the coat for cash, obviously, then take your cut and leave the rest of the money and the suitcase in the same locker when you come back. You can give the key to Floss.'

After he'd given me a few tips on selling techniques, we shook hands. 'It'll be like a holiday, only with benefits,' he added. 'I'll telephone every evening to see how you're getting on.'

Floss had finished her sweets by then and was sitting on her hands, gazing into space. Chalkie looked at her approvingly. 'She's handy to have around, my daughter, and the older she gets, the handier she'll be. I've got big plans for my little girl.'

I should have done more for Floss, I knew that. Chalkie was neglecting and exploiting her, and I should have put a stop to it.

Yet I daren't risk involving the authorities and she was useful to me, too, though I'm ashamed to admit that now.

'Could you keep an eye on our flat while I'm away?' I asked her, once Chalkie had sloped off. 'Telephone me at once if you spot anything strange – your father will have the number.' She gave me one of her inscrutable stares. 'Please? I'm worried about Miss Claude, that's all.'

She looked down, scuffing the dirt with her shoe. 'I'm not a snitch.'

'I'm not asking you to tell tales. Just let me know if anyone's hanging around.'

I felt anxious about leaving Claude on her own but I needed to get away from London and couldn't take her with me. She wasn't in danger, anyway; if my worst fears were realised, our visiting art dealer wouldn't be interested in her. Or so I thought then, in my innocence.

* * *

I took a bus from the station straight back to the exchange to tell Miss Ryan I'd just heard my mother had had a stroke and I was needed urgently at home. It was almost true, after all. She gave me a week's compassionate leave, saying I would be missed, and I hurried home to tell Claude I'd be going away for a little while. It took me a while to pluck up the courage to open our back door – very quietly, so I could find out if she were alone. She was lying on her bed with her legs up on a cushion, reading, and seemed quite unperturbed to hear of my plans.

'Of course I'll be all right. If anything should happen, which it won't, I'll call the midwife. Or ask Mrs Hoffman for help. We're the best of chums since Floss brought her that rabbit last week. She actually smiled at me this morning.'

I smoothed the counterpane. 'And the art dealer man didn't come back?'

'No. Why would he?'

'If he does, would you let me know straight away? Floss will have the telephone number of my hotel.'

'Your hotel,' she repeated wistfully. 'What I wouldn't give for a few days somewhere swanky.'

'If I do this favour for Chalkie,' I said, 'we'll have enough money to get out of London for a while. I'll come back for you and we can take the week off somewhere. A breath of fresh air would do you the world of good.' Her face looked puffy and as pale as unbaked dough, and her ankles were swollen. 'If you have to go to hospital, will you leave me a note?'

'Of course,' she replied absent-mindedly, going back to her book. She'd shown little interest in what I'd actually be doing in Cheltenham and I hadn't gone into detail; the less she knew the better, for her sake.

After another disturbed night, I left early the next morning. Pulling the heavy door shut behind me, I had the strangest feeling that I would never set foot in Victoria Mansions again. Maybe I wouldn't make it as far as Cheltenham; maybe I would never come back.

Chalkie had told me to wear the fur as soon as possible but there were too many policemen walking around Paddington station to risk it. No doubt the coat featured on some list of stolen property; if it was as wonderful as he made out, they were bound to be suspicious. I collected the suitcase from left luggage and boarded the Cheltenham train, where a kind gentleman helped me stow it on the luggage rack of our first-class compartment. I sat by the window, my nerves stretched tauter than violin strings, and when at last the train began to move, I couldn't help letting out a sigh of relief.

The woman sitting opposite caught my eye. 'Marvellous to

be leaving the city, isn't it?' she said. 'I don't think I could have stuck it out another day. Did you hear about the latest explosion? I can't believe gas had anything to do with it.'

She wore a pointed green hat festooned with pom-poms, like a tiny Christmas tree. I shook my head with a regretful smile, taking out my book to forestall conversation. She leaned back, disappointed, and unwrapped a barley sugar.

A flap of the safety netting had come loose so I worked it further open to look into the back gardens of terraced houses, with their concrete shelters and vegetable patches, their boarded-up windows and tarpaulins bulging over damaged roofs. We passed Nissen huts squatting behind barbed wire, a recreation ground packed with abandoned cars, one ugly munitions dump after another, until gradually the barren city gave way to shorn fields under a clear grey sky. The landscape became familiar; I could feel the sharpness of stubble underfoot, smell the ditches knee-deep in brackish water, hear the harsh cries of rooks. Thank God, at least those days were behind me. Perhaps this would become the pattern of my life: fleeing from one place to the next, never quite fitting in anywhere.

The kind gentleman had fallen asleep, so I lifted down my suitcase from the rack and took it into the corridor to slip on the coat. It was certainly gorgeous: a dark, glossy sable that fell to mid-calf. I went back to my seat and settled into the coat's cushiony depths like a broody hen. This must be how those women felt, the ones I'd seen running down the steps of grand houses along the riverbank or walking out of smart hotels in Mayfair. They might not have been so very different from me, after all.

I caught the pom-pom lady staring at me. 'Lovely day, isn't it?' I said, fanning myself with a newspaper.

'Far too hot for a coat like that,' she remarked.

It was a useful lesson to learn. She thought I was showing

off; I should treat the fur as carelessly as my old cardigan, to show I took such luxury for granted.

* * *

Cheltenham lay in a valley surrounded by hills, basking in faded gentility. The taxi took me down wide streets, past fine Regency houses overlooking a park where men played football and mothers sat watching their children. The place had been bombed in 1940, the driver told me, but most of the damage seemed to have been repaired. Despite the usual posters exhorting everyone to do the right thing, life seemed almost normal, which was extraordinary in itself. The hotel receptionist greeted me with a smile, handed over the key to my room and summoned the porter to carry my suitcase. He must have found it strangely light.

I lay down on the bed, letting the hotel wrap itself around me in a cocoon of flowery cretonne and plush carpet, and slept for what remained of the afternoon. That evening, I sipped my brown Windsor soup in solitary splendour, wishing Claude had been with me and things were like they used to be. We could have laughed about the other guests: the sisters who wore the same twin-sets in different colours and spoke to each other in whispers; the deaf elderly mother and her exasperated daughter; the red-nosed majors drinking brandy in the bar after their wives had retired for the evening.

After an early dinner, I took my coat for a walk. The town had been heaving with Americans until a few months ago, the waitress had told me with a wistful look; now they had all gone, leaving a terrible mess behind. Cheltenham didn't look too messy to me. What sort of life could one lead in a town like this after the war? I imagined cycling to some quiet job – in a library, perhaps, or a primary school – with a cat waiting for me at home, and an allotment to occupy the long, empty hours.

People were filing out of a modern red-brick church at the end of evening service. On an impulse, I headed through the open doors and sat in a pew near the back. It was draughty and spartan inside, and I was glad of the coat. There were few concessions to comfort or distraction: no embroidered hassocks, stained-glass windows or wall hangings, no plaques commemorating the war dead. The altar was decorated for harvest festival with a collection of moulting corn dollies, a few wizened apples, some rosehip sprays and three tins of Spam. A woman in a cloche hat trimmed with a feather was walking up and down the pews, collecting hymn books. I twisted my legs aside to let her pass and she glanced at me, her eyes overshadowed by the low brim.

The vicar returned from dismissing his parishioners, rubbing his hands together, and smiled at me. 'I'm allowed to sit here, aren't I?' I asked gracelessly.

'Of course,' he replied. 'We shall be tidying up for at least another half hour. Are you in need of ministry?'

I refused but thanked him, a little more politely. 'Oh well. Let me know if you change your mind,' he said, and wandered off.

I sat for a while longer, listening to the echoes of other people's conversations with God. 'Do come again,' the vicar called as I was leaving. 'Our door is always open, metaphorically if not literally.'

The woman with the hymn books turned to look. She nodded and the feather in her hat swooped like a pointing finger, marking me out.

* * *

Four hundred guineas seemed like a lot of money to me but Chalkie was confident the coat would fetch at least three hundred and fifty. Winter was coming and new furs were impossible to buy, he said; anyone who already had one was hanging on to it. I slept under the sable at night, feeling as though an exotic animal were keeping me company. We had all been starved of beauty for so long that it was a joy simply to look at something so extravagantly lush, to feel the silk lining cool against my skin and the weight of dense fur hanging from my shoulders. I wanted some extraordinary woman to claim the coat: 'my coat', as I began to think of it.

Replies to the advertisement were trickling in and in due course a succession of Cheltenham's society ladies met me in the hotel lobby. Chalkie had told me how to draw attention to the fur's finer points: the quality of the pelts and the skill with which they had been sewn together, the fact one could stroke the sable in any direction and it would retain its softness. A short opening in the lining showed the underside, a butter-soft suede, which could be inspected on request. My prospective buyers agreed the quality was outstanding but no one wanted to pay for it. Two hundred pounds was the only offer I received, and Chalkie didn't think much of that.

In between appointments, I read magazines in the guests' sitting room or strolled about the town, always ending up at the church. I could sit quietly there without having to account for myself, and the vicar didn't seem to mind. Sometimes he would be in attendance, sometimes not, but the woman in the cloche hat was a constant presence. 'Margaret,' I heard him call her. 'Thank you so much, Margaret. What would we do without you?' And she would nod solemnly, accepting her due.

She seemed to be a general dogsbody, keeping flower vases topped up with water, changing hymn numbers in the wooden wall rack, polishing silver chalices and candlesticks. One morning a bossy woman arrived with an armful of dahlias and commandeered Margaret's help in arranging them, sending her traipsing back and forth to fetch foliage from her car or scissors from the vestry.

I watched Margaret carry out these menial tasks with unfailing dignity. She always wore the hat, which emphasised her square jaw and beaky nose, and usually a gabardine mackintosh, belted at the waist. Woollen stockings sagged around her spindly calves and long narrow feet, swollen with bunions. They must have been painful. She kept a pair of carpet slippers in the vestibule, and I found the soft shuffle of her steps soothing. I must have interested her too, because I'd often catch her staring at me. On the third or fourth day of my trip, I offered to help her lay out the prayer books for a funeral that afternoon: a man of ninety-three, it turned out, who'd gone to bed one night and never woken up. I'd forgotten such deaths were possible.

'You can wait in the vestibule with me once the service begins,' Margaret offered in her deep, sonorous voice, and I felt absurdly flattered.

The vestibule was even draughtier than the body of the church. We sat on folding chairs, listening to the organ wheezing away and snatches of prayer floating through the open door. I read a yellowing leaflet advising what to do in the event of a gas attack. When I looked up, Margaret was watching me, her hands buried under her armpits to warm them.

'I've not seen a coat like that for a while,' she said.

'Beautiful, isn't it?' I stretched out my arms and she leaned forward to run her hand down one sleeve, as though stroking a cat.

'I'd wear it all the time, too, if it was mine. No sense in keeping things for best these days.'

I told her the coat didn't actually belong to me: I was selling it for a friend. It seemed wrong to lie to Margaret, or perhaps merely unnecessary. I could see her digesting this piece of information, like a cow chewing the cud.

'Do you want to try it on?' She was about to refuse but I'd already taken off the coat and thrust it into her arms. 'Go on. Just for fun.'

She held the sable up to her face and inhaled its softness, as I liked to do. Then she stood up to put it on over her mac, wrapping it around herself. 'My husband promised me a fur,' she said. 'That's why I married him. Thirty-seven years I waited, and now he's gone.'

'I'm sure he'd have bought you one if he could.'

'No, he wouldn't. He hated spending money.' She looked down at the sable. 'You could be anyone in a coat like this.'

The fur softened her angularity, emphasising the pallor of her worn skin and the darkness of her eyes. Now she looked noble, even tragic: a *Mater Dolorosa*.

'What do you think about when you sit here?' she asked suddenly, as though it were a perfectly ordinary question.

'My life, I suppose,' I replied after a while. 'Do you believe it's possible to do a bad thing and still be a good person?'

'I don't know. You should talk to the vicar about that.' She took off the coat and spread it out over the back of the chair, inspecting the seams. 'How much are you asking?'

'But what do you think?'

'Depends how sorry you are, I suppose. The Bible says God forgives sinners who truly repent. Is there a label anywhere?'

I showed her where it was, near the bottom of the lining – not that it would tell her much, being written in Cyrillic script. Shivering, I snatched up the coat and put it back on.

'So what's the price?' Margaret repeated.

'Four hundred guineas,' I said, to put an end to the conversation.

'And is that fair, in your opinion?'

'You'd have to pay at least seven hundred in a showroom.' I let the fur's warmth seep into my bones. 'Our Father, which art in Heaven,' boomed the vicar, with a few uncertain voices lagging behind. The service would soon be over. After I'd helped Margaret tidy up, it would be time for sherry and dinner at the hotel, and the end of another aimless day. How would Claude be spending the evening? There had been no word from Floss so I had to assume all was well in Victoria Mansions.

'All right then,' Margaret said. When I asked her what she meant, she said, 'I'll pay the asking price.'

'Really?' She must have been joking, surely. Perhaps her mind was going.

'Really.' She stroked the sleeve again. 'I'll bring the cash tomorrow. My husband told me to put up a stained-glass window in his memory but I'm holding the purse strings now and I'd sooner have this coat.'

'If you're serious, you can have it for three fifty,' I said.

'I don't want charity,' she replied. 'If it's worth four hundred, then that's what I'll give you.'

At least I tried. I've often thought about Margaret, patrolling the church in my sable; especially during that terrible winter after the war, when elderly people were dropping like flies. Maybe one day I'll go back to Cheltenham to see if she's still there and tell her what I've learned about forgiveness – although I doubt she'd be interested.

* * *

I couldn't wait to give Chalkie the news of my success, but he didn't ring at the usual time that evening. When the hotel receptionist put through a call to my room after dinner, Floss was on the end of the line instead. 'It's Dad,' she burst out. 'He's been arrested at the Three Horseshoes and taken down the nick. What shall I do?'

'Keep calm, that's the first thing.' Though I was on the verge of panic myself. 'Do you know why?'

'Must be the cards. His mate Kenny was carted off too and they're in it together. Mam told him no good would come of gambling and that's what I'm always saying too, but will he listen? And now look what's happened!' I'd never heard her talk so much in one go. 'What am I going to do?' she repeated, her voice rising. 'I'm all on me own and scared to go to the den at night.'

'Listen, I'm coming back tomorrow. Can you ask to stay with one of your neighbours?'

'Suppose so.' She sounded doubtful.

'If you can't find anyone who'll have you, go to our flat and ask Miss Claude whether you can sleep in my bedroom. Tell her you've spoken to me and I've given permission. I'll meet you there tomorrow afternoon and we can decide on a plan.'

'Thanks, Miss. Come as soon as you can, won't you?'

I told her I'd aim to be back by lunchtime. 'It'll be all right, I promise. If the worst comes to the worst, find someone from the WVS to help you.'

'You must be joking,' she said. 'Oh, I nearly forgot. Dad sent a message. You're to give the money to me instead of leaving it in that locker. He says throw away the key, to be on the safe side.'

* * *

I didn't get much sleep that night, worrying about all the things that were bound to go wrong the next day. Margaret might not turn up with the money, or she might have tipped off the police, or a detective might arrest me when I got off the train at

Paddington. What if Chalkie had confessed about selling the coat? All those options seemed perfectly possible, even likely. Yet in the morning, I found Margaret standing alone on the church steps at the time we'd agreed. We went to the vestry, where she counted out the money and I handed over the fur, wishing her much joy of it. I tucked the notes in my brassiere, Chalkie's money in one cup and my share in the other (including the extra fifty guineas Margaret had insisted on paying), and took a taxi to the station with the last of my petty cash to catch the next London train. The journey seemed to take for ever. As we approached the station, I hid in the lavatory, only emerging once everyone had disembarked. Then I hung around on the platform for ten minutes or so, as vulnerable without the coat as a sheep after shearing, before heading for the Underground.

The city felt teeming and dangerous after five days in Cheltenham. I would go to the flat, give Floss the money, pack a few things and leave again for Leamington Spa the same day. I'd already found two or three places to stay in the town from my hours spent with *The Lady* magazine in the hotel lobby, and would head there whether Claude came with me or not. And as for my job, well, that was the least of my worries; I could ring Miss Ryan and tell her my mother had taken a turn for the worse. Sweat beaded my forehead, despite the cold wind whipping my legs as I hurried towards Victoria Mansions, and dread clenched my stomach into knots. My carefully constructed life seemed about to unravel.

In too much of a state to be careful, I rushed into our flat through the front door, calling for Claude as I dropped my suitcase in the hall and tore off my hat and gloves. There was no reply. I opened the drawing-room door and found her standing by the mantelpiece.

She wasn't alone: a man sat on the sofa, his legs

nonchalantly crossed and one arm stretched along the back of the cushion. He turned to meet my gaze.

'Goodness, Fabia,' he said, with the charming, crooked smile that made me so terribly afraid, 'I would hardly have recognised you. Our ugly duckling seems to have turned into a swan.'

Claude stared at him, and then at me. 'Do you two know each other?'

'I'll say.' He was still smiling. 'Will you tell her, darling, or shall I?'

I couldn't speak. It was as much as I could do to hold myself upright.

'I'll do the honours then.' He turned to Claude. 'Frankly, I'm a little hurt this will come as a surprise, but Fabia is my wife.'

I sank into the nearest chair. There was no point trying to run; the game was up.

17

MY NEMESIS

London, September 1944

Claude had laughed, but her face changed as she looked at me. 'My God, don't say it's true.'

I couldn't meet her eye. Fumbling for a cigarette gave me a reason to drop my gaze and a moment to think, but my hands were trembling too much to risk lighting one. The sight of my dearly beloved had brought back the old familiar panic. Anthony's hair had been bleached by the sun and his face was so deeply tanned that his pale-blue eyes were more startling than ever. He'd been in khaki the last time I'd seen him, but now he wore civvies: a salt-and-pepper three-piece suit and jaunty red tie. He was a good-looking man, one had to admit. 'Handsome devil,' people say lightly; never was an expression more accurate than in his case. I made myself acknowledge his presence, the force of his will and the power he would always hold over me. Yet I had changed in the year we'd been apart. The spark of resistance burning inside me grew stronger as I sat there, contemplating my fate and deciding whether to accept it.

I was angry with Claude, too – furious, in fact. She had been lying to me for days, and now look what had happened.

'I'm sorry I had to make up a story, Pamela,' Anthony was saying to her. 'You understand though? I had to find out the truth for myself. My wife has always been unstable yet I refused to believe she could sink so low.' He shook his head, staring down at his clasped hands. 'It's one thing to leave me, but to abandon my mother without so much as a backward glance...' He shot me a look of pained reproach. 'How could you, Fabia? A woman who's been so kind to you, who loved you like the daughter she never had.'

This was too much; I laughed out loud. His jaw tightened and I caught the flash of fury on his face before he could suppress it. 'You see?' he told Claude, quickly regaining control. 'She's unhinged.'

An energy was flowing between them that I didn't understand. How many times had he been to the flat before? They meant something to each other, I could tell, and my fury burned brighter.

'Why didn't you mention the fact you were married?' she asked, turning her gaze on me.

'Because it was safer for you not to know,' I replied. 'And I wanted to forget it myself.'

Anthony let out a bitter laugh. 'So much for the vows we made in the sight of God.' He was playing the part of a wronged husband to perfection. I wondered how long it would amuse him, and what was the point of this charade.

'You told me your wife was dead,' Claude said to him, 'and that you'd loved her dearly. You don't seem surprised to see her – or particularly pleased either.'

Anthony jumped to his feet. 'Because of her treachery!' He loomed over my chair, his voice trembling with suppressed emotion. 'I went through hell thinking you were dead, Fabia, trying to comfort Mother and deal with the house – which seems to be falling down, incidentally – while all the time you were holed up here, living the life of Riley.'

It was a struggle to keep my expression blank. Claude had been stupid to believe his lies but I knew how convincing he could be; it was her betrayal that stung so bitterly. How could she have entertained a stranger in my flat and then lied to me about it?

'How did you find me?' I asked. 'Just as a matter of interest.'

'Your handbag was eventually returned to me,' he said, throwing himself into a chair. 'I found a letter from your solicitor inside, with details of your inheritance. It seemed scarcely credible so I had to come and see for myself.'

'And you let him in for a cosy chat,' I said to Claude. She tossed her head and looked away.

'Do you know, I almost wish you had died,' Anthony went on. 'At least then I could remember you with some affection. Now our marriage feels like a lie from the start.'

He was certainly laying it on thick. For whose benefit? I wondered. It could only have been Claude's, unless he was simply entertaining himself. Or perhaps he was rehearsing the line he would take when he brought me home: the prodigal wife, ripe for further humiliation.

'So many lies.' Claude rose from the chair with some difficulty, walked to the window and turned her back on us.

Anthony glanced at her sharply. She felt betrayed, too, I realised. He must have made her some kind of promise and now she was doubting he'd keep his word. He had to make women fall for him, that was his favourite sport.

I stood up and joined her by the window. 'What did he say? Let me guess. That he couldn't sleep for thinking about you, that you were unlike anyone he'd ever met, that you fascinated him in a way no other woman had before.' How cheap the words sounded in my mouth! Claude glared at me as an angry flush crept up her neck. I was hurting her, and I didn't care. 'That it didn't matter what size you were, it was your mind as much as your body he–'

'Enough!' Anthony sprang towards me, his face contorted with rage. I'd made him angry enough to lose control, and that was victory of a kind. Let him kill me, I didn't mind. A quick death would be preferable to the slow drip, drip of casual violence he'd inflict on me in private.

'That he would look after you, and make your life perfect?' I went on, my voice rising as my husband dragged me off by the wrists. 'That you would never–'

He drove his fingernails into my skin so sharply that he drew blood; the pain made me gasp, but it cleared my head. I smiled as he threw me back on to the sofa and raised his palm to slap me. He drew back, breathing heavily, stared at me for a second, then lowered his hand and backed away.

'I shall ask for a divorce,' I said, stupidly.

He brought a hip flask from his pocket and took a swig. 'You're a dead woman, remember? If you come back to life and take me on, you'll be ruined. Deserting the Land Army, living under false pretences, stealing an identity card – they'll lock you up for years.'

So Claude had told him everything; that hurt more than the wounds on my arms. He would have tricked her into blurting it all out but she'd done for me nevertheless.

'Dear God, why did I ever try to find you?' Anthony had begun pacing up and down. 'I should have thanked my lucky stars you'd gone.' He drank from the flask again, wiping his mouth with the back of his hand, and glanced around the room. 'This flat will come to me, you realise, as your next of kin.'

I could see him calculating how best to turn the situation to his advantage, weighing the pleasure of tormenting me in the future against the satisfaction of taking everything I owned. He couldn't bear to think I might have the upper hand in any respect. It occurred to me that, had we been on our own, he might well have tried to kill me; everyone thought I was dead anyway so he'd probably have got away with it. Claude was my protection.

I took a cigarette out of my handbag and lit it without asking his permission, then offered the packet to her. She ignored me.

'This is what we'll do,' Anthony said abruptly. 'I shall let you stay dead. Walk out of here immediately and we'll never see each other again.'

'And let you inherit this flat as well as my house?'

'Of course, that's the deal. You can start again somewhere else and I won't interfere. It's up to you: either accept my offer or I'll take you to the nearest police station.' He laughed. 'I could have you committed to an asylum, come to that.'

The room was very quiet. A cylinder of ash fell off my cigarette to land on the rug. I rubbed it in with my shoe; ash was good for carpets, someone had once told me. The seconds dragged by.

'All right then. I'll go.' Because really, what choice did I have?

Anthony nodded, regarding me with contempt.

'And what about me?' came a voice from the corner.

I jumped, and so did he. We must have both forgotten Claude was there.

'Pamela,' he began, in that phoney voice, 'I'm so sorry you had to get caught up in this sordid business. I'm sure it was all Fabia's idea, and of course I won't tell anyone about your involvement.'

'But can I stay here on my own?' she asked. 'Until it's time for me to go to the maternity home, I mean?'

'I don't see why not.' He took his time, considering. 'I can't expect you to clear out straight away, given your circumstances.'

'And afterwards?' she persisted.

I stared at her, incredulous.

'Hard to say. My leave ends tomorrow and who knows when I'll be back in Blighty again.' He smiled. 'Let's take it one day at a time.'

'Don't have anything to do with him!' I burst out, even though I hated Claude for what she'd done to me. 'You've seen what he's like – he'll destroy you for the fun of it.'

Anthony snorted. 'Pamela, the choice is yours. As far as I'm concerned, you can stay in this flat for as long as you like. I won't tell anyone you're here, I promise.'

He smiled at her and she smiled back: reluctantly at first, but with a gathering warmth that made the bile rise in my throat. How could she?

I stood up. 'At least let us say goodbye in private.'

He laughed then, sticking his hands in his trouser pockets and jingling some coins. 'Oh, so that's how it is. Certainly not! I won't let you spill poison in Pamela's ear. I'll escort you to the door and Pam can wave goodbye if she feels like it. Come on now, there's a good girl.'

Claude wouldn't meet my eye, though I willed her to look at me. If she had expressed some regret, I might have forgiven her even then, but her face was blank. I gathered up my handbag and walked out of my sitting room for the last time with my head high and my gaze fixed straight ahead. In the hall, my hat and gloves lay on the table, and the empty suitcase where I had dropped it.

'You may take your things,' Anthony offered generously, following behind.

I put on my hat, looking at myself in the mirror as I adjusted it, and Claude behind me, watching him. She was going to let me go without a word.

Anthony came closer. 'Poor old Fabia,' he said softly in my ear. 'You have a pash on her, don't you? I love your pet names. Cecil and Claude, too funny.'

He stepped back and laughed, jingling coins in his pocket again: a habit I'd always found irritating. Claude went to him and they stood side by side to see me go, like hosts waving off a guest who's overstayed her welcome. I reached for my gloves, first one and then the other.

'"O fat white woman whom nobody loves",' Anthony recited tenderly, '"why do you walk through the fields in gloves, missing so much and so much?"' He smiled. 'Well, you might not be so fat anymore and there aren't many fields around here but I'd say the rest of it's fairly accurate.'

He'd taunted me with the poem so often that it should no longer have had any impact, but I was wound up so tightly that a wave of instinctive, uncontrollable rage swept me away. And I was worried for Claude, of course. Knowing him as I did, how could I leave the two of them alone together?

This is what happened next, as far as I recall.

I picked up the suitcase and swung it with all my strength into his solar plexus. With a grunt, he doubled over, unable to free his hands from his pockets, and staggered back into the hall table, knocking over the lamp. Claude had to jump out of the way. By the time he'd recovered sufficiently to come charging towards me, I'd seized a walking stick from the elephant-foot stand. This was my home territory and I had the advantage of surprise; he was blind with anger, but mine had made me cunning. The moment he lunged, I speared him with it, aiming under his breastbone and up, as though I were tossing a particularly heavy bale of straw. The impact ran along my arm, jarring my whole body, but the blow was enough to lift him off his feet and send him flying backwards through the air.

He slammed against the wall in the corner and teetered there for a moment, struggling to regain his balance. To one side of him lay the doorway to the bathroom; to the other, that rectangle of deeper darkness at the mouth of the cellar. For a second, he hung on the air, arms clutching at nothing and his jacket flying open, before gravity sent him toppling back into the void. I can still hear the crack as his body smashed against some obstacle beneath, the thud as it landed, and the silence that followed. The final, awful silence.

A clatter made us jump but it was only the walking stick falling out of my hands. I remember slumping against the wall, and Claude staring at me with her hand to her mouth. Time passed. It seemed important to restore some kind of order. I tottered across the hall to pick up the lamp and set it back on the table. She shrank back as I approached the cellar steps. Clutching my arms across my chest, I bent over to listen, straining to hear the slightest sound from below. Any minute now he would come crawling up, bloody and wild, to confront us. Yet the only sound was my own breath, midway between a sob and a moan.

I turned to Claude. 'I didn't mean to – honestly.'

But she only stared back at me with frantic eyes.

'I did it for you, to keep you safe,' I said. 'I couldn't let you go with him.'

'What? You think I should be grateful?' Breaking free, she began to laugh, so wildly that I had to slap her face to make her stop. She leaned against the wall, one hand to her cheek.

'We must decide what to do.' I pressed my palms into my eye sockets.

'You should telephone for an ambulance,' she said, still holding her face. 'We can say he tripped. That's possible, isn't it?'

'Are you mad? No one will believe it was an accident, not when they find out he's my husband.' I picked up my handbag and rummaged through it for cigarettes. It took us several attempts to light them, matches spilling over the floor.

'If the police get involved, it will all come out,' I told her. 'You realise that? They'll drag you into it, blacken your name as well as mine.'

She took a deep drag on her cigarette. 'You'll have to go down there and see if he's – you know.'

Alive or dead: both possibilities were equally awful.

I dug my fingernails into my palms. 'I can't.'

'Yes, you damn well can. You made this happen.'

'To save you! Why did you let him in here in the first place? How could you have betrayed me after everything I've done for you?'

We were gnawing at each other, like wounded dogs in a fight. She took the torch from the hall table, put her hand on the small of my back and thrust me towards the cellar entrance. 'We're wasting time. Go on, get it over with.'

Standing at the top of the steps, I suddenly recalled our first evening in the flat, when we had gone to fetch wine from the cellar. We had been so happy then. How had it come to this? I shone the torch down into the pool of darkness, holding my breath. Not a sound; nothing moved.

'I can't go down there,' I whispered.

'You have to. One step at a time.' She pushed me forward. 'Take it slowly.'

So I put my foot on the first stair and inched down, keeping close to the wall as there was no handrail. Halfway along, I held up the torch to the pipe with a bolt sticking out that gleamed in the light; when I touched it, my finger came away dark and wet. I wiped my hand on my frock and sank down on my haunches, thinking I might be sick. Screw your courage to the sticking place, and we'll not fail. There had been a dreadful accident and we were dealing with the situation as best we could. Down to the cellar to fetch some coal and look what I found. He must have tripped and fallen. It's easy to lose your footing in the dark. A dreadful accident and it wasn't my fault.

I couldn't see the body at first. He had fallen to one side of the steps and lay on his front, thank God, legs sprawled apart. Most undignified. A dark, shining puddle was swelling silently and steadily beneath his head across the cellar floor. He must have struck the bolt and dropped to the ground from there; judging by the unnatural angle of his neck, it had to be broken. He was unmistakeably dead. Terrible to admit this now but at the time, I felt a tremendous surge of relief – until the realisation of what had happened struck home.

Somehow, I managed to stagger back up the stairs to where Claude was waiting. 'He's gone,' I told her. 'It would have been quick. We'd better leave through the kitchen. I know a place we can go while we decide what to do.'

And then somebody knocked on our front door; a soft, insistent tap. Claude jumped, walked quickly and silently to her bedroom and closed the door behind her. I was strangely calm – as though all along I had been waiting for the moment of discovery and now, with a ghastly inevitability, here it was. So this is what would happen. I'd have to let events take their course. Straightening my shoulders, I went to answer the summons.

Floss was standing there. 'I called round the back but nobody answered,' she said. 'What's going on?'

'Nothing much.' I tried to gather my thoughts.

She looked at me curiously. 'You got the money?'

Of course; now I remembered. 'Come through to the kitchen and you shall have it.'

I pushed her in front of me across the hall, away from the mouth of the cellar. What would she see? A stick on the floor, my suitcase tipped over. I might have seemed jumpy and strange, but that could lead her to any number of conclusions.

'Are you all right?' she asked, as I reached into my frock for the money.

I attempted a laugh. 'Why shouldn't I be?'

'No particular reason.' She shrugged. 'There might have been some bother, that's all.' I stared at her, terrified. 'Selling the coat, I mean,' she added.

Gradually, everything was coming back to me. 'Did you stay here last night?' I asked, handing over Chalkie's wodge of notes.

She shook her head, counting them out one by one with agonising deliberation. 'Miss Claude said it wasn't convenient.'

I tried to focus, to concentrate on Floss so I didn't have to think about anything else. I would help her now, and she would be grateful and take my side. She had gone back to the Peabody Buildings the previous night, she told me when she'd finished her laborious task of counting, and found somewhere to sleep. A shelter, most probably. There were dark circles under her eyes and her hair was even more of a mess than usual.

'So where shall I go now?' she asked. 'I'm scared the police are going to come.'

I fished out a handful of notes from the other cup of my brassiere and gave them to her. 'Take this. You don't have to count it now.'

Her eyes were like saucers. 'What do you want me to do?'

'Find someone from the Salvation Army. You know what the uniform looks like?' She nodded. 'Tell them your mother's dead and your father's been arrested, and you're all alone.

They'll take you somewhere you'll be fed and looked after properly. You can't carry on like this, Floss. It isn't right.'

'Is the money for them?'

'No, it's for you, to tide you over. You can say it's from your mum if anyone asks.'

'So you don't want nothin' in exchange?' Quickly, she tucked away the cash in another pocket before I could change my mind. 'Ta, Miss.'

'Actually, there is one thing,' I said. 'Would you mind if Miss Claude and I stayed in your den tonight?' I couldn't abandon Claude, no matter how she'd treated me.

'Course not,' she said, getting up. 'Told you it would come in handy one day.'

I unlocked the kitchen door to hustle her out, but she lingered on the step. 'There's been a man here,' she said abruptly, in a rush. 'He came last night and I seen him a couple of times before.'

Oh, Floss! It was too late now to tell me that. 'Why didn't you telephone? You were meant to be keeping an eye on the place.'

'I know,' she muttered, 'but Miss Claude made me swear not to. I gave her my word. You won't tell her I've broken it, will you?'

I took a deep breath. 'It's all right. That man's gone and he won't be coming back.' I bent down to look in her eyes. 'And we're leaving too, Miss Claude and I. You won't see us again. Be a good girl, won't you? Go to school and stop pinching things or you'll end up in trouble.'

She bit her lip. 'But I have to do what Dad says.'

'No, you don't.' I gave her shoulders a shake. 'This is your chance to get away. Don't waste it.'

She gave me one of her inscrutable stares. 'And don't

mention us to anyone, will you?' I added. 'Just pretend we never existed.'

'Don't worry, Miss. There's all sorts of things I know and I never tell.' She dropped her eyes. 'Not usually, anyway.'

After she had gone, I drank a cup of water, splashed my face, combed my hair and lit another cigarette. One minute I felt hot, the next deathly cold. Tremors shook my body from head to foot. I had no concept of time: the seconds might have been minutes, the minutes, hours. At last I walked down the corridor and knocked on Claude's bedroom door. She didn't reply. I knocked again, and pushed it open.

The room was empty. She had gone.

18

LOOKING BACK

High Wycombe, November 1952

'I should have thought,' she says, 'that I am the very last person you would want to see again.'

We're standing under a pergola, looking out into the sodden garden. It's not actually raining but the ground is covered in puddles and drops are falling intermittently from the branching vines overhead. Claude's taken a coat from a peg by the door but I'm shivering in a thin jacket, rubbing my arms against the cold.

'There are things you need to know,' I tell her, 'and questions I'd like to ask.'

She raises her eyebrows. 'Really? And what makes you think I'll answer them?'

'Because we were friends! Cecil and Claude, the two of us against the world. Remember? I stood by you when nobody else would and in return, you betrayed me.'

She actually winces, and I despise her for it. 'You lied to me from the start,' she says, 'acting the innocent virgin when you were married all along. That's not how friends behave. And then you–' She stops and shakes her head. 'Well, we don't need to go into all that.'

'But don't you see, I couldn't tell you about my husband. The less you knew, the better. I wanted to blot him out, to pretend he never existed, and then you brought him into our home. You were thinking of going off with him, weren't you? Don't try to deny it. I don't blame you, I know how persuasive he could be, but he'd have made your life unbearable, just like he did mine. He pretended to love women but he hated them, deep down. Even his mother – although I can't blame him for that.' I dig my fingernails into my palms and add, more quietly, 'Anyway, it was an accident. I'm not sorry he's dead but I never intended to kill him.'

'I was there, remember? I saw your face.' She looks away. 'But I don't know why you're bringing that nightmare up again. I've managed to put it out of my mind.'

I take out my cigarette case and, seeing her eye it, offer her one. She hesitates before accepting, bending her head to my lighter.

'I suppose you know what happened to Victoria Mansions?' I ask, stamping my frozen feet. She shakes her head and doesn't look particularly interested when I tell her.

'So where are you living now?' she asks, for form's sake.

'I've got a flat in Cheyne Walk, overlooking the river. It's not a patch on this place but I'm comfortable there, and beholden to nobody. I pay my own way. I'll probably be made a partner in the business next year.'

'Bully for you.'

Furious tears come to my eyes and I have to look away, grass and trees blurring into a haze of grey and green.

'I'm glad you're doing well,' she says after a while, 'but seeing you out of the blue brings back a host of painful memories. Surely you can understand that?'

197

I can't admit those days were the most vivid and exciting of my life and everything that's happened to me since has seemed trivial in comparison, that I feel a pale imitation of the girl I was then, like the watery coffee we used to drink in the war. I mutter something banal about happy memories too.

'We had fun, didn't we?' I go on. 'Despite all the worry and those wretched doodles. Do you remember that pub we used to go to in the World's End where you could get a slice off the joint and vegetables for ninepence?' I hate myself for pleading with her but I can't seem to stop.

'There weren't any joints. Not by that stage of the war.'

'Yes, but they'd killed the pig! Surely you remember? The street pig, who lived in somebody's backyard? The police heard him squealing and took him into custody, but Chalkie's lot stole him back and he was butchered in the pub cellar. You said it was the best meal you'd ever had.'

She shakes her head. 'Are you sure you aren't muddling me up with somebody else?'

'Of course not. Who else could it have been? Come on, what about the time we burnt a cork to use for mascara, and ended up looking like we'd got two black eyes?'

She looks at me for a while without speaking and then she asks, more gently, 'Why are you here?'

'Because I can't forgive you,' I reply, surprising myself as well as her.

'Forgive *me*?' she repeats. 'Whatever for?'

'For abandoning me when I needed you most. I did everything for you – gave you a home, paid your way, cheered you up when you were miserable – and you took my kindness and threw it back in my face, as though I were nothing.' I drop my cigarette butt in a puddle. 'I'd never have treated you like that.'

'Oh, you looked after me all right,' she replies, 'but you let me know what a tremendous sacrifice you were making, and how lucky I was that you were so kind-hearted and generous. I was a fallen woman, and you loved having me around so you could feel superior. How can you talk to me about forgiveness after what you did?'

'I saved you, that's what I did.' All I want is for her to acknowledge the truth; she doesn't even have to apologise.

She walks a few paces away then turns to face me again, her eyes cold. 'We have nothing more to say to each other. I should like you to leave.'

We return to the house without speaking so I can collect my briefcase. She's not going to get away with it that easily though.

'There's just one other thing,' I tell her, as she holds open the drawing-room door for me to pass through. 'I've found the baby.'

She freezes. 'What baby?'

'Yours, of course.' I smile to show I mean no harm. 'Well, she's not a baby anymore, is she? I've got to know her a little. Such an interesting child, although not quite what I expected.'

I may be down, but I'm not out.

19

CLINGING ON

London, September 1944–August 1945

'Do you think I'd have looked at you twice if you didn't have money?' my husband used to say. 'Pity you turned out to be such a crashing bore.'

But I didn't have money, that was the problem – only a crumbling house I'd inherited from my parents without any means of maintaining it. Anthony was seduced by the turrets, the wood panelling, the drive lined with rhododendron bushes that ended in a turning circle for carriages; too dazzled to notice the woodworm and rising damp, the cracked roof tiles and antiquated plumbing. He thought he could install his mother on one floor, put me on another and carry on living as he pleased. It was bound to end in disaster. He had no idea about managing property or staff and, to tell you the truth, he wasn't very bright. Yet I was the bigger fool to fall for his lies in the first place.

We met in 1941, at a drinks party in the officers' mess of a nearby training camp. Cocktail parties are my idea of hell but for some reason, I accepted the invitation that had been issued to all of us Land Girls. My mother had died only a few months before so I was feeling lonely and unsettled, wanting my life to change but not knowing how. Be careful what you wish for, as they say. Anyway, after an hour spent shrieking banalities in that stuffy, crowded room, I developed a crashing headache and went outside for some fresh air, thinking I might lurk there until the bus arrived to take us back. Anthony noticed and followed to see if I was all right. I have no idea why. Looking back, I picture him as a shark, circling the water until it scents blood. He offered to drive me home and I was so desperate to leave that I accepted.

'I was looking for an excuse to get out of there myself,' he told me in the motor car. 'Can't stand that sort of thing. Far sooner be soldiering than making small talk.'

He would have had his pick of all the girls that evening so I assumed he wasn't attracted to me. For that reason, I felt less nervous around him than the sort of men I usually ended up with – the rejects, to put it bluntly – so we got along pretty well. Anthony could make himself agreeable when he chose. My house was looking particularly lovely on that summer evening, its fading splendour flattered by the dusk, and I could tell he was impressed. The gardens were still beautiful then. They'd been my mother's pride and joy; I can see her now in my mind's eye, wandering down the path in her battered straw hat, secateurs in hand and a trug over her arm. She cared more about her tree peonies than she ever did about me.

Anthony escorted me to the front door and didn't seem inclined to jump back into the car, so I invited him in for a drink. We stood in the drawing room, watching swallows chase each other through the inky blue sky, and he laughed at everything I said. I became emboldened, intoxicated by his company as much as the whisky. The house reminded him of his grandparents' home, he said – an outrageous lie, I was to discover, since his grandfather had owned a bakery in Walsall and lived in the flat above – and asked whether I'd mind giving him a guided tour. He found me fascinating, he told me before he finally left that night, and I was stupid enough to believe him. As if a man who looked like a matinée idol would ever have courted me without some ulterior motive!

He set about the task with a will because his regiment was about to be sent overseas; we were engaged three weeks later and married a fortnight after that. Ours would be an unconventional partnership, he said, because we were intelligent, sophisticated people who didn't follow the herd. We would have separate bedrooms and be free to lead our own lives (I wasn't entirely sure what that implied), coming together in the morning for coffee and a crossword puzzle, perhaps, and evening drinks before our shared supper. We would be companions, best friends, soulmates. He'd help with the upkeep of the house and gardens, and I could organise our domestic arrangements. He made the plan sound idyllic, and he was so respectful: sometimes he would kiss my hand, or the top of my head. It seems extraordinary now, but he made me feel secure. I would feel safer with a man about the place, he said, taking care of everything.

Our wedding was one of those rushed wartime affairs, with icing over a cardboard cake and a new hat to smarten up my best costume. There were only a few guests: Aunt Ivy and a couple of schoolfriends on my side, and a few fellow officers on his – plus his mother, of course, who was already installed in my house by then. Anthony said he couldn't bear to leave me alone in that big house when he went abroad; we would be company for each other, and he liked to think of his two favourite girls together.

Mrs Heythornthwaite – Phyllis – came from Bristol, which had been heavily bombed. Her house had been destroyed in a raid and she'd been living in temporary accommodation, so Anthony must have thought it the ideal solution to have her move in with me. I'd be saddled with looking after her as she declined (she was already becoming frail) and she would keep an eye on me while he was away. Not that she seemed particularly pleased with the move to Suffolk. She complained from morning to night, until the stroke put an end to that. Everything disappointed her: the cold, the damp, the wind, the heat, the flies, the smell of manure, the isolation... you name it. Bristol was a paradise on earth in comparison.

'You can always go back there,' I told her once, goaded beyond endurance.

Instead, she asked her former neighbour, Mrs Cleverly, to stay. Valerie Cleverly; she could have been a character from a nursery rhyme. A stout woman twice the size of Phyllis, with an enormous bosom and curly white hair. I'd hear them talking in the kitchen when I returned from the farm, Phyllis's peevish whine punctuated by sympathetic murmurs from Valerie. If I entered the room, they'd fall silent or start chatting about the weather. I didn't mind. Mrs Cleverly entertained Phyllis, she'd brought her ration book with her and seemed to enjoy shopping, so she was actually quite useful. However, Anthony came home unexpectedly on leave when Valerie was in residence and made it very clear she wasn't welcome. His mother should have asked his permission before inviting guests to the house, he said, and Mrs Cleverly was dispatched back to Bristol on the first train the next morning. I almost felt sorry for Phyllis. Anthony never raised a hand to her but she was almost as frightened of him as I was.

I'd quickly discovered what an appalling mistake I'd made. We hadn't bothered with a honeymoon but spent the rest of my new husband's leave at home, and there I soon got the measure of him. He became angry at the size of my monthly allowance from my parents' estate ('paltry') and things went from bad to worse from that moment on. There were no chummy drinks or crossword puzzles: he seemed to find the very sight of me infuriating. One day he took off somewhere in the car and came back late in the evening, in a foul temper. His mother and I had both retired to our rooms and I could hear him crashing about downstairs, swearing. The next thing I knew, he'd burst into my bedroom without knocking and forced himself upon me. I can't bear to recall the incident in any detail, only that it was the most degrading and humiliating attack one could possibly imagine. He stank of alcohol and his eyes were bloodshot; he was like a wild animal.

'That'll teach you,' he said afterwards, buttoning himself up. 'I probably won't bother you again in this way but just remember: I can, whenever I feel like it. We're married, after all.' And he gave that awful crooked smile.

I started locking my bedroom door at night. Sometimes I would see the doorknob slowly turn and hold my breath, but after a while his footsteps would retreat down the landing and he never assaulted me again in that way. I became used to everyday, minor acts of cruelty instead: a punch in the stomach or a yank of the hair. He was careful never to leave marks where they could be seen: once even stubbing out his cigarette on the birthmark at the nape of my neck. His moods were terrifyingly unpredictable. Sometimes a drumming of his fingers or a tic at the corner of his eye would alert me there was trouble ahead; at others, he would fly into a rage without any warning. Thankfully, he was only home for weekends at first, then abroad for most of 1942 and 1943 – Egypt and then Italy – with only a brief period of leave at the beginning of 1944. Anthony was very good at fighting; he was mentioned twice in dispatches. I wonder whether he enjoyed having a legitimate reason to unleash all that savagery, instead of venting his fury privately on some pathetic female. The idea of having him home for good when the war was over appalled me.

Knowing the sort of man he was, I couldn't have let Claude throw in her lot with him, no matter how badly she'd treated me. And I still thought of her as my friend at that point, despite her behaviour. Left alone in the flat that terrible day, I came close to losing my mind. I ran upstairs and outside into the rain to look for her, rushing like a madwoman this way and that through the gardens and along the streets of our square, the breath tearing at my chest. I remember a warden stopping me to ask what was the matter, but not what I replied. Yet I must have recovered some sort of control, because I ended up at home again, sitting on the edge of Claude's bed. She had only slipped out for a moment, I told myself; if I kept absolutely still and tried to fix my mind on nothing at all, she would soon be back.

When I had at last accepted that was not going to happen, I got up and walked out of her bedroom and into the sitting room. I picked up Anthony's hat from the coffee table, went back down the hall and hurled it down the cellar steps with my eyes shut. Stumbling over the walking stick, I wiped that with a towel and threw it down too. Then I packed the few clothes I possessed. Claude's portrait stood in the living room, its face to the wall, so I put it in the suitcase, before returning to her room to see if she might have left any clues as to where she had gone. She hadn't taken much with her, as far as I could tell: the photograph of her sister from the bedside table, her haversack and a few clothes. Feeling under her pillow to see if her nightshirt were there, I found a small red notebook which I put into my pocket to examine later.

Footsteps on the floor above made me suddenly frantic to escape, so I rushed through the back door and along the road to

Floss's den. Impossible to stay there though: the view of our backyard was too disturbing. As soon as darkness fell, I crept through the night to the Underground station. A poster in the ticket office advertised a deep-level shelter at Clapham so I took a southbound train and holed up there for a few days, like an animal in its lair. I hardly slept, didn't eat, couldn't look anyone in the face. Whenever I closed my eyes, I would see that bloodied corpse crawling up from the cellar to confront me. Nobody took much notice of my distress. I wasn't alone in waking from nightmares, nor the only one carrying all my worldly goods in a suitcase.

Eventually I summoned the courage to call in at the exchange and tell Miss Ryan things had not turned out well at home. She took one look at me and said I could have another week's compassionate leave. I spent it sitting in the shelter or on a Clapham Common bench, rigid with terror. People would have been looking for Anthony Heythornthwaite; his body must have been discovered by now. He might have told someone where he was going, or left his car parked outside Victoria Mansions. I couldn't remember whether I'd locked our front door. What if Mrs Hoffman had heard the commotion and come to investigate? Or Guy Cavendish had come downstairs, looking for me? And Floss... Floss, who knew so many things, might change her mind about never telling. Sooner or later, the police would track me down.

When my leave was up, I went back to the exchange frightened of my own shadow. If anyone brushed against me in the street or called my name unexpectedly, I had to struggle not to scream. And then shortly after I'd returned to work, I put a hand in my coat pocket one morning and came across the red notebook I'd found underneath Claude's pillow. It turned out to be a diary, as I'd suspected, which I read with mounting disbelief. A dreadful creature referred to as 'C' featured prominently in the narrative. At first I couldn't believe Claude was referring to me, but when she sneered at my household rules and fondness for the novels of Angela Thirkell, there could be no doubt.

I can't breathe in the flat when C's there, she'd written, *she sucks all the air out of it. Always watching me with her eagle eyes, making a mental note of everything I say or do, as though she can peer inside my head to see what I'm thinking. Not sure I can last another day here, let alone weeks.*

At last, I saw her true character and the extent of her treachery. That first weekend when she'd returned from home with her sister Pamela's identity card, I learned she'd confessed to her parents she was pregnant and asked them to take her in. They'd thrown her out of the house; she had come back to Victoria Mansions because she had no alternative, rather than because she wanted to. She took my kindness completely for granted.

Occasionally she wrote that she'd had a better day and acknowledged I'd done her some small favour, but most of her diary entries were concerned with how miserable and lonely she was, and how insufferable she found me. Around the time of our trip to Godalming, she had simply written, *Can't see any light at the end of the tunnel. Very low.*

Life wasn't all doom and gloom though. Her later entries mentioned someone known as 'S' who managed to cheer her up a little. *Met S in Kensington Gardens*, she'd written on one occasion. *Had a good chat and a few laughs.* And a couple of weeks later, *S and I went to a concert at lunchtime. Things might be looking up?*

There were also a few references to 'Y', whom I took to mean Jan. *Drinks with Y in the Grapes*, put her in a good mood for a couple of days, and then in late August, *Y won some money on the horses and treated me to lunch in Soho. Spaghetti with onions! Ghastly indigestion but worth it.*

Why hadn't she told me she was doing all these things with other people? I wouldn't have minded. The fact she was keeping secrets from me was what really hurt. There was no mention of Anthony. The last diary entry read, *C going away to Cheltenham, thank God. With a bit of luck she might stay there.*

A final twist of the knife. For the second time in my life, someone I'd trusted with my most tender, private feelings had betrayed me – and the worst of it was, I couldn't have it out with her. All that justified resentment festered inside me until I was driven almost mad; even Mrs Shaw noticed my sullen fury and asked me if anything were the matter. Like her, I would have welcomed annihilation. It didn't matter to me whether I lived or died, whether the war would be over by Christmas or drag on for another six years. Claude had treated me appallingly and there was nothing I could do about it. The world seemed a very dark place.

When the V-2 rockets were finally admitted to exist, I scarcely lifted my head. Elsie on the switchboard knew all about the damage they caused. 'They're packed with that much explosive, there's no bodies to pick up,' she whispered. 'The ambulances go away empty. All that's left is a stain on the ground.' And Mrs Shaw had sighed wistfully.

By then I had emerged from the deep Underground shelter to take a room opposite Miss Ryan's in Holland Park. I worked as many shifts as she could give me and walked back to the hostel every evening, to lie fully dressed on my bed with the light on. At least my room had electricity and a door I could bolt top and bottom. The days passed somehow, and October arrived in a gust of wind. Claude would have gone into the maternity home by now. I had telephoned the place in Leamington Spa several times over the course of a month but they had no record of a Pamela or Stella Atkins shortly due to give birth. She could have been anywhere. I imagined her lying awake at night in some dreary dormitory while the other girls shifted and snored. What image would come to her mind when she thought of me? Did she feel any remorse? Probably not.

I don't remember much about life in the hostel: mainly queuing with a towel over my shoulder for the bathroom and trying to avoid Miss Ryan. She had been a reassuring presence at first, with that air of the Home Counties about her, despite the siren suit she would change into of an evening. Yet she was too greedy for my company, too keen on inviting me for drinks in her room or sandwiches by the Serpentine and hinting she would recommend me for promotion. I couldn't let anyone come too close, let alone her. The other girls my age thought me an odd fish, I could tell, and steered clear of us both.

Once a week, I would take the Underground to Sloane Square as dusk fell and stand in the gardens opposite our flat for an hour or so. I never saw Floss, which I hoped meant she was safely far away, and sadly I didn't see Guy Cavendish either. I wasn't brave enough to walk through the front door, braving Mrs Hoffman, and run upstairs to find him; it took all my courage merely to watch from the shelter of the trees.

One damp autumn evening, I turned into the square with my head down to find that 117 Victoria Mansions no longer existed. There were no cranes, no police dogs and no rescue workers; no one was trapped and no large masonry needed to be removed. Instead, only a vast absence confronted me. I found myself staring through a gap in the middle of the long building, as though a giant tooth had been extracted. On either side of the void, pipes jutted like hardened arteries from a skeleton of broken timber, and the rooms of our neighbours' homes lay open to view. I could see their unmade beds in wallpapered rooms, unplumped cushions, tables laid for meals that would never be eaten, a clock waiting to be wound on the mantelpiece above a grate with the fire laid, ready to be lit. Nothing remained of our flat, or those on the floors above. A whole section of the roof and its chimney pots had gone, together with the staircases and flats beneath, and probably their inhabitants too – everything had been pulverised into rubble no bigger than a pebble and blown in great heaps into the gardens. Beyond the crater, the tenement building where Floss had her hideout rose up, as though proud of its squalor.

A warden was keeping watch by the rope barrier, although there was nothing accessible to steal. 'I used to live here,' I told him, overwhelmed by an urge to talk. 'Our flat was just behind where you're standing.'

He turned around to look. 'Had a lucky escape, haven't you?'

'I'll say.' The scene of my crime had been obliterated; now only Claude would know what I had done. Later I would mourn when I read Mr Cavendish's name on the casualty list outside Chelsea Town Hall: Guy Cavendish, who had been so kind to me when I was feeling wretched, whom I had left without saying a word of thanks. There was no mention of Mrs Hoffman; she must have moved away by then, as Chalkie had predicted. I had also been saved. Some sort of existence had been restored to me; I would have to get through it one way or another.

* * *

October turned into a squally November. Claude must have had the baby by then; I tried not to think about her but she seemed to be always hovering at my shoulder, just out of reach. I missed and loathed her in equal measure. She appeared constantly in my dreams, where I could at last confront her.

How dare she treat me so badly and then simply disappear? Walking beside the river, I imagined the cold clutch of the water dragging me down. Oblivion, that's what I wanted: a break from the burden of being myself. But I hadn't the guts. Instead, I volunteered for the Red Cross and spent that Christmas working in a soup kitchen, gave blood, knitted scarves, pushed about a man in a wheelchair.

Doodlebugs and V-2s fell in quick succession at the start of the new year and carried on in waves through the spring. Meanwhile, daffodils appeared in Green Park and the deckchair attendant returned. At the end of April, Hitler committed suicide and the war was over – in Europe, at least. Yet it was hard to look ahead with much optimism. We'd been waiting so long for the end that it felt like an anticlimax, and peace only emphasised my loneliness.

I went into work as usual on VE Day and joined the crowds in Piccadilly at the end of my shift, tagging along with various parties: a family from Walthamstow with a granny and twin babies asleep in a pram, three drunk but friendly GIs with a gaggle of Wrens, a group of Land Girls from Kent, believe it or not. I passed myself from one group to another, as though changing partners in an eightsome reel. People were climbing up lamp-posts, dancing in a conga through the doors of the Ritz, splashing about the lake in St James's Park. They looked ridiculous. Only the bonfires blazing under trees in Hyde Park made any sort of sense; I sat huddled in a deckchair under an abandoned greatcoat, staring into the flames. What had they been for, those long years of destruction and loss?

News began to emerge of the death camps in Germany. I couldn't bear to look at the pictures of emaciated bodies piled in obscene mountains, nor the pathetic heaps of belongings. Yet at least I was managing to survive. The morning after VE Day, Mrs Shaw taped up the windows and doors of her flat in Chalk

Farm, pinned a typewritten note on the door to warn the neighbours about gas and lay down with her head in the oven. Miss Ryan and I went to her funeral and the GPO sent a wreath, although she hadn't come into work for a fortnight. I should have visited to find out what was wrong but that probably wouldn't have made much difference; I couldn't have brought her any comfort.

20

MARKING TIME

London, 1945–1952

Later that summer, Miss Ryan told me she was retiring to live with her cousin in Bognor Regis, and said she had recommended me to Miss Magee as her successor. I didn't want the job though. By then, I was tired of listening to other people's conversations; meaningless chatter held no interest for me anymore. Browsing the Situations Vacant column in a newspaper one day, I saw a position advertised in the soft-furnishing department at Peter Jones and applied for it there and then. The store was a link to the life I'd led before: a life that seemed increasingly remote, as though it had been a dream. Perhaps one day I might see Claude walking across Sloane Square, hips swinging and skirt slapping against her legs. Miss Ryan understood my need for a new start and wrote me a glowing reference. Although I had no experience of selling, I was sufficiently educated and well-spoken to make a good impression at the interview, and was offered the job a week later. It came with staff accommodation at a reduced rent in a building behind the store.

We were referred to as Partners at Peter Jones but I was a shop assistant, nevertheless. I didn't mind the work. Not at first, anyway. The room sets made me feel as though the world were an ordered place once again, where families sat around dining-room tables and switched on lamps without a thought to the blackout. Stock was scarce but the utility designs were acceptable and the new streamlined look suited our modern building, with its acres of steel and glass. I learned how to sell; when to give customers space to make up their minds and when to drop a casual comment to clinch the deal. Although I tried not to rub it in, I was clearly a cut above the other girls on the shop floor – some of whom struggled to write a customer's details in the order book.

Not long after I'd joined the company, the Americans dropped an atomic bomb on a city in Japan. Thousands were killed, and then thousands more when another place was bombed three days later. The heat was said to have been so intense, some people simply vanished, as though they had never existed. I couldn't let myself think about death on such a vast scale; it was easier to concentrate on cushion covers, lining fabric and Petersham braid. The Japanese surrendered soon after that. More lives would have been lost had the war in the Far East dragged on, that's what everyone said in the staff canteen, and the Japs had done terrible things to our POWs. All the same, VJ Day was a subdued affair. No one felt much like celebrating – least of all me.

I was lucky to have ended up at Peter Jones. My wages weren't bad and the staff were well-treated. There were staff outings and trips to the theatre, and a weekly gazette brought news from the various stores in the partnership, which we were encouraged to think of as family. In my spare time, I took to exploring the city again, looking for signs of renewal: a row of prefab houses here, a scaffolding tower there. Cigarettes were even harder to find than during the war and half the pubs I passed in the evening were closed because they'd run dry, but walking took my mind off the lack of food and other consolations. London was still full of women and old men, because the young ones were off doing their National Service – not that I cared.

To disguise the emptiness inside, I started paying more attention to my appearance. A girl who worked on the haberdashery counter and boarded with me, Jocelyn, took me in hand. We weren't allowed to wear make-up at work for fear of outshining 'Madam', but in the evenings, she showed me how to outline my eyes in black with a little flick at the corner, like the models on the cover of *Vogue*. Surrounded by fabric all day, I bought a sewing machine to make my own clothes. The stallholders in Berwick Street Market would keep remnants for me, and once I found a red velvet curtain in a skip behind the Windmill Theatre, which I turned into an evening gown. Not that I had any occasion to wear it. Jocelyn had a fiancé; sometimes they invited me out for a drink but it wasn't much fun playing gooseberry.

I couldn't be bothered to make friends. The people around me seemed like shadows, preoccupied with such trivial concerns. To while away the long Sunday afternoons, I walked along the river or through the parks to Shepherd Market. What of Jan? The house in Shepherd Street was boarded up and I didn't recognise anyone in the pub to ask for news of him. I wrote to the overseas broadcasting department of the BBC to ask whether Jan Fitzgerald still worked there, but the person who replied didn't know him and said she'd been unable to find any record of the name. Perhaps he'd been only a ghost too. It might have been reckless to want to see him again, yet I needed to talk to someone who'd known me then. Sometimes it seemed as though I'd dreamed up the flat in Victoria Mansions, and everything that had happened there.

Our first peacetime Christmas came and went: so eagerly anticipated yet something of a damp squib. I ate mock turkey on Christmas Eve in the staff canteen and spent the next day helping out at a Salvation Army hostel, where veterans of the Great War were joined by survivors of the Second for one day of comradeship and company. The winter was dreary, and I was glad to spend my days at work in the warm glare of fluorescent lighting. By the spring, however, I'd had enough of the selling floor. The rules and restrictions that had once been a comfort now seemed ridiculously constraining, and I was losing patience with the women who idled away their afternoons choosing a yard of ribbon. The long pearly days filled me with a restless energy. When the store closed on Saturday afternoons and Sundays, I worked for an antique dealer in Kensington High Street, re-upholstering chairs and sofas, mending cushions and altering curtains. He taught me about furniture and we would sometimes go to country-house sales together, where I picked up more tricks of the trade by watching what he bid for and seeing how he handled himself.

Seeing I was bored, my manager suggested I apply for a job as a buyer; one of the sharp young men and women who went all over the country, looking for new products to sell in the store. Some of them had university degrees. Yet I didn't want to get above myself; the company workrooms were more appealing, with their atmosphere of quiet industry. Eventually I found a position in the upholstery department, cutting out and stitching loose covers. Those sorts of jobs used to be reserved for men but women had taken over during the war and now we were accepted – grudgingly though. I could feel the old boys watching as I sliced into the damask and brocade, willing me to make a mistake, and my scissors and weights would vanish if I took my eyes off them for a second. Yet I wasn't there to make friends. When the men discovered I could do the work as well as any of them, and better than most, they left me alone. Even at lunchtime, when I sat by myself in the canteen.

I stuck it out for six months before the manager took me aside to ask whether I'd be interested in visiting people at home to cut patterns for their loose covers *in situ*. It was a step up the ladder, he said, and a job that would suit me perfectly, given my experience of dealing with 'the lady customers'. The men were probably trying to get rid of me but I didn't care. I had the use of a small van which I'd load up each morning with my tools and rolls of fabric, then off I'd drive all over London, revelling in the empty streets and my commercial petrol coupons. Sometimes a maid would answer the door but more often than not, the lady of the house would show me through to the sitting room. I was treated with more respect than I had been on the selling floor; usually offered tea or a glass of water, and often a woman on her own with the children would keep me chatting. There wasn't so much of that 'round the back for the tradesmen's entrance'. Rationing and shortages were worse than ever – even bread was rationed now – and there was still a sense we were all in it together.

Going into other people's houses helped me feel part of society again. I liked looking at their photographs and invitations on the mantelpiece, smelling their suppers on the stove, patting their dogs. I developed a persona: discreet, polished, scrupulously honest. If I found so much as a threepenny bit down the side of the sofa, I'd make a point of returning it. My evolution continued. The fat days were well and truly behind me; a man could have circled my waist with both hands if he'd felt so inclined – and if I'd felt inclined to let him. I'd also moved out of staff digs and was renting the attic of a house in Cheyne Walk from an elderly widow, the mother of one of my customers, who wanted somebody else under the same roof at night. I painted the rooms mustard yellow and filled them with mismatched rugs and furniture picked up from market stalls for next to nothing. At first, Claude's portrait hung by the window, soaking up the afternoon sunlight, but after a while I relegated the painting to a cupboard. I couldn't bring myself to get rid of it altogether; one day, I'd find her again and make her account for herself. I did throw her diary on the fire one evening after one too many whiskies, though I'd read it so many times, I knew it more or less by heart.

I was managing. When I threw out yards of billowing calico and waited for it to settle, I felt at peace. There was a rhythm to the task: measuring, cutting, fitting, pinning, tacking. A kind of magic, too, turning a faded hulk into something clean and fresh. Work got me through the appalling winter of '47, when the countryside ground to a halt, half the power stations shut down and my clothes froze over the back of the chair. That spring, I met Noel Berridge and took another step forward. I knew him by name: he was the designer of choice for all the society ladies, if only so they could boast about him to their friends, and he had a showroom in Knightsbridge with extraordinary window displays.

At the time, I was working in a grand house in Cadogan Square. The woman who lived there, a Mrs Jellicoe, had chosen Berridges for the wallpaper and curtains, but had come to Peter Jones for her upholstery since we were quicker and, more to the point, cheaper. The decorators were tidying up as I was cutting a pattern for the sofa when Noel Berridge himself appeared to sign off the job. It was a welcome interruption, as Mrs Jellicoe and I were in the middle of a heated discussion about trims. She wanted to reuse yards of some ancient tatting from the loft and I was doing my best to change her mind.

Suddenly Noel Berridge was there, scorning my opinions on fringing. Impeccably dressed in a pin-striped suit with a white carnation in the buttonhole, he had piercing blue eyes and the most perfectly waved grey hair; I couldn't take my eyes off it. He didn't seem overly impressed with me, however. After inspecting the sofa, he pointed out a couple of darts that needed adjustment and took issue with Mrs Jellicoe's choice of fabric. Then to round off the fiasco, he caught me having a cigarette in the kitchen at lunchtime with the housekeeper and ticked me off before disappearing in a chauffeur-driven Wolseley. When I'd finished for the day, however, I found a note tucked under the windscreen wiper of my van: *I'm short-staffed at present. If you give up that filthy habit, you can come and work for me. NB.*

I'm still not sure why he wanted me, let alone why I agreed to take the job. Perhaps we each recognised a fellow imposter. Noel's upper-class accent slips when he's had a few drinks, and there are rumours about the company he keeps and what goes on at the parties in his flat above the showroom. Yet we can't be the only ones accustomed to secrecy these days. I often look into the faces of passing strangers and wonder what they have to hide.

* * *

My job at Berridges soon became all-absorbing, for which I was grateful. Noel made me spend three months machining loose covers in the workshop next door to the showroom before I graduated to hand finishing, and because I stayed late most nights for want of anything better to do, we saw a fair amount of each other. The workshop was the nerve centre of the business, where Noel had his office and orders were made up. When the manageress left to get married, he offered me her job. Some of the women didn't take kindly to being told what to do by a young upstart, but with Noel's backing, I got rid of the troublemakers and introduced a bonus scheme. I discovered a talent for managing the girls: I was polite and fair, and didn't care in the slightest whether or not they liked me. In fact, I could quite understand if they didn't. All that mattered was finishing the orders on time and to the highest possible standard. This was my domain, the place where I felt safe and could see proof of my worth.

As the months went by, Noel and I ended up working more closely together. When everyone else left early on Friday afternoons, he'd ask me into his office for a drink so we could discuss new projects. I felt able to express my ideas, although he frequently disagreed with them, and soon we began talking more generally about the business. After I'd spent a year or so managing the workshop and we'd built up a good relationship, he started taking me out with him in the Wolseley on site visits: ostensibly to measure up and advise clients about fabric, but also to chat to them and handle the social niceties. I became his assistant, with a secretary of my own to deal with administration, and filled the emptiness at my core with hard work and ambition.

Time rolled on and suddenly 1950 was upon us. Everyone was looking forward instead of back and at last I managed to forget the brief, intense period I had spent with Claude for days at a time. The past lay out of sight, folded over itself like layers of rock beneath the earth's crust. I never let myself think about Anthony; he was a monster who had tortured me long enough. He must have broken into the flat, looking for me, and fallen down the stairs: that's what I would say if his body were ever found and I were ever traced. I didn't think about his mother either. She must have died by then and it would have been hypocritical to grieve; we'd never liked each other.

The following year, I was busier than ever: Berridges was

asked to design a room display for the Homes and Gardens pavilion at the Festival of Britain exhibition on the South Bank, a little further upriver from my rooms in Cheyne Walk, and our business expanded. I thought of Claude briefly when the king died and Princess Elizabeth became queen, and then when identity cards were abolished soon afterwards and I could finally burn Mary Hale's. I felt liberated, almost safe. Yet locking up the workshop one evening a few months ago, I bumped into two policewomen strolling along the street. Any encounter with the law still made me anxious, so I prepared to hurry past with my head down.

'Hang on a minute,' one of them said.

I steeled myself to look her in the face. She was young and clear-skinned; not pretty, exactly, but easy on the eye. 'What for?' I asked baldly. 'It's late and I need to get home.'

'Don't you recognise me?'

I had no idea who she could have been. One of the girls from the Gerrard Street switchboard, perhaps, or a fellow assistant at Peter Jones? Nobody I wanted to talk to, at any rate.

'I'd know you anywhere, Miss Cecil,' she went on. 'Even with your hair like that, and so thin. It's me, Floss.'

Good God, so it was. Now I recognised her teeth, although she had grown into them at last. She turned to her companion. 'Go on ahead, Brenda. I'll catch you up in a minute.'

We were left alone. I stared at her dumbly. She looked so pleased to have found me but all I could think about was the last time we had been together, the two of us in the kitchen at Victoria Mansions.

'So what are you up to these days?' she asked.

I tried to pull myself together. 'This is where I work, at Berridges.' Then cursed myself for having given that away.

She inspected the sign above the door. 'Ooh, very posh.'

I forced myself to meet her eye. 'You look well, Floss. I can't believe you're old enough to join the police though.'

'I'm not, strictly speaking.' She gave me one of her old winks. 'I've come to an arrangement with Brenda and borrowed a year off of her. But I was always grown-up for my age, wasn't I? And the Sally Army did a grand job of making me respectable.'

'They certainly did.' Now I could return her smile. 'But a policewoman! Really?'

She laughed. 'Well, you know what they say. Takes a thief to catch a thief.'

'Look after yourself,' I said, anxious to get away. 'Goodbye, Floss. I'm glad things have worked out for you.'

She laid a hand on my arm. 'You don't need to be afraid, Miss. I'm not a snitch and you were always good to me. Do you remember when I first got my monthlies and thought I was going to die?' A vague memory of some unpleasantness swam to the surface of my mind. 'You took me to the chemist and got me sorted out,' she went on, 'and then we saw *Mrs Miniver* at the pictures.'

'Are you sure?' That didn't sound like me; perhaps she'd gone with Claude instead.

But Floss was adamant I had taken her. 'I used to think of you two as my big sisters,' she said. 'You looked out for me and I'll never forget it. I won't cause you any trouble.'

I affected a laugh. 'That's nice to know.'

'Do you still see Miss Claude?'

I told her we'd lost touch and she nodded, as though that didn't come as a surprise. 'I often wonder what happened to her, with the baby and everything. I suppose we'll never know.'

When I asked after Chalkie, she said that he'd died in prison – unexpectedly, of a heart attack. 'So now I've got nobody left, but that's all right. The force is my family now.' She grinned. 'Bit more reliable than the old man.'

On a whim, I suggested that we meet for a drink sometime after work, and we fixed a date. Why shouldn't we talk about the old days? It might be interesting to find out whether she knew any more about what Claude had been up to, all those years ago.

* * *

Floss in mufti was even more surprising than Floss in uniform. She wore tight slacks rolled up to mid-calf and a lacy white shirt under a jacket with a tight waist and a diamanté brooch on the lapel. It was clearly a look, and not one I could have carried off. We met one evening in a pub near the house she shared with Brenda in Fulham: one of the new prefabs. She drank beer while I drank gin, and we both smoked cigarettes. It felt odd at first, getting to know her as an adult. We talked for a while about her job and mine, and then once the ice was broken, we could go back to the past.

When I asked her what she remembered, she came up with a few disjointed fragments: the lunch we'd had in a British restaurant (which she'd thought the height of sophistication), the unexploded bomb lying for days behind Hanover Mansions, the time a Ministry of Food inspector had caught the butcher giving her an extra rasher of bacon.

'I used to wonder what you and Claude got up to when I was out at work,' I said with a light-hearted smile.

She shrugged. 'Nothing much. Mostly we just hung around the flat. She was keen on schoolwork, made me read out loud and practise handwriting. She found an atlas somewhere and we did geography: names of capital cities, rivers, that sort of thing. And she taught me arithmetic.'

'I would have helped if I'd known.'

'But you didn't have time, not with working all day.' Her wide, innocent eyes looked into mine. 'Can't have been easy.'

'No, it wasn't.' I felt a sudden rush of warmth towards her. 'But we couldn't have managed without you, Floss. Do you remember when you ran into that building and pulled Claude out?'

'That's what made me want to be a policewoman,' she told me. 'Well, actually I wanted to be a fireman but they wouldn't have me so I joined the police instead.'

'You saved her life,' I said. 'Not that you got any thanks for it, I bet.'

'We helped each other. It's like we three were destined to meet, don't you think? And now you and I have met again.' She grinned. 'I don't believe in coincidences. Must be fate.'

I bought another round of drinks, with a whisky chaser for Floss. She said I shouldn't have but drank it all the same, and lit another cigarette while she ruminated.

'She must have been lonely, Miss Claude, and worried about the baby. There was that friend she used to visit but, apart from her, she didn't have anyone except you and me.'

'Which friend do you mean?' I asked casually.

'The woman who lived in South Kensington, off the Cromwell Road. A mews house, it was, with blue shutters. Mrs Thompson, or Johnson, or Watson – something like that. She was in the family way as well. I suppose that's how they met. Didn't you know her too?'

'Oh, yes.' I pretended to see the light. 'The name rings a faint bell. I went there once, I think. Remind me which mews?'

'The name of a county, I think. Dorset, or maybe Devon.' Floss took a swig of beer. 'I never went inside. Used to hang about in the street until Miss Claude came out and then we went home. I suppose they didn't want me eavesdropping. Nice little house, it was, with a horse-head door-knocker. I used to picture the two of them all cosy together, drinking tea from china cups and eating fancy biscuits.' She laughed. 'I had an overactive imagination when I was a kid.'

She'd certainly hidden that well, young Floss with her poker face. How little we show other people of our essential selves! Yet Claude and I had seen each other at our very worst, as well as our best and bravest. There was a bond between us that couldn't be forgotten or denied.

21

ON THE TRAIL

London and Surrey, September 1952

There was no Devon or Dorset Mews in Kensington, I discovered after some extensive research with an *A to* Z, but I found a Cornwall Gardens, with a passage across the middle that might have been taken for a mews. I went there one weekday afternoon and sure enough, walked into a short, cobbled street lined with houses that would once have been stables. One of them had blue shutters, window boxes overflowing with pansies and a brass horse-head door-knocker. I could imagine Floss kicking her heels in the lane outside it until Claude re-emerged. This Mrs Thompson or Watson, or whoever she was, might have invited her in for a glass of squash.

I rapped on the door, which was quickly answered by a young woman in a cherry-print frock with an apron over it and a duster in her hand. She had a round, rather vapid face and curly blonde hair scooped up in a scarf. I introduced myself as Miss Jones and told her I was keen to find a friend from the ATS I'd lost touch with since the war: one Pamela Atkins.

'She mentioned you a couple of times, Mrs Thompson,' I finished up, 'so I just wondered whether you'd heard from her recently.'

'Mrs Johnson,' the girl said, 'but do call me Susy. I'm afraid I haven't seen Pam since then, either.' She thought for a few seconds before adding, 'I might have a letter from her somewhere though. I'm sure I had her address at one point. Won't you come in while I take a look?'

She held open the door for me and I stepped directly into a small room, stuffed full to bursting with ornaments. Porcelain shepherdesses and ladies in crinolines peeped coyly from display cabinets and side tables, while a string of china lambs gambolled either side of an ornate Delft clock on the mantelpiece, and Toby jugs grinned down from a shelf underneath the cornice. There was hardly space for a chair and low sofa under the window.

'Goodness, what a marvellous collection,' I said, edging carefully towards a seat.

'It seems to grow overnight.' She gave a self-conscious laugh, taking off her apron. 'Anyone would think they were breeding.'

I wondered whether she'd had all these nick-nacks when Claude came to visit – although surely they wouldn't have lasted five minutes during the raids.

'Pamela told me you were expecting a baby too,' I said. 'You and she must have had lots to talk about.'

'Oh, we did.' Susy's eyes lit up. 'She was such fun! So much pep about her. I should love to know what she's up to these days.'

'Me too!' I said matily. 'That's why I'm trying to trace her. This letter: where was she when she wrote it?'

'Now let me think.' Susy tapped one manicured fingernail against her lips. How could Claude have put up with her for five minutes? 'She hadn't had the baby by then, because I would have remembered whether it was a boy or a girl. I had a daughter, Lesley. Pam and I were due at roughly the same time, and we used to imagine how lovely it would be if our children could play together. Her little one must be coming up for eight now, like mine.'

'I thought Pamela was going to give the baby up for adoption though. Because of her – situation.'

Susy looked at me sharply. 'She didn't want to.'

'Of course, but one has to be realistic.' I softened my voice. 'It must have been hard for her, going off to that maternity home all on her own. Was it in Leamington Spa, or have I dreamed that?'

'I'm not sure.' Susy threaded her way through the display to a spindly desk and opened the drawer, causing the figurines lined up on top to rattle alarmingly. She shuffled through various papers, muttering under her breath, while I made encouraging remarks about how kind it was of her to go to so much trouble.

Met S in Kensington Gardens, I remembered from the diary. *Had a good chat and a few laughs.* I bet they bloody did – at my expense, no doubt.

'Ah, here we are!' She'd found a Liberty-print address book, stuffed with loose notes and envelopes. 'I don't have her address in the book, I'm afraid, but there might be...' She held the book by its spine and shook it so that various scraps of paper fluttered out, read them, then shook her head. 'No, sorry. Nothing doing. I must have had her details once because I seem to recall passing them on to someone else.'

'Really? Who would that have been?'

She shrugged. 'Not sure. Another friend, maybe? It was years ago.'

I tried another tack. 'Can you remember anything she said in the letter?'

Susy knelt back on her heels. 'Well, she was mainly writing to thank me for having her to stay. She spent a week here, you see, when the girl she was living with threw her out.'

I nearly fell off the sofa. 'Threw her out? I never heard about that.'

'Oh, yes.' Susy nodded, smoothing the cherry-print cotton over her knees. 'They'd had some sort of altercation, though I never got to the bottom of it. I gather she was rather difficult, this girl – something of a prickly pear. Anyway, poor Pam turned up out of the blue in an awful state, with a few clothes stuffed into a haversack. Of course, I was happy to take her in. My husband was away and it was cosy, the two of us waiting for our babies together. I was a few weeks further along the way than she was, so I went off to the country to have Lesley and she went–' She put her finger to her lips again, pondering. 'That's it! She went to her sister's.'

'But I thought her sister was dead?'

'Really?' Susy frowned, then her face cleared. 'Oh, I tell a lie, it was her sister-in-law. Her brother was away in the forces but his wife let her stay. Pam might have had the baby there, I suppose. I can't recall what plans she'd made.'

'And where was that, exactly?'

'I'm not sure. One of the university towns, I think. Oxford or Cambridge, or maybe Durham. You seem very keen to get hold of her. Does she owe you money?' She grinned, showing a lot of teeth.

I smiled back. 'Goodness, nothing like that. But as you said, she was a lot of fun, and our friendship meant a lot to me.'

'Oh, same here! If you do find her, would you write and tell me her address? I'd love to hear her news.' Susy got to her feet. 'You were clever to track me down, I must say. Excellent sleuthing.'

'Pam told me about your darling house with the blue

shutters.' My face was beginning to ache from the effort of smiling. 'How did you meet, as a matter of interest?'

'Oh, quite by chance. We got talking one day on a bench in Hyde Park and hit it off straight away.' She glanced at the clock on the mantelpiece. 'I'm sorry, but I must be going. Time to pick Lesley up from school.'

'Thank you so much, Mrs Johnson. Susy.' I stood up too, holding myself very still in case I broke something or went on the rampage. 'You've been a great help.'

* * *

This was what Claude did, I realised, walking back to Berridges in a temper: she picked people up on a whim – even ghastly creatures like Susy Johnson – and dropped them when they were no longer of any use. 'Something of a prickly pear' indeed! When I thought about all the times I'd brought her cups of tea in bed, shown an interest in her endless ailments, devised little treats and excursions to cheer her up, it made me mad enough to spit. How dare she tell random acquaintances I was 'difficult'! She'd had a brother in the forces, too, if Susy was to be believed, and never once mentioned him to me. I'd slipped a small figurine from Susy's collection into my pocket and set about it at home with a rolling pin. Once the simpering chimney sweep had been reduced to powder, I felt a little calmer. It was ridiculous to become so worked up but, as I might have mentioned, I can be hot-headed and injustice always makes me angry. Claude wasn't worth another second of my time, I decided.

We were so busy at work that I managed to succeed in putting her out of my mind for a few weeks until, leafing through *The Times* early one morning, I read an announcement that Colonel Gerald Blenkinsop had died; a solicitor in

Godalming had the funeral details. It had to be him. I doubted there were two Gerald Blenkinsops in England, let alone Godalming. Perhaps Claude was looking at this same announcement even now and shuddering at the memory of that dreadful day. Or perhaps she was looking at it and wondering whether to give Mrs Blenkinsop one last shot at being a grandmother, if she had somehow contrived to keep the baby. I telephoned the solicitor's office as soon as it opened, cancelled a couple of appointments and made my arrangements to remember a dear friend, or so I told Noel. The chance of confronting Claude put paid to all my good intentions.

Funerals of people one doesn't know well can be strangely enjoyable, I've found, depending not only on the choice of hymns or quality of refreshments. There's a sense of completeness in contemplating a life that's come full circle, and a feeling of relief and companionship among the mourners. Besides, there are fewer social obligations at a funeral than a wedding or christening; the oddest sort of behaviour can be put down to grief. I chose a dark suit and pillbox hat with a veil and set off for Godalming in a state of some anticipation.

One wouldn't have thought the Colonel Blenkinsop described at his funeral and the man who'd received us at The Willows eight years before were the same person. He was virtually a saint, to judge from the eulogy, tireless in his work for the community and various charities, a generous and convivial host. Brief mention was made of his only son, a war hero who'd given his life for his country in true Blenkinsop fashion. I'd been scouring the pews for Claude since I arrived and looked around particularly closely at that point, but there was no sign of her. It had been an outside chance she would come to the ceremony, even if she'd spotted the announcement, yet worth a try all the same. When the service was over, we filed to a nearby hotel, where pork pies and pallid cucumber sandwiches (disappointing) awaited us in the conservatory. Skulking in a corner, I observed Mrs Blenkinsop from a distance. The colour in her cheeks and air of animation surprised me; widowhood seemed to suit her. She must have sensed me watching and caught my eye, and the next thing I knew, she was advancing towards me. I braced myself, prepared for trouble.

'What are you doing here?' she asked.

'I've come to express my condolences,' I replied. 'Colonel Blenkinsop and I–'

'Rubbish. I know exactly who you are. You have a distinctive face and I remember it clearly. The details of your previous visit are etched on my memory, unfortunately. Have you come to make a scene?'

It seemed wisest to tell the truth. 'I thought my friend might have been here. Pamela Atkins. Stella, I mean. We've lost touch and–'

'Well, that's hardly likely, is it?' Mrs Blenkinsop interrupted. 'Given the reception she got last time.'

'I suppose not. But I'm keen to find her and it seemed worth a try. I don't suppose she ever wrote to you? After the baby was born, perhaps?'

'She did not.' Mrs Blenkinsop glanced around to make sure no one was eavesdropping and said, in a slightly softer tone, 'Gerald had his reasons for sending her off with a flea in her ear and he was my husband so of course I couldn't say anything, but she has been on my conscience, I must admit. He was a man of firm opinions but he could be a little harsh when provoked.'

Too late now for regrets. I hardened my heart, remembering how she had stood in the doorway, wringing her hands while her husband said those awful things. 'I knew Stella well. She wasn't a tart.'

Mrs Blenkinsop looked shifty. 'Possibly not. As a matter of fact, the last time we saw Peter, he did tell me he'd met somebody else. He was going to end the engagement with Esme when she came home on leave, but he was killed before they could meet. But my husband said this affair had probably been just a fling, and then when this girl Stella wrote to us...' She shook her head. 'Her spelling left something to be desired, and she actually thought we'd be pleased to hear of her predicament! Obviously, we couldn't let her tarnish Peter's name and break poor Esme's heart all over again.'

'What about Stella's heart though?'

'Oh, I can't imagine she grieved for long, a girl like that. She'd have found it easy enough to replace him. Well, goodbye, young lady.' Somewhat pointedly, she eyed the plate of soggy sandwiches I was clutching. 'I hope you haven't had an entirely wasted journey.'

I thought constantly about Claude over the next few days. My equilibrium had been shaken; I lost patience with clients, made careless mistakes when adding up estimates and ordered twice as much as we needed of the wrong fabric. She haunted me. I realised my life would always seem incomplete, unfulfilled, until I'd found her and we'd had it out, face to face. Trying to sleep one night, I suddenly sat bolt upright in bed, remembering the address on her identity card: Cedar Lane, St Albans. That was where her sister had lived, and her parents might still be there. I had no idea of the number. And anyway, what would I say if Mr or Mrs Atkins opened the door? It might be wiser not to let Claude know anyone was looking for her. I took the train to St Albans the next weekend, all the same, and then a taxi to Cedar Lane. It was a depressing street, lined with ugly pebbledashed houses lurking behind desolate front gardens; not the sort of place where strangers asking questions would be welcome. I told the taxi driver to turn around and take me back to the station. The task seemed hopeless. I was an amateur, blundering about in search of clues.

The following Sunday, I invited Floss and Brenda – a stocky, taciturn girl with a menacing air – to my flat for tea. Floss wandered about, wide-eyed, picking things up and exclaiming over them. 'This is just like your old place,' she said, although it wasn't at all. Victoria Mansions had been an underground lair, furnished with only the few odds and ends we'd managed to salvage. Now I'm up high and airy in Cheyne Walk, with some decent furniture and a chair at the window to watch barges sailing up and down the river. Traffic became busier once they started building the site for the Festival of Britain, further upstream, and it's stayed busy ever since.

'We should give our house a going-over,' Floss told Brenda, who was sullenly eating a scone. 'A lick of paint and a few cushions and you wouldn't recognise it. What d'you say?'

Brenda said she thought it wasn't worth the effort but if Floss was dead set on decorating, she wouldn't stand in her way.

'I'll help, if you like,' I offered. 'There's often fabric left over at the end of a job that you could have cheap. And paint too.'

Floss beamed. 'Thanks, Miss. It was my lucky day, running into you again.'

'Mine too.' She was a rewarding person to do things for, so appreciative and loyal. I liked looking at myself through her eyes – as I had been then, and as I was now.

* * *

A couple of weeks later, one of our clients happened to change her mind about some hand-painted wallpaper that the manufacturer refused to take back. I didn't know whether it was the sort of thing Floss would like, being on the chintzy side, but the quality was excellent and there were four rolls going for free so I left a message for her at the police station, offering to bring round a sample. She rang me back, delighted, and we fixed a time that weekend. Those boxy little prefabs, like overgrown dolls' houses, had been springing up all over the place after the war; it would be interesting to see one from the inside.

Floss showed me around, pointing out various features: the bathroom and separate lavatory, the neat kitchen with its electric cooker, fridge and fold-down table, the boiler that provided hot water and central heating, and a wash copper for the laundry. 'To think I'd live in a house with all the mod cons!' she said. 'I keep pinching myself, honestly.'

It wasn't as bad as I'd feared; in fact, so clean and convenient, having everything to hand, and gardens front and back with tomatoes and runner beans among the marigolds.

'Cup of tea?' Floss asked, and I remembered how she had entertained me in her tumbledown den with sugared milk out of a jam jar. She'd come a long way since then. The furniture was basic utility, but the carpets weren't bad and we decided wallpaper would spruce up the sitting room no end.

'We'll make it look like a gypsy caravan,' I said. 'That's the style to aim for: romantic and cottagey. I can find some sprigged cotton for the curtains.' They would have to be light, since there were only wires stretched across the windows instead of proper tracks.

'A gypsy caravan! Do you hear that, Brenda?' Floss asked, giggling, and Brenda allowed herself a small, grim smile before she went off to make the tea.

'I loved your place in Victoria Mansions,' Floss said. 'The way you'd arranged everything, and all those little touches. Do you remember that cigarette box?'

'Of course.' I'd pinched it as a souvenir from a bar in a hotel Guy Cavendish had once taken me to. 'Although we never had many cigarettes to put in it.'

'Look, we've got one now. Fully stocked.' Floss offered it to me and flicked a Bakelite table lighter.

'You know what happened to Victoria Mansions, I suppose?' I asked.

She nodded. 'Just as well you got out when you did.'

I couldn't resist prodding her to see if she would give anything away. 'Did you ever wonder why we left so suddenly?'

'It wasn't my place then, and I can't see it matters now. You must have had your reasons, you and–' She hesitated. 'Seems odd to think of her as Miss Claude still. What was her real name?'

'Stella,' I replied. 'Stella Atkins. And I'm Margot. You don't need to call me Miss Hall, not now we're proper friends.'

She blushed but luckily Brenda came in at that point with the tea and a plate of digestives, so that created a diversion. 'I used to wonder whether you were spies,' Floss said, once the tea had been poured. 'Or whether Miss Claude – Stella, I mean – was having a baby with someone important, so that was why you had to hide away.' She blew on her tea before taking a sip. 'She sent me a postcard after you'd gone, and I wrote back but I never heard any more. I suppose once she'd had the baby, she wanted to forget about anyone who'd known her then.'

'But how could she have sent you a postcard?' I asked. 'How did she know where you were?'

'I went to see that friend of hers, in the house with the blue shutters. She gave me Miss Claude's address and I wrote to tell her mine. I didn't expect to hear back, not really, so it was a nice surprise to get her card. I've kept it all this time.'

I placed my cup deliberately back in its saucer. 'I should love to see that card, if you don't mind.'

'Course not. I'll fetch it in a second.'

I had to contain my impatience while she sipped her tea and talked about inconsequential things. At last she went off to find the postcard, leaving Brenda and me stranded in an uneasy silence. I was too agitated to make small talk. 'Better clear the tea things, I suppose,' Brenda muttered eventually, loading up the tray.

Floss came back with a biscuit tin – the same one she'd used to store her wartime treasures – laid it down on the coffee table and proceeded to open it with great ceremony. She glanced at the postcard before handing it over. There was a picture of the Radcliffe Camera in Oxford on the front. On the back, Claude had written: *Thanks for your letter, Flo. Sorry I didn't get to say goodbye. Keep up with your schoolwork, be good, and if you can't be good, be careful! C x*

She'd drawn a little picture of that man with his nose over the wall who'd popped up everywhere during the war, and written, *Wot, no sugar?* underneath.

Floss was still rooting around in the tin. She came up with a square of tightly folded paper which she passed to me. 'That was her address at the time, but I don't think she stayed there long. Like I said, I wrote again but she never replied. Can't bear to throw it away, somehow.'

I stared at the faded, creased writing: 414 Banbury Road, Oxford.

Well, it was a start.

22

JANET

Oxford, October 1952

Banbury Road was a long one, heading north out of Oxford or south towards the city, depending on one's perspective. I drove there one Saturday in the Morris Minor I'd bought when petrol rationing ended, and discovered number 414 conveniently close to a parade of shops. The house was screened from the road by a tall hedge, but a café on the other side of the road at least gave me a view of the gate. After walking along that stretch of the pavement two or three times, I settled down in the café with a pot of tea, a newspaper and an Eccles cake to watch for any comings or goings. I wore a headscarf and carried a shopping basket so no one took any notice of me. It was a sunny autumn day and students were everywhere, young men and women, too, dashing about on bicycles. I felt young myself, despite the headscarf, and suddenly full of hope. We were all worried about Russia and the threat of nuclear confrontation, but the last war seemed to belong to a different age and my future shone bright with possibility. I'd been wondering about starting my own business for a while. Noel was too conservative to appreciate the new designers with their modern, clean aesthetic, but I knew what discerning people were looking for these days.

My eye was suddenly caught by movement on the other side of the road. Two people emerged through the gate of number 414: an ordinary-looking woman in a tweed coat, holding the hand of a girl aged about seven or eight, rather plump, wearing a school mac belted at the waist and a beret from which two chestnut plaits dangled, like bell ropes. They crossed the road and walked past the window in which I was sitting, so I was able to get a good look at them. The woman seemed preoccupied, a little harassed, consulting a piece of paper in her hand that I assumed was a shopping list. The girl looked pleased with herself, as though she were making secret and delicious plans.

I paid for my order, left the tearoom immediately and followed the pair at a discreet distance. About a hundred yards further down the road, they separated: the woman joining a queue outside a grocer's shop and the girl carrying on to a newsagent's on the next corner. I quickened my pace and hurried after her, arriving at the shop in time to hear her ask, 'May I have my comic and a penny bar of chocolate, please?'

'What's it called again, Janet?' the shopkeeper asked, turning to leaf through a stack behind the counter.

'*Girl*,' she replied (an uncompromising title), waiting without any sign of impatience. I couldn't see her face and her back gave nothing away but, all of a sudden, one chubby hand had sneaked out and she'd pinched a chew from a box on the shelf.

The man turned back. 'That'll be fivepence ha'penny.' He tore a coupon from her ration book before handing over the comic and chocolate bar.

'And two fruit salad chews, please.' She tucked the comic

under her arm, gave him a coin and pocketed her loot. I stared at her as she passed by but she kept her eyes lowered.

Hastily, I bought a packet of cigarettes and hurried to catch her up. 'Excuse me, young lady,' I began, out of breath. She turned to look at me with a blank, impassive expression, and I noticed a bulge in her freckled cheek. 'I saw you steal that sweet just now.'

She swallowed. 'What sweet?'

'The chew you took from that box on the counter. The one you've just eaten.'

'No, I didn't.'

'Yes, you did! I was right behind you.' It was ridiculous, arguing over a farthing chew, yet I admired her nerve.

'Why didn't you say something then?'

'Because I could hardly believe my eyes. I should make you go back to the shop right now and apologise.'

'Are you going to?' She squinted up at me into the sun.

'I'm not sure.' I folded my arms. 'Maybe I should tell your mother what you did. She's at the shops, isn't she? I saw you together just now.'

That rattled her. 'Please don't tell,' she said, dropping the cheeky attitude. 'It was a mistake and I'll never do it again, I promise.'

'You'd better not.' I glared at her, pursing my lips as though making up my mind. 'All right then. It'll be our little secret. But you could end up in serious trouble if you carry on like this. I'm only ticking you off for your own good.'

'I'm sorry, honestly.'

I could tell she didn't mean it; already she'd retreated into herself again. I scrutinised her closely; the freckles, the hair, the round hazel eyes. 'How old are you, Janet?'

'Seven. I'll be eight next month.'

'And what's your last name?' I saw her hesitate, wondering

whether to invent something. 'It's all right,' I added, 'I'm not going to tell anyone what you did. I should just like to know, that's all.'

'Atkins,' she said quickly. 'But I have to be going. My mother will worry if I'm not back soon.'

'Of course.' I forced myself to smile as though I liked her. 'And I'm Miss Smith. Bye for now. Don't worry, my lips are sealed.'

I pretended to draw a zipper over them in a light-hearted way but she was already hurrying off. I watched her go: Janet Atkins, with the key to a mystery in her cunning little hand.

* * *

I found a modest but clean bed and breakfast further along the Banbury Road and booked myself a room overnight, exploring Oxford in the afternoon before supper in a timber-beamed café off the High. The ancient colleges drowsing behind secret doorways were untouched; there was a rumour Hitler had been planning to make the city his new capital after the planned German invasion and that was why it had never been bombed. How narrowly we'd escaped!

In the morning, I ate a surprisingly good breakfast and strolled down the road to the sound of bells pealing from neighbouring spires. I'd have bet good money on Mrs Atkins being a churchgoer and so it turned out: from my vantage point across the road, I saw a party of three emerge single file from number 414. Mr Atkins led the way, chest out and shoulders back in the best military fashion. He was all parcelled up in a loden overcoat and Homburg hat, a clipped ginger moustache bristling above his lip. Mrs Atkins followed in her Sunday best, turning occasionally to remonstrate with Janet who was lagging behind, scuffing the pavement with her outdoor shoes. I waited until they'd passed by before crossing the road and tagging along, and we walked in tandem to a church about half a mile away. I was quite safe; Janet was in a world of her own and her parents would have had no idea who I was.

I sat a couple of pews behind them in the church, absorbing a sense of who they were from the little I could see. Mrs Atkins sat closer to Janet than to her husband, and was constantly distracted by her daughter: nudging her to sit up straight, finding the right page in her hymn book, frowning at her for fidgeting. She seemed a precise, pernickety sort of woman. Mr Atkins sat stiff and unmoving, as though he were a waxwork or had fallen into a trance. Claude's brother, then, though he had little of her exuberance. I wondered what he'd been like when they were growing up, whether he'd been a bully or babied by his sisters. He'd certainly done well for himself; a house on the Banbury Road was a far cry from the pebbledash terrace in St Albans.

The vicar was an elderly man in glasses with a languid, non-committal delivery who seemed to be boring himself as much as his congregation. After twenty interminable minutes, a frantically cheerful woman announced it was time for Sunday school, whereupon various children stood up and straggled out of the pews to assemble by a side door. Janet needed a furtive slap on the leg from her mother before she consented to join them. They were being marshalled into pairs but none of the others wanted to hold her hand. Finally losing patience, the jolly woman thrust a small blonde girl in Janet's direction and left them to get on with it.

I could sense Janet's resentment from halfway down the church and warmed to her. I've never felt particularly easy in the company of children; in my opinion they're either dull or precocious and it's hard to say which is worse. (Floss had been an exception but she was always in a category of her own.)

Janet, however, reminded me of myself as a girl. I could imagine the thoughts running through her head as she glowered at the other girls and boys. Her hair glimmered in the shadowy nave of the church before she and her reluctant partner disappeared through the door to receive their instruction and I stood up too. I'd got what I came for, and there were plans to be made.

I drove back to London that morning, stopping for lunch at a pub by the river, and the next day booked myself a week's holiday as soon as work commitments allowed. Noel looked surprised but he couldn't object, since I hadn't taken any time off for at least a year and a half. I said something about 'staying with friends in the country' in a tone that discouraged further questions, though I could tell he was itching to ask. Anyway, I needed a break. It would be good to take stock, to reflect on the life I'd made for myself and consider the future, and Oxford was as good a place to do it as any. A single woman could wander round those medieval streets feeling soulful rather than superfluous.

As soon as I arrived back in the city, I found a pet shop and bought a puppy: a fluffy white one, small enough to carry about in a covered basket. The woman who ran the bed and breakfast, Mrs Williams, was most particular about rules and wouldn't have reacted well to a pet. Children liked animals, didn't they? The other thing I knew about Janet was that she had a sweet tooth; luckily I had plenty of ration coupons. Armed with the dog and a bag of sweets, I set off to make friends.

For the first few days, I watched Janet from a distance to familiarise myself with her routine. She'd emerge from the gateway of number 414 at eight each morning and walk half a mile up the road to knock on the door of her friend's house. The friend would often keep her waiting on the doorstep before emerging in a rush, her coat unbuttoned and her bag gaping open. Janet, on the other hand, was always neat: her shoes polished, her mac belted, her satchel buckled, her spindly plaits impeccable. One would have thought she'd never put a foot wrong, although I knew differently. She and her friend – curly hair, glasses, thin legs and large feet – then walked another mile or so to arrive at the school gates by a quarter to nine. If it looked as though they were going to be late, Janet would forge ahead. The friend was chatty, easily distracted by cats, cars or passers-by, while Janet plodded remorselessly on, her eyes fixed straight ahead. I wondered whether a puppy would be enough to engage her; I might have had more luck leading a giraffe down the street.

The puppy was also turning out to be a terrific nuisance. He had an irritating high-pitched bark and tiny needle-sharp teeth which he used to devastating effect on my shoes, my handbag, the bed leg and the steering wheel of my car, to name a few of his favourite toys. He also left foul messes everywhere, despite being endlessly paraded outside to do his business. Luckily the carpet in my room was a serviceable dark brown but, even so, I had to do a lot of work with lavatory paper and Jeyes disinfectant, and Mrs Williams must have thought I had tummy troubles from the number of times I visited the bathroom. After the first sleepless night, I made the wretched creature sleep in my car, having lined the seats and footwells with newspaper – inadequately, as it turned out. I'd thought having something to look after might be fun, but the puppy and I were locked in a battle of wills and I was losing. After each fresh atrocity, he would stare at me triumphantly with his black button eyes shining.

After our morning Janet patrol, I would leave the puppy in my car and walk into town, stopping off wherever took my fancy along the way. I spent hours in the Pitt Rivers Museum, browsing the fascinating collections of Oxford University, walked around Christ Church Meadow and sat in the Bodleian

Library, reading *Country Life* or *The Lady*. I'd lunch in a café or tearoom, then liberate the dog and take him for a walk until the time came for us to observe Janet's return journey at a quarter to four. Sometimes her friend was with her, sometimes she was alone. She often took a detour through a small park on the way home where she might sit on a bench, reading a comic.

One day she attempted to climb a tree. Propping her satchel against the trunk, she managed to clamber on to the lower branch where she stood, gazing up into the canopy, before slumping back on her bottom again. For a while she teetered there, looking down at the ground. It must have seemed alarmingly far away and my stomach lurched in sympathy. Then abruptly she flopped out of the tree like an ungainly fledgling turfed out of the nest, landing in a heap on the grass.

'Janet, is that you?' I called, emerging from behind a bush with the puppy in tow. 'It's me, Miss Smith. Goodness! Are you all right?'

She gave me a brief glance as she scrambled to her feet and replied she was, brushing leaves and shards of twig from her mac.

'That was quite a drop,' I said. 'You should sit down for a while to get over the shock.' She stared at me suspiciously. 'You can play with my puppy if you like,' I added.

The wretched creature chose that moment to squat and relieve himself on the path, smirking at us as he did so.

'No, thank you,' she replied. 'I don't like dogs.'

So that was three pounds down the drain. 'Well, let's find somewhere to sit anyway,' I said, stepping away from the stench. 'Would you like a sweet? I've some liquorice allsorts in my pocket.'

'What's your puppy called?' she asked, following me willingly.

'Snowy.' It was the first name that came into my head.

'Like Tintin's dog?'

'Probably.' I had no idea what she was talking about. 'Now let's sit on this bench till you get your breath back. You can tell me what you did at school today.' I held out the bag of Allsorts and she helped herself to a handful while Snowy scrabbled at a patch of earth.

'Not much. Writing and stuff. We had Music and Movement this afternoon in the hall.' She stood up, still chewing, and waved her arms stiffly in the air like a traffic policeman. 'That's becoming a tree. May I have some more Liquorice Allsorts, please?'

'Of course.' We were making some progress. 'You know, I was an only child too. I used to invent all sorts of games when I was your age.'

'I'm not an only child,' she said thickly, a trail of brown slime dribbling down her chin. 'I've got a brother, Terry. He's away at boarding school.'

'And how old is he?'

'Thirteen. Why do you want to know?'

I shrugged. 'No reason in particular, just chatting. I don't have any children but I have a–' I was about to claim a niece until I remembered the only-child complication, 'a god-daughter about your age. And I had a lovely aunt, Aunt Ivy. We were very close.'

Janet was gazing longingly at my pocket. 'You'd better not have too many sweets or you won't eat your tea. Maybe one more.' I held out the bag, asking casually, 'Do you have any aunts or uncles?'

She nodded, her hand hovering over the sweets before pouncing on a pink bobbly jelly.

'And what are their names?'

'Uncle Eric and Aunt Betty, Aunty Susan, Uncle Henry and Aunt Stella.'

'I have an Aunt Stella too, as well as Aunt Ivy!' I exclaimed. 'Isn't that a coincidence? My Aunt Stella's quite a dragon. What's yours like?'

'All right, I suppose.' Janet glanced at me warily.

'And do you see a lot of her? Does she live close by?'

'Look at your dog!' she shrieked suddenly. 'He's doing a wee on my satchel!'

'Oh dear. Naughty thing!' I wiped her bag on the grass while Snowy gambolled around me, yapping joyfully.

'Thanks for the Allsorts.' Janet took the satchel from me, holding it at arm's length, and marched away.

'Wait a minute.' I hurried after her. 'I want to ask about your Aunt Stella. Does she often come to visit?'

'I'm not supposed to talk to strangers.'

'But you know me. I'm Miss Smith, remember? We met outside the sweet shop.'

She turned to stare at me. 'Why do you care so much about my family?'

'Oh, I don't, not really. I just wanted to chat, that's all.' I shrugged, holding up my palms in a gesture of supplication. 'I'm here on holiday, you see, and I don't know anyone else in Oxford. I was only trying to be friendly.'

Janet slung the satchel over her shoulder and took to her heels, the bag bouncing against her plump bottom as she ran. Snowy chased after her, checking to see whether I objected. When I didn't, he sat down and began to lick his private parts.

At least I didn't have to put up with the ghastly thing a minute longer. I left him tied to the park railings and did what might have been quicker in the first place: drove back to London, contacted a private detective recommended by Floss and asked him to look into the birth and probable adoption of Janet Atkins, born somewhere near Oxford, some time in November 1944.

* * *

This was how I imagined the story: after listening to Susy Johnson prattle about their little ones playing together, Claude changes her mind about having her baby taken away by a stranger and asks her sister-in-law whether she can stay until after she's given birth. She might not raise the idea of adoption straight away, or even at all. Maybe she'll drop a few hints. The Atkins' already have one child, a boy of five or six at the time. Perhaps they've been trying for another without success, perhaps Mr Atkins has been away for too long to fulfil his husbandly duties, or perhaps they only ever wanted one child but the sight of Claude's newborn daughter simply melts Mrs Atkins' heart. (No doubt Janet was more appealing as a baby.) At any rate, the child isn't put up for adoption and when Mr Atkins is released from military service, he's presented with an addition to the family. Janet will have been in the household for at least six months and probably more by then, long enough to have established herself. 'A daddy's girl,' Mrs Atkins might tell her husband, 'the little sister for Terry we always wanted.' Now Claude knows where her daughter is and can watch her grow up. The fiction is maintained that she is Janet's aunt; only she and the Atkins know the truth.

And now I do, too. The detective confirmed my guesswork was accurate – at least, as far as the facts are concerned.

23

A WATCHING BRIEF

Oxford, High Wycombe and London, November 1952

Information is readily available if you know where to look: adoption papers, birth, death and marriage certificates, census records, and now these new national insurance numbers. Somewhere there must be a death certificate for Fabia Heythornthwaite, although I'm not sure how long a person has to be missing before they're declared dead. I don't feel like Fabia Heythornthwaite anymore, thank God. I was Fabia Russell-Jones before I married but I don't feel much like her, either: that gauche, awkward girl who couldn't speak to a man without blushing. I was Cecil for a while and now I'm Margot Hall. (I changed my last name slightly, too, just to be on the safe side.) Who is she? Perhaps I'll only find out later, looking back. Claude is Stella again, because of course she couldn't carry on using her dead sister's name once she was back in the bosom of her family. She's also Mrs Henry Lycett. Respectable at last, and all because of me. I never did get to ask her those questions I had in mind, although that's probably just as well. Because essentially, they all boil down to one: did you ever care about me at all? And maybe I don't want to hear the answer.

She had spoken so viciously to me in the garden of her desirable residence that I drove back to London in a state of shock. I'd discovered where she lived all by myself, although no doubt the private investigator would have found that out for me too. He'd told me the exact date of Janet Atkins' birth: November 14th, which this year was a Friday. It seemed likely Claude would pay her daughter a visit, if not on the day itself then some time over the weekend. The Banbury Road bed and breakfast was fully booked, according to Mrs Williams (though I think that might have been down to Snowy's depredations), so I splashed out on two nights at the Randolph instead. The hotel was undergoing building work; I complained about the noise and had ten pounds knocked off my bill, making it almost reasonable. Then it was back to wandering up and down the Banbury Road and lurking in the café to watch the goings-on at number 414.

I'd missed Janet's return from school on Friday afternoon, having arrived late in Oxford because of the traffic, but around five in the afternoon, her curly-haired friend arrived at the gate in a frilly dress that didn't suit her at all, along with a woman I presumed was her mother and an older girl who might have been her sister. The mother left shortly afterwards and although I missed seeing the girls emerge at the end of the party, I was certain no other guests had arrived. The next morning, however, I struck gold. A sporty two-seater Morgan drew up and parked on the road a short distance from number 414, and a woman in a sheepskin coat got out, carrying a parcel wrapped in pink spotted paper. She headed towards the house but, by the time I'd left the café and made my way there, she was disappearing through the front door so I only caught a fleeting glimpse of her from behind. I retreated to wait in the café, where the waitress had become used to my comings and goings. (I was passing myself off as an eccentric academic on a research trip.)

An hour or so later, I watched as this woman and Janet walked down the road together. My heart turned over. It was definitely Claude. Older and slimmer, because she wasn't pregnant anymore, but with that mobile, expressive face I would have known anywhere. Janet was talking, her face lifted, and Claude was looking down at her as though the lumpy girl were a luscious strawberry or a cream cake she wanted to devour in one gulp. She put her arm around Janet's shoulder and gave her a brief, fierce squeeze, then thrust her hands back in the pockets of her coat.

I'd seen enough. There was no point following them to the park or the sweet shop or wherever they were going. Instead, I hurried in the opposite direction to fetch my car from the Randolph, parked it as close behind Claude's as possible and settled down to wait. When she climbed back into the car a couple of hours later, I was ready to follow at a discreet distance. Her Morgan could have left my Morris Minor far behind, but luckily she was a surprisingly cautious driver and I kept the bright-red car in view without too much effort as we drove east out of Oxford. I had to drop further back when she turned off the main road after an hour or so, but she wouldn't have noticed the anonymous grey saloon chugging along in her wake. She led me up a hill and then down a quiet road with wide grass verges and tasteful house names on plaques or slices of wood – rather like the Blenkinsops' neighbourhood in Godalming, in fact. Just as that thought occurred to me, I had to brake sharply to avoid slamming into the back of the Morgan, which was waiting to turn right across the flow of traffic, into a driveway with pillars on either side.

Parking a little further down the road, I hurried back on foot to investigate. Greystones, that's what Claude's house is called.

Hovering by the gate, I saw her car parked on the drive; she'd already disappeared. As I watched, a man emerged from the house, whistling, opened the garage doors and got into the car to back it inside. I could imagine her running into the house, hanging up her coat and calling, 'Park the car for me, would you, darling? You know how I hate reversing.'

I retreated behind the pillar before he could catch me lurking.

'Can I help you?' someone called, and I turned to see a man in overalls, bending over a lawnmower on the verge a couple of houses away.

'I'm lost,' I replied, laughing at my ineptitude. 'Could you tell me the name of this road? And the nearest town? I haven't the faintest idea where I am.'

He was only too happy to oblige: we were in Acre Lane, on the outskirts of High Wycombe. *Women drivers*, I could see him thinking. *Shouldn't be allowed on the road.*

* * *

So I had found her, as I always dreamed I would. What next? I hugged my secret close for a while, thinking about Claude in her elegant house with the carefree, whistling Henry. 'Uncle Henry and Aunt Stella,' Janet had told me. He probably played golf. They'd invite friends from the club or neighbours around for dinner, and none of them would have any idea what she was really like as she sat at the end of the table, taking the credit for her housekeeper's cooking. Of course, she wouldn't have to work for a living. Perhaps she indulged in a spot of gardening, or sat on a committee for some worthy charity, or made jam for the WI. If she'd had any more children, no doubt there would be a nanny to look after them. Everything would be taken care of.

I looked at my own life from the outside, as a stranger might, and wondered how Claude would judge me. I'm efficient, practical, unflappable. 'My second-in-command,' Noel calls me. 'The indispensable Miss Hall.' I have an eye for arranging furniture or paintings and excellent taste, although I can't afford to indulge it as much as I'd like in my own home. I know which tones will harmonise with each other and where an accent colour will have most effect – the *coup de rouge*, as the French call it, that will make a room sing. I enjoy talking to clients, finding out how they want their homes to look and turning their half-baked, impractical ideas into reality so they feel they've done all the work themselves. I become their confidante, sharing every aspect of their lives, from the food on their table to the clothes in their wardrobe and the pyjamas under their pillow.

People would think me successful. I rent a small but charming flat in a fashionable part of town with a river view and some decent antiques, I have important connections within the industry and a few good friends: the Hunters from a couple of doors down who always invite me round at Christmas; Michael Bassano, a friend of Noel's who shares my passion for Impressionist painters; Sarah and Emma, who used to work for Berridges and have stayed in touch. I'm godmother to Sarah's son. Or is it Emma's? I can never remember. I'm slim and not unattractive, and still some way off forty. Men often ask me out, even those whose wives have invited me into their homes. Naturally I never accept. The past is always with me, a warning voice in my ear.

It might have been wiser to walk away with the knowledge I'd gained and leave Claude to rot in suburbia, but I couldn't help brooding over this snatched glimpse into her world. She walked with me through the day, like a tack in the sole of my shoe. In the end, I typed a letter on Berridges' headed paper. It announced the company was offering a free, no-obligation design consultation to owners of particularly fine houses in the

Home Counties, in return for permission to use photographs of any future work for publicity purposes. I addressed the letter to the homeowner at Greystones, Acre Lane, High Wycombe, and signed it, 'pp Noel Berridge'. I opened all his post and could weed out any reply she might make. There was no way of knowing whether she would take the bait but the chances were pretty high; everyone likes something for nothing, and the letter would surely appeal to her vanity.

So it turned out. A few days later, Mrs Henry Lycett wrote back to say she would be delighted to meet at our earliest convenience and provided her telephone number so a date and time could be arranged. I let my assistant handle the details, and the die was cast. I drove to High Wycombe in a Berridges' van to meet Claude, and she was vile.

How could she have treated me so cruelly? I've asked myself that question a hundred times, and the only answer I can come up with is guilt. Guilt with a helping of shame. She must have been so frightened I'd tell Henry about her past that she lashed out, and to hell with the consequences. To hell with loyalty and gratitude, too, and any sense of obligation. Yet I was someone to be reckoned with now; she couldn't humiliate me and get away with it so easily. She needed to know I wasn't going anywhere. At the beginning of December I sent a Christmas card (a print of Pissarro's *Old Chelsea Bridge*) to Mrs Henry Lycett 'and family', wishing them a peaceful and prosperous new year. Marvellous to have seen her, I wrote inside; we mustn't leave it so long next time! And I printed my home address underneath.

I wasn't really expecting her to reply, so it was a surprise to receive her card a week later (a winsome robin with holly in its beak). She was coming to London for a spot of Christmas shopping the next Saturday, she wrote in her customary scrawl, and wondered whether we could meet for lunch. Very short notice and she would quite understand if I couldn't make it, but she would hope to see me at Rules in Covent Garden at twelve thirty.

She's evidently come to her senses. I'll be dignified and magnanimous, and hear her out. I won't ask for much: the occasional invitation to dinner or drinks, maybe a play or exhibition in town. A small part in her life, that's all I want. And really, that's the least she owes me.

24

RULES

London, December 1952

I'm expecting her to be late but when I arrive at Rules, five minutes after the appointed time, she's already installed at a table near the window. We can be seen, if not heard; the other diners are some distance away and a frosted glass partition between them and us gives the illusion of privacy. I wonder, as I walk towards her, if she has requested this table in particular, and whether she comes here often. Then I wonder how to greet her, but she solves the question for me, waving from the red velvet banquette.

'Hello. Forgive me for not getting up but this seat's not letting me go in a hurry.'

'Don't worry, please.' I give my coat to the hovering waiter and take a chair opposite. The clear winter light is full in my face and I regret not having come earlier to choose the best seat. 'Had a good morning shopping?' I can't see any bags but she might well have handed them in at the cloakroom.

She looks a lot smarter than the couple of times I've seen her to date, and I'm flattered she's made the effort. Her hair is swept back under a fur-trimmed beret, she's wearing pearl earrings to match her choker and her lipstick has been perfectly applied. Her demeanour has changed, too; she's calm, pleasant, controlled. I feel at a disadvantage, my nose red from the cold and my hair a little dishevelled. Too late now to go to the Ladies'. I tuck a limp strand behind my ear.

'Thank goodness that ghastly smog has cleared,' she says. 'I read about it in the newspaper. It must have been simply dreadful, trying to get about.'

'Impossible! Honestly, one couldn't see one's feet, looking down.'

The waiter approaches with menus and asks whether we'd like a drink. I order a dry Martini and she says that sounds lovely and she'll have one too. The words dance in front of my eyes. How can I think about eating and speak to her at the same time?

I lay down the menu. 'Blundering about in the fog reminded me of the blackout, actually. Do you remember? Falling off the pavement and linking arms with complete strangers – it took me right back.'

A shadow crosses her face, just for a second, and then she talks some more about the weather, and what a funny name for a restaurant but apparently it was founded by a man called Thomas Rule in 1798. The waiter returns with our drinks, a basket of bread rolls and a slab of golden butter on a saucer. Outside, black umbrellas bob along the street as people hurry through snow that's turning to sleet. Inside, the atmosphere is warm and welcoming, the pink-shaded lamp above our table shedding a rosy glow over the silver cutlery and crystal glasses. Should we go halves on the bill or will she pay the whole thing? This meal is bound to be expensive. She orders pea soup and fish pie; it's my turn to say that sounds lovely and I'll have the same.

'And a bottle of Sancerre,' she tells the waiter, handing back the menu. She cocks an eyebrow at me. 'If that's all right with you?'

'Perfectly.' The Martini gives me courage. 'Since when did you become a wine buff?'

'Oh, one picks things up. Henry says you can't go wrong with Sancerre.'

I take out my cigarette and the waiter springs forward with a lighter. The service is perfect: attentive yet unobtrusive. We sit back and smoke, looking at each other. She's not going to apologise.

'I'm surprised you invited me to lunch, considering the last time we met,' I say, in a casually neutral tone.

She takes a sip of her Martini; I've already drained mine and am hoping the wine will soon arrive. 'I wanted to tell you about my life,' she says, 'to save you the trouble of ferreting it all out for yourself.'

But now the wine is here and our waiter is making a song and dance about showing her the bottle, uncorking it and pouring her a mouthful to taste. Eventually he fills our glasses and retreats. She takes a sip and watches me, biding her time.

'So how did you meet your husband?' I ask, bridling under her scrutiny.

'I taught his children. Henry's a widower, as you may already know, and he has two sons. They've just arrived home from boarding school for the holidays.'

'I can't imagine you as a teacher.' Although then I remember Floss telling me about Claude having helped her with geography and arithmetic. I was surprised she'd had the patience.

'Oh, I loved it,' she says. 'I needed a job with

accommodation and teaching beats nursing or housekeeping in my book.'

I wait for her to ask me about my career until it becomes clear she won't. My role – for now – is to listen to her talk. With a flourish, the waiter places our brimming soup bowls on the spotless tablecloth. I take a spoonful and burn my tongue.

'I spoke to Janet the other day.' She breaks a bread roll apart. 'Apparently she recently met a tall, thin lady called Miss Smith who gave her sweets. I assume that was you? She said this lady had a dog. I can't picture you with a pet. But then again, we haven't been in touch for such a long time, and how well did we know each other in the first place? We can't have lived in that flat for more than a couple of months.' She looks at me steadily. 'I visited Victoria Mansions the other day. I'd no idea the place had been bombed. A V-2, I suppose?'

I nod. 'Mr Cavendish was killed. Awful, isn't it? And I lost everything, had to start again from scratch.'

She doesn't care about that. 'About Janet,' she begins. 'I didn't go to a maternity home to have my baby because the district nurse told me how they treat unmarried mothers in hospital. They leave you to labour on your own without any help, then take your baby away as soon as it's born and have it adopted without letting you say goodbye. "So you don't get upset", they say. They bind your breasts when the milk comes in and too bad if you get an infection. You have to be punished, you see, so you'll remember not to be wicked again. I went to my sister-in-law instead, and gave birth in her spare room with a nice young midwife. As you seem to have discovered. I suppose you hired a private detective.'

'As if I'd do such a thing. As a matter of fact, I bumped into Floss a few months ago.'

'Floss?' Her face lights up. 'What an extraordinary coincidence. How is she?'

'She's become a policewoman, would you believe.'

Claude laughs. 'Of course she has. Perfect! But how did she know where I was?'

'That friend of yours gave her your brother's address in the Banbury Road all those years ago and she'd kept it ever since.'

'What friend?'

'You know perfectly well. Susy Johnson, who lives in Cornwall Gardens and whom you used to visit on the sly. She has a daughter called Lesley, in case you're interested, and she'd love to see you again. Perhaps Lesley and Janet could be friends.'

She gazes at me steadily again. 'What a strange woman you are. Still, it's good to have news of Floss.' She shakes her head. 'A policewoman! Whatever would Chalkie say?'

I don't want to talk about Chalkie. 'Floss would love to see you. We could meet up, the three of us, have a drink together some time.'

'No, I don't think so.'

'I won't tell anyone about Janet, if that's what's bothering you.'

'I'm not worried,' she says. 'Henry already knows and he's the only one I care about. He guessed, actually, some time ago, and he doesn't mind. He's a lovely man. I suppose you think I don't deserve him.'

'Of course not.' But that is exactly what I am thinking. Everything's turned out pretty well for her, hasn't it? She sits there in her pearls, drinking wine in one of the best restaurants in London with an adoring husband waiting for her at home, and hasn't the courtesy to ask me a single question about myself. She can't even pretend to care how I've managed over the years. I push aside my soup bowl and light a cigarette, ignoring the hovering waiter. Damn her!

'I found your diary,' I tell her. 'The one you kept while you were living in my flat. How could you write such awful things?'

She blushes, embarrassed for the first time. 'Writing a diary was my release. I'm sorry if what you read was upsetting but those were my private thoughts.'

'I knew all along you were unhappy. I was only trying to help.'

'I didn't mean to be cruel.' She leans back for the waiter to take her bowl and continues, after he's gone, 'We were thrown together in such close proximity and you were too much for me.'

'What do you mean by that?'

'Too intense,' she says. 'You never left me alone for a second. You'd have eaten me up, given half a chance.'

'I took care of you! Nobody else was going to, were they? I actually saved your life, may I remind you.'

She frowns. 'Really? I don't remember that.'

'You don't remember me pulling you out of a building that was about to collapse?' I give a bitter laugh. 'Well, perhaps I shouldn't have bothered.'

'All I can bear to remember from that day is Floss running towards me with a look of grim determination on her dear little face.'

'So you're determined to write me out of history?'

'If only I could,' she replies.

We sit in silence as the waiter produces our plates of fish pie under silver domes, which he whips away with a flourish, wishing us *bon appetit*. We stare at the mound of food. Claude picks up her fork and spears a prawn; I toy with a mound of mashed potato.

'What about Janet?' I ask abruptly. 'I shouldn't imagine she's been told the truth about her Aunt Stella.'

The colour rises in Claude's cheeks. 'Janet is a child, she doesn't need to know. It would only upset her. And Cynthia, too. She's been a good mother, in her own way. I won't have you punishing them for what you see as my sins.'

She's rattled, I can tell. I pour myself some more wine, noticing she's hardly touched hers.

'I still have Guy Cavendish's painting of you,' I say. 'Would you like it back? His work fetches a lot of money these days.'

'Then perhaps you should sell it.' She gives up the pretence of eating, lays down her fork and leans back against the seat. 'I wonder what else you'd like to know. Well, you've seen my house, so I don't need to tell you about that. Henry and I lead a quiet life, on the whole. Turns out I love gardening, and that keeps me busy. We go to the theatre in Oxford occasionally, and for long walks in the Chiltern Hills, and take the boys camping during the school holidays. I've become a prison visitor at a young offenders' institute in Aylesbury. I go there twice a week. And I see Janet once a month, besides Christmas and birthdays. So that's me in a nutshell. Very dull, I'm afraid.'

'Aren't you at all interested in my life?' I ask.

'No, not really.'

'Then why invite me here? Why go through this charade?'

She pushes her plate aside and catches the waiter's eye. 'I'm too full for pudding, aren't you? Let's just have coffee.'

Then she blots her mouth with a napkin, takes out a compact and reapplies her lipstick, smacking her lips together while she looks at herself in the tiny mirror. How vulgar, I hear Mother say.

'I asked you here to tell you this is the last time we shall meet.' She lights a cigarette and leans back against the banquette, her back ramrod straight and her arms stretched out on the table. 'I've taken a leaf out of your book, you see, and done some digging myself.'

'Oh, yes?' I'm not alarmed, not yet.

She empties the last of the wine into my glass. 'Fabia

Heythornthwaite is such an unusual name. I contacted the Land Army and they gave me your old address, after a bit of prompting. Of course, it was Phyllis Heythornthwaite's address too. And it still is.'

My stomach begins to churn. The waiter brings our coffee but even the smell of it makes me feel sick. I clasp my sweaty hands in my lap. The restaurant is stuffy and the window won't open. I consider a trip to the Ladies' but am not sure my legs will hold me up.

Claude looks at me across her coffee cup. 'You may be interested to hear she's not dead yet, your mother-in-law. Tough old bird, isn't she? She's living there with a companion, Mrs Cleverly. They're great pals. And Ellen still comes in every day to cook the lunch and do a bit of dusting. They spend most of their time in the kitchen, next to the Aga. It's a draughty old house and freezing cold, but of course you know that already.'

She's taking her time, relishing every word. My head swims.

'I told them you and I had been great pals in the Land Army and we had a long talk about the old days. With Ellen and Mrs Cleverly mostly, although Mrs Heythornthwaite can follow every word.'

I close my eyes. The past is rushing to greet me; I hear the old ladies' whispers and see the furtive, frightened glances.

'We got on so well, they invited me to stay for lunch. I helped Ellen wash up afterwards and we continued the conversation. Ellen says the old lady's speech is improving, although she's still very hard to make out because of her... stroke.' She stubs out the cigarette half-smoked, screwing the butt round and round the ashtray. Here it comes.

'Except she didn't have a stroke, did she?'

I open my mouth but can't manage to speak.

'No, it was a brain injury. The poor thing fell down the stairs one night and hit her head on the stone floor.' Her eyes are

263

bright and hard. 'Which is something of a coincidence, isn't it, when you think what happened to her son. Of course, I didn't mention that, although no doubt it would be a relief for Mrs Heythornthwaite to hear the story. She must want to lay Anthony to rest. Perhaps I'll tell her some other time.'

She takes a sip of coffee, leaving a bright-red stain on the rim of the cup. 'She's an extraordinary woman, your mother-in-law. They don't make them like that anymore. Ellen said she wasn't found until the morning, so she must have spent hours lying on those cold flagstones. Strange you didn't hear her fall, wasn't it? She would have made quite a noise and according to Ellen, your bedroom was right at the top of the staircase.'

Bile rises in my throat. I swallow and force myself to meet her gaze.

'Ellen always had her doubts about our Fabia,' Claude goes on. '"Good riddance to bad rubbish", those were her very words. She and old Mrs Heythornthwaite drank half a bottle of sherry when they heard you were dead, apparently, and it wasn't for the shock. I gather she'd already told the police about her suspicions but there wasn't much they could do without evidence. They could hardly put Phyllis Heythornthwaite on the stand, given her condition.'

I find my voice at last. 'It was an accident. If you repeat any of this malicious gossip, I'll–'

She leans forward. 'You'll what? Sue me for slander? I don't think so.' She opens her handbag, takes a five-pound note out of her purse and tucks it under her saucer. 'That should cover our bill. There'll probably be enough for a glass of brandy too. You look as though you need one.'

'I can't believe you'd take Ellen's word over mine,' I say, with a stab at dignity. 'She's a char, and a lazy one at that.'

'I liked her. And I know you only too well, remember? You may call yourself Margot Hall and dress like a mannequin but

I've seen what's underneath and it's nasty, through and through. If you approach me or any of my family again, I shall go straight to the police and tell them all about you. There's no point trying to hide. You might look different now but that birthmark at the nape of your neck won't disappear.'

My hand flies there unconsciously.

'By the way,' she adds, almost as an afterthought, 'have you visited Victoria Mansions recently?' When I don't reply, she says, 'You should. I went there last week and couldn't believe my eyes. Work's just started on a new block of flats to fill in the gap on that side of the square. They'll be digging the foundations next week, the foreman told me. So maybe Mrs Heythornthwaite is about to find out what happened to her son after all. Still, I could always fill in the details for her.'

'How could you?' I whisper. 'After everything I've done for you.'

'Goodbye, Fabia,' she says, and gives me a grim smile. 'I trust this is the last we'll see of each other.'

She slides along the banquette, stands up and edges past me, keeping the widest possible distance between us. I watch her collect her coat, drape it over her shoulders and walk out into the rain. She tilts back her head, lifts her face to the sky for a moment, and then she's gone.

EPILOGUE

New York, February 1964

A canapé? I simply couldn't, although they are delicious. I have to watch my weight, unfortunately. But I will have another drink, if you absolutely insist. Thank you so much. I adore *your* accent too! You Americans still sound exotic to me, even after ten years. It'll be eleven this summer, actually. Isn't it extraordinary how time flies?

Oh, I love it here, couldn't imagine living anywhere else. English stately homes can be splendid, of course, but they're freezing in winter and stifling in the summer. And a place of any size is impossible to run these days, one can't get the staff. I've grown used to my creature comforts, couldn't do without air conditioning and central heating now. And your wonderful food! Do you know, meat was still rationed when I left England? As soon as I arrived in New York, I went straight to a diner and ate the most enormous beefburger! I know, too funny for words. Cigarette? Here, have one of mine.

Yes, this house has turned out rather well. I'm glad you

approve. It was a collaborative process, of course. Mrs MacBride has such vision. Yes, she does have quite a penchant for animal fur, doesn't she? We've confined most of the leopard skin to the den, though I notice a few pieces have crept back in here. I might have to have words with her later, ha ha. I shall be starting on their fishing lodge as soon as I can find the time. Have you stayed there? Such an idyllic spot. There'll be plenty of tartan to reflect the family's heritage, and my business partner is sourcing some fabulous British antiques to send across the pond. I agree, it's the perfect arrangement – expansion into America was the next logical step for us. He and I are on the telephone to each other constantly so you can imagine the bills, but communication is vital.

No, I haven't been back to the mother country in person. Not once, no. Well, I haven't any family left over there and I'm not overly keen on flying, it still seems unnatural. Besides, I've made my home here. I've a dear little flat – sorry, apartment! – overlooking Central Park, although I'm always travelling and don't spend nearly as much time there as I'd like. In fact, I'm off to Maine tomorrow. Of course, I couldn't refuse Kathleen's kind invitation for this evening. Seeing the result of all our hard work makes my job worthwhile. Do take one of my cards, although I'm afraid I haven't a spare minute until the autumn. Sorry, the fall. Silly me, you'd think I'd remember by now! Old habits die hard, don't they? Here, your glass needs topping up – let me catch the waiter's eye. And just a splash for myself, thank you. Maybe a drop more. Perfect.

As I was saying, work is my passion. I'm terribly dull, really. No, seriously, I am. Business is my life blood, and I love dealing with Americans, you're so straightforward and ambitious. Just like me, in fact. You don't care where a person's been, you're only interested in where they're going. So refreshing. Yes, the British are supposed to have a great sense of humour. And one mustn't forget Shakespeare, you're right. No, I'm afraid I don't understand the Beatles at all. They look like four ordinary, scruffy youths to me and I don't find them funny, they just seem terrifically cheeky. Rude, actually. And the hysteria! One can't hear a note of their music for all those silly girls screaming, which is probably a blessing. You're a fan? Well, each to his own, ha ha. If we all had the same tastes, the world would be a very dreary place.

I didn't realise you'd spent any time in the UK. When was that? Fascinating. I'm glad people were hospitable. We were all so grateful to America during the war, of course. Me? Oh, I worked in a munitions factory. Frightfully boring but I was glad to do my bit. Heavens, is that the time? I must dash. So lovely to talk to you.

Yes, Margot Friedenberg, that's my name. Miss, actually. I'm divorced. Well, in fact, the marriage was annulled. We both realised it was a mistake immediately, although I'm sure you don't want to hear about that. Goodbye then. I've really enjoyed getting to know you, Mr Templeton. Mr Templeman, of course. Do forgive me for rushing away. Maine tomorrow and I haven't even thought about packing.

No rest for the wicked, ha ha!

THE END

ACKNOWLEDGEMENTS

Terry Pratchett once said that more than half the skill of writing lies in tricking the book out of your own head. Well, this one was particularly reluctant to emerge. I started thinking about Cecil and Claude during a Creative Writing MA at London's City University, and my thanks are due to Jonathan Myerson, who ran the course with such intelligence and good humour, to Lucy Caldwell and Claire Allan, and to my fellow students, who also taught me so much. I must have rewritten the story at least five or six times since then and I'm grateful to all those who read and helped improve my early drafts, particularly Jane Allberry, Julie Bull, Anthony Cartwright, Rachael Gibbon, Debra Hills, Belinda Lovell, Jacqueline O'Mahoney, Leanne Salisbury, Hilary Stallibrass, Sallyanne Sweeney and Kate Worsley. I should also like to thank Amy Weller and the UK Ladies Peloton Book Group for their friendship and support. The greatest thanks of all are due to my wonderful editor and agent, Nicky Lovick, who believed in this story and encouraged me to have one last shot at getting it right. Without her guidance and conviction, this novel would never have seen the light of day, and I owe her more than I can express without gushing.

I'm also indebted to Betsy Reavley and the wonderful team at Bloodhound Books, including Better Book Design, who gave Cecil and Claude such a glorious cover for their sortie into the outside world, and Abbie Rutherford, for her eagle-eyed yet sensitive copy editing. And as ever, to my husband and sons, without whom the world would be a very dreary place.

A NOTE FROM THE PUBLISHER

Thank you for reading this book. If you enjoyed it please do consider leaving a review on Amazon to help others find it too.

We hate typos. All of our books have been rigorously edited and proofread, but sometimes mistakes do slip through. If you have spotted a typo, please do let us know and we can get it amended within hours.

info@bloodhoundbooks.com